Gun for Hire

GW00457630

Thomas Waugh

Nothing to Lose first published 2016 by Endeavour Press Ltd.
Darkness Visible first published 2017 by Endeavour Press
Ltd.
Ready for Anything first published 2017 by Endeavour Press
Ltd.

This edition published 2018 by Sharpe Books.

Table of Contents

Nothing To Lose

Thomas Waugh

"A murderer is regarded by the conventional world as something almost monstrous, but a murderer to himself is only an ordinary man."
Graham Greene, *The Ministry of Fear.*

"Good Lord above, can't you see I'm pining?
Tears all in my eyes
Send down that cloud with a silver lining
Lift me to Paradise
Show me that river, take me across
And wash all my troubles away
Like that lucky old sun, give me nothin' to do
But roll around Heaven all day."
Haven Gillespie, *That Lucky Old Sun.*

1.

It was late. Cold. But Michael Devlin's heart was colder.

Frost dusted the cars, hedges and slate rooftops alike. The moon was dim and sickle-shaped. Pink-grey clouds, like tumours, blotted out the stars. It was a fine night — for killing.

Smoke pirouetted up from Devlin's cigarette as he followed Martin Pound, Conservative Member of Parliament for Wiltshire South, down the quiet street, full of attractive terrace houses, in Chiswick. Pound was heading for his London home (taxpayers had bought the property but the minister intended to pocket the robust profit when he sold it on). Devlin's window of opportunity would close when the MP reached his drive. But it only takes a moment to assassinate someone. Devlin had stalked his prey since the minister had left his club in Piccadilly and got on the tube. Pound liked to use public transport. He liked being recognised by members of the public, especially young women.

The clip-clop of Pound's polished oxford brogues, no doubt purchased in Jermyn Street along with the rest of his wardrobe, sounded like horses' hooves upon the concrete. Devlin's footsteps were quieter and quicker. He carefully pulled out a black-handled kitchen knife from the inside pocket of his dark blue suit. His orders — given to him by Oliver Porter — were to use a knife instead of a gun.

Talking out on the terrace of the National Liberal Club, Porter had briefed Devlin about the contract: *"Make it look like a street crime. A random act. There have, fortunately for us, been a number of stabbings in the area over the past few months. The nature of the crime shouldn't raise too much suspicion."* The two men had been friends, and business associates, for several years now. Oliver Porter had his manicured fingers in several pies and served as a middle-man for all manner of spooks, gangsters and commercial organisations. Porter 'fixed things'. He had encouraged Devlin to continue to use his skill and training after he came out of the army. The well-connected ex-officer was comfortable moving in both the underworld and the upper echelons of society. Business was business.

Porter had explained to Devlin that the politician owed some businessmen a large sum of money. *"Pound lives beyond his means and has a nasty gambling habit. And he has borrowed capital from some even nastier people."* Pound had become embroiled in a business deal for the notorious gangsters, the Parker brothers, and though he had paid off a substantial amount of his debt to them, his creditors were still not happy. Now he was threatening to confess all to the authorities, unless his debt was written off.

Devlin wasn't particularly concerned with his victim's sins or the reasons behind the contract. Everybody sins, and everybody dies. He flicked his cigarette butt into a drain. There were no cameras on the street, and no lights on in the homes which flanked the road they walked down. Devlin's iron-wrought, work-hardened features barely changed as he put his hand over the minister's face and silenced his scream. His other hand curled around him like a snake and buried the knife into his chest, puncturing his lungs. The minister shot out an arm, his hand outstretched, but then he slumped to the floor like a puppet whose strings had been cut. To give credence to the scenario of a street crime Devlin stabbed the politician several more times. The minister's woollen overcoat soaked up the blood, which oozed out of his body. Devlin took the man's wallet and jewellery, as any good mugger would.

Devlin proceeded to calmly walk down the street. He wiped the handle of the kitchen knife, so as not to leave any prints, and tossed the weapon into a bush in the nearby park.

He walked for half a mile — the bitter chill in the air didn't bother him — and then hailed a black taxi to take him to Rotherhithe. Devlin was a polite but forgettable fare. He made a modicum of small talk, but for the most part thumbed his way through the last chapters of Turgenev's *Home of the Gentry*. He got out the cab near Southwark Park and walked half a mile back towards Tower Bridge and his apartment. On his way he sent a brief text message to Oliver Porter: *Job done.*

2.

Devlin's fifth floor apartment was located off Tooley Street and overlooked both Tower Bridge and an attractive square containing shops, a fountain and a bronze statue of Charles Dickens. Aside from the endless rows of bulging bookcases the apartment had an air of emptiness about it. It looked as if the occupier was either moving out or waiting for someone to move in. There was a leather sofa and widescreen television in the living room, but no ornaments or photographs – and only one framed picture on the wall. The apartment lacked a woman's touch. The bathroom contained a mere half a dozen items and the bedroom was equally spartan – save for more books and a collection of silver-framed photographs of his late wife, Holly, on top of a chest of drawers.

Michael Devlin's build and looks were average. "You have a wonderfully anonymous, forgettable face," Oliver Porter had remarked when he made his pitch for the ex-soldier to become a contract killer five years ago. His hair was shortish and light brown. His hairline was receding and small patches of white hair were creeping into his stubble. If you looked closely at the forty-year-old you would have noticed one eyebrow was slightly shorter, from where a bullet in Afghanistan had struck a piece of masonry and a stone shard had injured him just above the eye. All the other scars he had brought back from the war remained unseen.

Devlin had been born in London, a Bernardo's child. He had lived in a number of foster homes, but never settled. Although he seldom struck the first blow Devlin regularly fought with his classmates and fellow foster children. Eventually he found a piece of normality when he was fostered out to a couple — Bob and Mary Woodford — who lived just outside of Rochester. His resentment towards the world subsided and he threw himself into his studies. But although Devlin read voraciously, the idea of university never appealed to him. 9-11 happened and Devlin decided to join the army. He wanted to do something. Help someone. Devlin served briefly in Northern Ireland before being posted to Iraq and then Afghanistan. After two tours in Helmand his former commanding officer offered Devlin a job as a security consultant for an investment bank. Devlin left the army and, shortly afterwards, met Holly. Life and love slotted into place. Happiness came – and went, when Holly died in a car accident. It was a hit and run. They never caught the driver.

So now Devlin drank heavily, kept himself to himself, read voraciously and occasionally killed people. Life was lived in the shadow of Holly, of an alternative present where she was alive. Devlin only accepted three or four jobs a year. Each job paid well and he lived relatively frugally. Having bought his apartment, his biggest expenditure was now paying the fees to the care home for Bob and Mary.

Devlin sat, slumped, on the sofa. He worked his way through a pack of cigarettes and turned his stereo to shuffle. Bob Dylan's 'Red River Shore' played in the background…

"Pretty maids all lined up
Outside my cabin door.
I've never wanted any of them wanting me
Except the girl from the Red River shore."

It was now after midnight. Friday, December 13th. Twelve days before Christmas. The blinds to Devlin's balcony window were open and he watched a young couple, in an apartment across the square, start to put up their Christmas decorations. This would be his fifth Christmas without Holly. His first the wrong side of forty.

Rain began to pepper the window. Soon it would sleet. A chill wind whistled through a gap in the warped balcony door. Devlin downed another inch of bourbon. Grief began to well up in his stomach again.

"Well, I can't escape from the memory
Of the one I'll always adore
All those nights when I lay in the arms
Of the girl from the Red River shore."

Devlin gazed up at the large framed print of Holbein's *The Ambassadors* on the wall. Tears moistened his hazel eyes. His hand shook a little as he lit another cigarette. Holly had given the picture to Devlin as a Christmas present. On their first date together she had taken him to the National Gallery. Holly had led him around each floor and exhibition, a whirlwind of enthusiasm and knowledge concerning iconic canvases by Turner, Constable, Gainsborough and the like. The climax of her tour was Holbein's *The Ambassadors*. The self-taught art lover (Holly had read as voraciously as Devlin) decoded some of the painting's messages for him: how the painting represented the spirit of the age — the growing division between church and state and the emergence of science and rationality over the spiritual. Holly had led a captivated Devlin around to the side of the painting to view the counterpane at the centre of the work of art from a different angle. The image of a macabre skull came into focus.

"For some people death lies at the heart of the painting," Holly had remarked, prettily tucking a strand of her long blonde hair behind her ear. "Death casts a shadow over everything and should lie at the forefront of everything. But my favourite part of the painting is this." She had pointed to the top left-hand corner of the canvas. A silver cross could be glimpsed behind the large red curtain, which served as the backdrop to the painting. "Despite the world's growing devotion to science, politics and philosophy I think the artist is saying that God and faith are behind everything."

"Philosophy cannot and should not give faith," Devlin had said, quoting Kierkegaard. The arguments of first cause, the intelligence of design, the scriptures or the divine hand of providence hadn't proven the existence of God for Devlin at that moment — the expression on her face had. Philosophy cannot give birth to faith. Faith gives birth to faith. And faith can give birth to goodness. Devlin believed that the soul was real. That love was real.

The depressed widower raised a corner of his mouth in a gesture towards a smile, recalling the scene. Devlin closed his eyes and tried to re-live the touch and taste of their first kiss, hear the gentle rustle of her silk blouse as it pressed against him and smell her favourite perfume (Chanel's Chance Eau Vive). God, he loved her. Memories of Holly sustained him, and damned him. Devlin poured himself another drink, hoping it would finally usher him off to sleep.

"Well, the sun went down on me a long time ago
I've had to pull back from the door
I wish I could have spent every hour of my life
With the girl from the Red River shore…"

3.

Martin Pound's body was found by his neighbour, Ernest Holland, who was out walking his wife's black labradoodle, Poppy. Ernest dutifully called the police. The call operator instructed him to wait by the body. Rather than praying for the departed soul of his neighbour Holland pleaded that no one would come along and see him with the unsightly corpse. He dreaded the sheer awkwardness of the scenario. What was one supposed to say? As much as the treasurer of the local rotary club had sympathy for the victim sprawled out before him, he did not want to become a victim of gossip.

Thankfully the murder of a prominent MP prompted a rapid response from the police and a nervy looking Earnest Holland did not have to stand sentry-like for too long before the emergency services arrived. The police ran a background check on the accountant to rule him out of their investigation before letting him go.

Virginia Pound was informed about her husband's murder. She agreed to accompany the police to the station to help with their enquiries. As distraught as she was the politician's wife still had the presence of mind to fix her hair and make-up and put on an appropriate black dress before she left the house, believing that the media would soon be thrusting cameras into her face. Virginia was a former journalist for the *Daily Express* and was as prepared as one could be for the oncoming storm.

The police called the security services and Home Secretary, among others. Their initial thoughts were that the murder was a tragic street crime. To their knowledge the minister was not in possession of any sensitive documents. His wife – and his mistress – had alibis.

***

Later that morning Virginia Pound ventured downstairs, into her husband's study. She opened the safe, concealed behind a large portrait of Disraeli, and went through some papers and files upon a memory stick.

The storm in a teacup was about to boil over...

4.

Emma Mills sat in her florist shop, at the base of Devlin's apartment block, perched on a wooden stool behind the counter. Her dog, Violet lay curled up, contented, on the floor by her side. The shop, *Rosebuds*, was a festive fiesta of colour and aromas. Frosted wreaths, smelling of pine and cinnamon, filled one of the windows. A tree — decorated with crystal baubles, fairy lights and foil-wrapped chocolates (which the florist gave out to any children accompanying their parents) — was topped off with a gleaming, porcelain angel resembling Grace Kelly. Yet the decorations were the poor cousins, in beauty and life, to the flowers populating the shop. The room teemed with handcrafted bouquets of bluebells, peach blossoms, wild roses, carnations, elegant orchids, lilacs, daisies, tulips and more. Turner and Monet would have envied the shop's palette.

Emma glanced again at the bouquet of lilies which sat waiting by the till. She tapped her foot in impatience. Every fortnight Devlin came into the shop and purchased a bouquet of lilies to place by his late wife's grave. An upturned copy of Graham Greene's *A Burnt-Out Case* lay on the counter. He had mentioned the book and recommended that Emma read it a month ago. She thought he might notice it and appreciate that she had taken on board his recommendation.

God, I'm like a teenage girl with a crush. Have you got so desperate that you're trying to send out signals to a widower whilst he's on his way to the cemetery to pay his respects to his wife? Get real.

Emma gently shook her head, chiding herself, and smirked at her ridiculous behaviour. She resisted taking the copy of the book off the counter though. She still wanted to impress him — and make him think about her.

The thirty year old florist was good natured and good humoured. A Louise Brooks bob framed a sweet, pretty face. A ribbon of scarlet lipstick ran around Emma's mouth and a thin line of black eye shadow accentuated her almond-shaped eyes. For the benefit of Devlin she undid an extra button on her purple polka dot dress (a dress which accentuated her enviable figure).

As per usual he was on time, and, as per usual, he wore the same charcoal grey suit (the suit he had worn to his wedding and also Holly's funeral). Violet scampered out from behind the counter and greeted her favourite customer, wagging her tail with excitement. Violet was as friendly and sweet-tempered as her owner. The black and white dog stood just under knee height. She was part beagle, part hound, part Staffordshire bull terrier. "But all mongrel," Emma would say. "Like me," Devlin had replied, having met the dog and its owner a year or so ago.

Devlin crouched down and scratched Violet behind the ear whilst retrieving a chew from his pocket with his other hand. He looked up at Emma and made a face to ask permission to give the treat to the dog. She smiled and nodded. Devlin smiled back – and not with the mechanical smile he usually offered up to the world. His grin melted his usually frozen features, but Emma couldn't fail to notice his eyes, red-rimmed with sleeplessness.

"Morning. How have you been?" he asked, whilst surveying the new layout of the shop.

21

"Busy, as you can see. If I have to put up another piece of tinsel I might hang myself with it. Thankfully everything's done now. How have you been?"

"I've been busy doing nothing — working my way through the pub's selection of guest Christmas ales," Devlin (half) joked. The assassin had explained away his lifestyle and lack of a job by saying that he lived off some good investments he made after leaving the army.

The sound was on mute but the news was on a small television at the end of the counter. A rosy-cheeked reporter was standing outside Martin Pound's house in Chiswick. A flurry of scrolling captions – and pictures of a tearful family – told the story.

"It's sad, isn't it?" Emma remarked, her face creased in sympathy.

"I must confess I find it difficult to mourn the death of a politician."

"No, I meant that it's sad for the family. Those children are now going to grow up without a father."

Devlin was going to reply that he had grown up without a father – and that it never did him any harm. But he refrained from saying anything. He felt somehow aggrieved that she was taking his victim's side over him. Violet, having finished her chew, jumped up at Devlin and licked his hand – but he failed to notice or respond. Sensing his awkwardness Emma decided to change the subject.

"Will you be popping in to the Nelson this evening?" she said, making reference to the apartment block's local pub, *The Admiral Nelson*.

"Probably. And you?"

"Definitely. My father's Irish. I'm beginning to think that I've inherited his tolerance – and addiction – to alcohol," Emma joked.

Devlin and Emma had met each other several times in the Nelson before. The first occasion had been on a sort of date, when he had realised that the florist was also a neighbour. They spent a long night together, over several drinks, talking about his time as a soldier, her plans for the shop and their favourite novels. Neither could remember the last time they had laughed so much. He enjoyed her company. But Devlin had made a promise to his dead wife that he would never fall in love or marry again. A sacred promise. Devlin felt guilty, feeling something for Emma. He couldn't just sleep with the florist and creep out before dawn, never to see her again. He didn't want to hurt her, promise something that he could never deliver on. And so they remained just friends, as much as Emma often signalled that she wanted more.

"I've got your flowers ready," Emma said, handing him the bunch of lilies.

"Thanks."

As he cradled the flowers Devlin noticed the copy of the book she had been reading. He wanted to say something. But didn't.

Emma craned her head and stared through a gap in her festive window display in order to watch Devlin walk across the square. Her face was creased in scrutiny. He was a puzzle — and she still couldn't put all the pieces together. Devlin sometimes told funny anecdotes about his time as a soldier, or spoke about military history, but what had he seen and done in the war? Had he killed anyone? She admired Devlin – and was attracted to him all the more – for still being devoted to his wife. He was being faithful to her, even in death. Most men are seldom faithful to their spouses when they are alive. But, even though she knew it was irrational and unkind, Emma resented Devlin's late wife for still having a hold over him.

Emma turned up the television in an attempt to stop thinking about him. The victim's wife was speaking. "This was no accident. The person behind my husband's murder will be brought to justice," Virginia Pound was declaring. Her face was a picture of disdain and determination as she glared straight down the barrel of the camera lens – and Emma fancied that she wouldn't have liked to be in the shoes of the killer right now.

5.

"That fuckin' ponce... Stupid fuckin' bitch... We can't be seen to be connected with this," George Parker spat, as he looked up at the television. The career criminal was sitting opposite his younger brother, Byron, in an Italian café they owned in Shoreditch. The café was closed whilst the owners discussed business. Two heavy set men, one white and one black, stood bouncer-like at the door, out of earshot. Jason and Leighton served as bodyguards, as well as drivers, to the Parker brothers.

The ceiling was yellow from the eatery's pre-smoking-ban days. Black and white photos of Sophia Loren, Gina Lollobrigida and Anita Ekberg livened up the sepia-tinged wallpaper. A signed colour photo of Trevor Brooking took pride of place on the counter, next to the flapjacks. The smell of bacon wafted through the establishment from where George Parker had ordered the manager to make him a sandwich. "And I want a proper bacon sandwich, with brown sauce. On white bread. None of your ciabatta or panini shit."

George Parker's flat, triangular face was shaped like an iron. He was a monster of a man, standing over six foot tall. An alloy of muscle and fat. His upper body was all shoulders and no neck. His nose had been broken on numerous occasions and zig-zagged across his face like a bolt of lightning. The fifty year old gangster's left eye was permanently bloodshot. Chubby, scarred fingers dripped with jewellery. A chunky, bejewelled Rolex jangled on his wrist. He was the eldest son of the notorious gangster, Ivan ("The

Terrible") Parker, and was part Irish, part Jewish and part Cockney. George Parker had had blood on his hands from an early age. He had broken his first jaw at fifteen and first kneecap at seventeen. At least nobody could accuse the gnarled-faced enforcer of breaking hearts. He liked to dominate women in and out of bed. Sex was an animalistic act for the Viagra-taking ex-boxer. Romance for George Parker was giving his wife or mistress his credit card and telling them to go out and buy something pretty. He demanded his wife remain faithful, whilst she turned a blind eye to his own infidelities – which included bedding his sister-in-law.

George Parker enjoyed having a good time. He called himself a larger than life figure and claimed that the crime writer Martina Cole had based a number of her main characters on him. He wore loud, shiny suits like those of talentless chat show hosts and overpaid footballers. He owned a yellow Rolls Royce, metallic blue Porsche Cayenne and white Jaguar XF. Not to be outdone by any Russian oligarch in Hampstead he had recently added several subterranean floors to his main house in Chislehurst. The property now possessed a snooker room, cinema and space dedicated to various pieces of West Ham memorabilia. George Parker had more money than sense – or taste.

George Parker had stood trial on two charges for murder, but had been acquitted. His first wife had been the bottle blonde actress, Shirley Dobbs, who the *Radio Times* once described as being like 'Barbara Windsor – but without the talent'. He had been shot three separate times over the years, but had survived. The last shooting incident involved his third wife firing a gun at him – but she only shot him in the leg. "God or my old man must be looking after me, bless his wicked soul," George had explained to the cameras outside Old Brompton Road hospital, after the shooting.

George and Byron Parker had business interests in central, east and south-east London. They had inherited a criminal empire from their father which revolved around drugs, prostitution, extortion and racketeering. Intimidation and violence were standard business practises. George Parker longed for the good old days, when he had driven around London with his father in his silver Bentley. There was no high like the adrenalin kick of power and violence – of drawing blood. George could scarce recall a year in his life when he hadn't killed a man, either with his bare hands or with the pearl-handled Browning pistol he carried with him at all times.

George still regularly frequented the clubs and restaurants of his youth (which he now co-owned with his brother). He had any new girl his escort agency hired sent to him first. He liked to test drive them. Drink lubricated his life and the former heavyweight champion of south-east London could never quite deliver a knock-out blow to his cocaine and gambling habits.

Byron Parker on the other hand, felt he needed double the patience and prudence of ordinary mortals to compensate for his elder sibling's foolhardiness. Few would have picked the two men sitting around the table as brothers. They were like chalk and cheese in dress, manner and build. Byron Parker looked like an accountant. His build was slight. His head was narrow, coffin-shaped. An often plaintive expression hung beneath a crop of thick black hair, flecked with grey. His suit was tailored, his nails manicured. He wore an elegant, antique Patek Philippe watch. Oliver Porter thought that his wire-framed glasses made him look like Heinrich Himmler.

Whereas George Parker liked to reminisce and yearned for a lost past Byron Parker focused upon the present and future. He had transformed his father's empire. Bettered it. The old revenue streams were drying up (and the Chinese and Eastern Europeans had cornered some markets due to the use of slave labour). It was now more profitable to rent out rooms in Soho to start-up tech companies than to use the spaces as brothels. Shoreditch had become similarly gentrified. The once grotty corner of London was now filled with Mummy- and Daddy-funded graduates who spent their working day – and leisure time – on Facebook and twitter. Pubs had turned into coffee shops or, equally hideously, gastro pubs. The new residents lauded the diversity of the area. Even after they moved out of London so that they could send their children to schools containing other nice, white, middle-class children they still spoke about their time living in East London as though it were a badge of honour or virtue. George Parker lamented some of the things the area had lost but he was compensated by the rise in rents and house prices. Various nightclubs and restaurants they owned in Shoreditch were proving worthwhile assets, and not just because they could be used to launder money. The Parker brothers made more money, legally, through their investments in the London property market than they did selling drugs nowadays. Their greatest enemy was the taxman and the rise in interest rates.

As Byron Parker grew ever more 'legitimate' his ambition grew to move in different, rarefied, circles. He had contacted Oliver Porter not just to resolve the problem of the loose-lipped politician. Porter could introduce him to the right people, facilitate memberships to the right clubs. He wanted his children to attend the best schools. His son would be a banker, not a criminal. Money could buy the finer things in life. Better food. Better clothes. Better friends. A good life was a prosperous life. He was fiercely loyal to his business partner, but Byron had out-grown the grunts and curses which served as conversation for his brother.

Byron Parker sat with a double espresso, a piece of biscotti and copy of *The Financial Times* in front of him. He obsessively straightened the cutlery on his side of the table. "Let's find out what is happening first, before we react in earnest. We have the necessary contacts with the police in the area to find out what the wife knows or doesn't know."

"We should have never have used that spiv of yours to get rid of Pound. We should have used our own people. I could have fuckin' put a knife in his chest for nothing. Why couldn't he just pay up? Silly bastard thought he was something special, threatening to blackmail us if we didn't write off his debts. Fucking politicians. Whores are more trustworthy. I'm not sure I trust this Porter friend of yours, either. He can use what he knows as leverage over us. And what do we know about the doer he used to take out Pound? Can we trust him? I don't want some bastard crawling out of the woodwork in a week's time, looking to exploit a situation."

Byron Parker subtly moved his plate away from the flecks of spittle which had shot out of his brother's mouth and landed on the table. His expression was pinched. He disapproved of his brother's ignorance and base manner – and he also felt that, behind his criticism of Porter, his business partner was criticising the way he had dealt with things.

"Porter's not to blame. And the job was carried out professionally. If it looks like we might be exposed in any way then we'll cross, or burn, that bridge when we come to it. Let's just find out what the wife knows first."

George Parker grunted in reply. Come what may he would take care of business.

6.

The cold numbed Devlin's face. He wished that it could numb his thoughts as well. Some of the newer recruits in Helmand had described the paratrooper as having ice in his veins, such was his coolness under fire and lack of remorse in killing the Taliban. But Devlin aspired to have nothing running through him, ice or fire. He envied the marble statues populating the cemetery. They didn't do harm to anyone and no harm came to them.

Low, leaden clouds besmirched the sky. Before him was a sea of grey and black headstones, occasionally pockmarked by the odd bouquet of flowers. Devlin walked quickly along one of the gravel paths in Garrett Lane cemetery, towards his late wife's grave. The army encouraged speed, efficiency – to be better than the enemy and civilians. Devlin had shaved that morning and polished his shoes as if he were attending a parade ground inspection.

Devlin bent down and pulled up the weeds upon the patch of grass around his wife's grave before placing the lilies next to the headstone. He used a handkerchief to wipe away the tiny flecks of mud on the classically-designed black, marble stone. Devlin read again the lines from Coleridge. Love and sorrow welled up in his chest.

"To be beloved is all I need
And whom I love I love indeed."

His loneliness seared, piercing his numbness. He wanted to tilt his head up to heaven and roar, have his body crack and crumble like a statue. The injustice of her death eclipsed any crime he may have committed, he believed. *I'm more sinned against than sinning*. Devlin's heart felt so heavy that he could have sunk into the sodden turf beneath his feet.

The sound of footsteps on the gravel attracted his attention. An old man shuffled by. His hair was snow-white, his expression glum and sunken. His skin seemed so powdery that Devlin feared a strong gust of wind might blow his features away. Both men nodded to one another and forced a perfunctory smile. The old man had put on his best suit too (which was now several sizes too big). Time and life had diminished him. No doubt he was a widower as well. Both men shared a similar haunted gaze, their eyes and souls hollowed out. Devlin experienced a strange presentiment of his future self. The hunched-over old man, wounded by the loss of his wife, was not long for the world. The young widower envied his elder. The thought of death brought a sense of consolation to the soldier. Devlin's face broke out in a sprained smile as he remembered a quote from Walt Whitman: "*To die is different from what any one supposed, and luckier.*"

***

Oliver Porter allowed his wife to sleep in. He made breakfast for his children and drove them to school in his recently bought Range Rover. Porter cherished his time with his children. Although not immune to bouts of selfishness and spite they were on the whole good-natured and contented. He was not making the same mistakes his father had made with him (which was not to say he wasn't making his own mistakes). During the thirty minute drive to their ferociously expensive school he asked them about their homework and what they would like to buy their mum and grandparents for Christmas. Porter was relieved – and enthused – to be back home. To be back to some kind of normality. A home cooked dinner by his wife and evening spent playing Risk or chess with his children was worth a hundred dinners at *The Ivy*. The routines of domestic life gave the ex-Guards officer structure. The mundane and familiar enriched his soul.

On his way home Porter stopped off at the village to order the goose and gammon for Christmas, from his local butcher. He also popped into the art shop and picked up two watercolours he had ordered, painted by a young local artist (the daughter of his postman). Porter's final visit was to the parish church, where he made a generous donation to the Christmas fund which provided food parcels for the elderly over the holidays. As much as the fixer liked to make money he also enjoyed spending it – and not necessarily on himself. Wealth is a great enabler of generosity.

The Range Rover crunched across the drive. The vision of his six bedroom Georgian house — its russet brickwork glowing in the pale sunlight — was a sight for sore eyes. The property was one of the most sought after in the area. On more than one occasion Porter had turned down exorbitant sums of money (from agents acting for football players, stand-up comedians and disc jockeys alike – the veritable royalty of the age) in offers to buy the house. They had moved in just over a decade ago. His wife had transformed the garden all by herself — and she, far more than him, was responsible for the much admired décor of the property. A large "shed" at the bottom of the garden served as Porter's office. The wooden outbuilding had its own specially adapted internet and phone connection, and a keypad lock prevented him from being disturbed. The domain was out of bounds to his children and even his wife. Work and family life needed to be kept separate, for various reasons.

A cup of tea and a bacon sandwich were waiting for him in the kitchen, as was his wife, when Porter got back home. Victoria was seven years younger than her husband. She was blonde, statuesque and well-bred but owned a healthy, broad sense of humour which allowed her to laugh at most things, including herself. She enjoyed the finer things in life but had enough character not to be a slave to them. Her family and interests (gardening, painting, charity work, shopping) kept her engaged and contented. Victoria was patient and understanding about Oliver's frequent periods away from home. She rarely asked about his work because, deep down, she didn't want to know the answers. Oliver had first met Victoria at a function for his regiment. She was the daughter of a brigadier. Both believed they had found themselves a catch and, within a year, they were married. Although some fellow officers called their barracks home Porter chose to take early retirement because he wanted to make a real home, with Victoria and his children.

Victoria switched on the news. The breaking story, that Virginia Pound had possible evidence proving that her husband's death was not the result of a mugging which had gone wrong, dominated the headlines. Victoria saw her husband's eyes harden and nostrils flare in what was, for Oliver, a disquieting expression. He pursed his lips — clamping his mouth shut for fear of betraying his raw anger and frustration.

"Is there something wrong, darling? Did you know the man?" Victoria said, her Home Counties accent awash with genuine concern.

"No. I may have met him in passing at a party though," Oliver replied, distracted by his own thoughts rather than his wife's words. The wheels of his mind turned as he tried to hammer out the ramifications of Virginia Pound's outburst. Firstly, it was conceivable that the Parker brothers may well send someone round to visit the widow – and it wouldn't be Santa. They would first interrogate her and retrieve any evidence linking them to her husband – and then they would silence her. Porter had seen a look of steely conviction in his eyes when Byron Parked had paraphrased Stalin to him over lunch: "Seven grams of lead to the head solves any problem." The Parkers may not be viewing the widow as the only loose end though, he thought to himself. Although Porter had an outstanding reputation for discretion he did not have a long-standing history and business relationship with the brothers. *They may consider me expendable.* Similarly Devlin may become a target. Without a shooter or fixer any case against the brothers would prove circumstantial, regardless of any evidence Virginia Pound might possess.

Porter sighed again. His phone felt heavy in his hands, like a gun, as he sent a message to Devlin, instructing him that they needed to meet up. He would have to travel back to London.

No rest for the wicked.

The season of peace and goodwill to all men couldn't start quite yet.

*

Devlin bowed his head before his wife's grave.

You must see everything — or nothing. Like God. If you would have made me promise that I would never kill again I would have kept my word. But that was a promise for another lifetime… Don't think less of me, although I think less of myself, for what I do. I wish I could talk about other, good things in my life. You kept my secrets and forgave me when you were alive. You're still doing it now. Please tell me you forgive me… Killing has become a job, as it was in the army. A doctor saves lives — it's his job. I get paid for taking lives. It's the same but different. Or at least that's what I tell myself. We all tell ourselves lots of things.

None of my victims are innocent. The world is a better place without an IRA brigade commander and corrupt Labour peer and pederast. Although what right do I have to be judge and executioner?

I'm not sure whether the job makes me feel numb or alive. But it makes me forget about you. I'm good at what I do. Porter says I've found my calling. We both know he's flattering me. But I have a moral switch, which I can turn on and off at will. The moral switch was always on when I was with you. But now I'm killer one minute, half decent human being the next.

Work gives me some respite. But then I feel guilty for forgetting about you. And the grief sets in again even more... You probably saw me with Emma today. She's just a friend, if that. I'll keep my promise. It's the only thing meaningful, honourable, I have left in my life.

The promise Devlin made to Holly on the evening of her funeral went bone deep. He swore that he would never marry or love again. He made it late at night, fuelled by love and alcohol. He made it to God as well as his wife, even though he cursed God's name for having taken her. It was a sacred pact, bigger and truer than life itself or his wedding vows. It was more important that any order he had been given as a soldier or any contract he had been offered by Porter, no matter how lucrative. All Devlin had was his grief and promise. If he didn't have those he would have nothing.

7.

The décor in *The Admiral Nelson* had barely changed over the past thirty years. Traditional pint glasses hung down from the horseshoe bar and a forlorn dartboard hung in the corner. The heavily veneered oak tables and beams were gnarled and cracking and the worn russet-coloured carpet was infused with the smell of tobacco from hundreds of lock-ins. A jukebox, which was seldom switched on, contained music by Fleetwood Mac, The Drifters, The Rolling Stones and Showaddywaddy. There was also a solitary album by Bon Jovi, for the 'younger' crowd. The floor was sticky and a number of planks creaked. But the regulars wouldn't have changed a thing, partly to put off other locals in the area from intruding upon their place of respite – a sanctuary from the modern world. Most of the young professionals in the area put their head in the door, cringed and walked away.

The landlord of the pub was a retired Scottish merchant seaman, Michael Robertson. He had bought the pub ten years ago, after he and his wife had been regulars for five years. The atmosphere was warm (as was the beer most of the time) due to the landlord's affable character. *The Admiral Nelson* had about a twenty-strong crowd of regular patrons. Thankfully they could drink for fifty. Everybody knew everybody else and, so long as you could take a joke and stand a round, it didn't matter who you were or where you came from – you were welcome.

Devlin entered the pub at around nine o-clock. Without a word the barmaid, Kylie, started to pour him a drink. The pint of the new Christmas guest ale was ready for Devlin before he even reached his regular stool at the bar.

"Thanks. Could I also have…"

Before Devlin had finished his sentence Kylie had proceeded to pour him a Jameson's and water. He finished off the round by buying the barmaid and landlord a drink. The latter sat down next to Devlin, one of his favourite regulars. Both men had spent many an evening drinking into the small hours. Michael Robertson was approaching sixty-five but a love of life, and alcohol, kept him young. His nose was as red as his eyes and his pot-belly now protruded out further than his once barrelled chest. His waxy skin sometimes looked as if it might fall off his face, but his smile routinely propped it up. His wife, Maureen, was Scottish Presbyterian. She could curdle her husband's blood with just a look, but still the old sailor had a roving eye for the ladies (fortunately or not for him they rarely gave him a second look). "I had a girl in every port when I was at sea. Luckily I knew where all the venereal clinics were in every port as well," he had joked to Devlin on more than one occasion.

Christmas songs played on a loop in the background, but not too intrusively.

"*I could've been someone.*
But so could anyone."

A couple of patrons swayed a little and mouthed the words. But the pub was quiet. It was the time of year for Christmas parties and work drinks – and Michael Robertson was not keen on hosting either.

"How are you, fella?" the landlord said, genuinely pleased to see the former soldier. Robertson appreciated Devlin's company and the amount of money the paratrooper spent in his pub.

"Fine, thanks. Where's Maureen tonight?"

"She's upstairs, watching one of her blasted soaps. But it could be worse, she could be down here watching me!" Robertson cheerfully explained. The sanguine landlord tipped his head back, laughed and downed his drink in one fluid, well-practised, motion.

After he had Kylie serve him another drink – and line another one up for Devlin – Robertson asked her to retrieve the small Christmas present he had bought his regular. Devlin picked up the wrapped hardback book. He thanked his friend awkwardly. He couldn't remember the last time that someone had bought him a gift. For the first time in a long time Devlin was touched.

"Just a little something, laddie. It's a thank you for all your support and for lending me half your military history library. I'm not sure if you'll like it. The lass Emma gave me some advice on what you might enjoy reading. She's a good sort, that girl. You could do a lot worse. She can hold her liquor too. Although in my past I liked women who could be under the table, or under me, after just half a bottle of wine. It saved time and money."

The landlord tilted his neck back again and let out another burst of laughter. But Devlin barely registered his drinking companion. Emma had walked through the door. She had changed into a black pencil skirt and had put on a new top, made of fine cashmere. She also wore a pair of silver droplet earrings, which had once belonged to her grandmother. Devlin had commented on how pretty they looked, many months ago. Her copy of Graham Greene's *A Burnt-Out Case* could be seen peeking out of her stylish leather handbag. Emma turned more than one head as she stood, slender and elegant, in the middle of the pub. Tinges of shyness highlighted rather than diminished her attractiveness. Devlin thought that she might be going out to a party and was just popping into the Nelson for one or two beforehand, or maybe she was going off on a date? Devlin didn't know quite how to feel about the prospect of Emma dating someone. He knew that he couldn't be with her, but he didn't necessarily want someone else to be with her either. At the very least any prospective date should treat her right, Devlin thought. *She deserves someone special... She deserves to be happy.* Devlin hoped that she could stay – and not just because of the way she was looking tonight.

The two figures smiled across the room as if they were the only ones present. Their eyes locked onto one another, neither quite sure which was most like a deer caught in the headlights. Something fell into place, like tumbler wheels in a vault door. Emma did and didn't want him to look at her in an amorous way. He never behaved in an inappropriate manner with her but there had been times when she wished that he wouldn't always play the gentleman. Sometimes a woman needs a good kiss, as a well as a kind word.

Emma was pleased to see that Devlin had changed his clothes. The suit would have reminded her of his late wife. He had changed into a dark blue polo shirt, jeans and – what with it being Bermondsey – a pair of white Reebok's. A black sports jacket sat on a stool next to him. Some may have judged the ex-soldier's face to be weathered (or even pained), but Emma thought he looked ruggedly handsome. He had a face that told a story – and one which concealed a story, too. It was also a face which reminded Emma of a painting she had received on her confirmation, when she was thirteen. Her aunt had bought her a series of illustrations depicting the story of Christ's crucifixion and resurrection. Devlin resembled the figure of the soldier who pierced the side of Jesus.

***

Devlin and Emma sat at their usual table in the corner, beneath a faded print of Turner's *The Fighting Temeraire*. Light shone from a teardrop-shaped bulb beneath a nineteen-seventies style lampshade. Devlin took sips from his drink even quicker than normal. His heart was beating a tiny bit faster than usual. He craved the taste of a cigarette in his mouth but he didn't want to rudely get up and abandon his friend.

Devlin was just about to compliment Emma on how nice she looked, but as he opened his mouth Kylie came over, bringing with her a couple of drinks courtesy of their landlord. Robertson raised a glass to his regulars from the bar and (unsubtly) winked at Devlin and nodded his head towards Emma.

The buxom barmaid, who was wearing a tight-fitting silk blouse and tighter-fitting short denim skirt, smiled at the former soldier far more than at the finely dressed florist. Devlin smiled back at the barmaid – but he did so a little cautiously. He hoped that Emma hadn't found out that he had slept with the fun-loving Bermondsey girl six months ago. They had just had sex, after a late night. Devlin knew that Kylie wasn't looking for anything more. And he had nothing else to give. Although Devlin had made a solemn promise to Holly and God that he would neither love nor marry again, he was a widower – not a priest or eunuch. He didn't want Emma to think he had rejected her in favour of the blonde barmaid. But if he had slept with Emma all those months ago he knew that it would've meant something to her. In the world Devlin had created for himself, killing and meaningless sex were no longer sins. But love was.

Devlin was even more embarrassed Kylie stroked him on the back and asked, with a flirtatious gleam in her eye, if she could do anything else for him.

"So do you have any exciting plans for Christmas?" Emma asked, once the barmaid had departed.

"I'm due to meet up with some old friends from the regiment," Devlin replied, lying. He was planning to stay at home on Christmas Day and work his way through a Bernard Cornwell novel and bottle of McClelland's. He didn't particularly care if people thought him lonely, but he felt awkward receiving any feigned sympathy. On the whole most people only really cared about themselves, Devlin believed. Nobody had seemed to genuinely care when Holly died. Everybody moved on easily enough, except Devlin. The cynical explanation for things was all too often the right one. Human beings are mainly selfish animals. "How about you? Where will you be spending Christmas?" he continued.

"I'll be heading back home for a couple of days and suffering my family. My mother will be especially keen to tell me how best to live my life. 'New year, new you,' she'll say. My father should be fine though, after his second glass of port. I'm looking forward to attending midnight mass in my old church. I'll take plenty of money so as to light plenty of penny candles and pray my mum loses her voice over Christmas. Have you ever attended midnight mass?"

"I have, but many years ago now. Even God doesn't have a good enough memory to recall the prayers I offered up back then, I imagine."

The chaplain attached to Devlin's regiment in Helmand had always been encouraging him to attend service. Occasionally they would talk about the Bible – but mostly they chatted about Camus and Chekhov. *The chaplain never gave up on me, even when I gave up on him.* Devlin wryly smiled to himself, recalling how the chaplain had once asked him what he felt when he shot an enemy. "Recoil," Devlin had matter-of-factly answered.

Emma tucked her hair behind her ears, perhaps to show off her silver earrings, and fingered the stem of her wine glass.

"Do you mind if I ask you something? I don't want to offend you though."

"I'm not easily offended."

"Do you believe in God?"

"I believe in God. I'm just not sure if he believes in me."

"He believes in everyone."

"He must be exhausted, believing in everyone for so long a time. It's made him the world's oldest – and greatest – holy fool. But ignore anything I say. I don't want you thinking I'm trying to offend you, Emma. As a soldier I'm just used to having a black sense of humour about things. Especially God."

Devlin's foot tapped the floor in anxiety. He craved a cigarette even more. He couldn't quite meet Emma's probing expression and averted his gaze to look out of the window. Flakes of snow shimmered under the glow of amber streetlamps. The cold called to him, like a siren song.

"I sometimes think God must have a black sense of humour too, given the state of humanity, so you're in good company," Emma said, trying to ease any awkwardness.

"You have a strong enough sense of faith for both of us. The world could use some more good Catholic girls like you."

"Well I'm not so sure about that. What does it mean to be a good Catholic girl nowadays? You need to feel melancholy, guilty and superstitious."

"Catholic girls have got plenty in common with soldiers, it seems," Devlin wryly remarked.

"Do you get to see your old friends from the regiment often?"

"When I can," Devlin answered, lying. Every month or so he received an invitation to a reunion or charity event. He would send his apologies and decline – and also send a cheque if the event was linked to a worthwhile cause. He had attended a few gatherings after Holly's death. One time he was asked to apply for SAS selection, by a former commanding officer. One time he was offered counselling. It was understandable that some blamed Devlin's retreat from the world on the war. But it was grief rather than PTSD which shaped his psyche. Devlin had no desire to trade combat stories with his former comrades. He already looked backwards enough in his life, in regards to Holly. But he couldn't move on either. He was in limbo. Devlin wanted to tell Emma that once you've been to one reunion you've been to them all. They usually ended in a drunken brawls – and that was just the wives and girlfriends.

Devlin wanted to talk to Emma about other things too. But he didn't.

8.

Midnight approached. The music in the pub was turned off. The snow had failed to settle outside but a frosty wind still howled through the narrow Dickensian alley which ran along one side of the pub. Emma had gone home. She didn't like to leave Violet alone for more than a few hours. There were times when she thought the mood music might be right between her and Devlin. They had laughed enough, drunk enough. But ultimately he only offered up a kind word, rather than a kiss, as they parted at the end of the evening.

Everyone else had called it a night too, bar Devlin and the landlord. Robertson proposed one last drink. He was in the process of locking the doors, so that his friend could smoke whilst they drank, when three late night revellers came into the pub.

They were city boys, derivative traders, who had strayed south of the river after a night celebrating their bonuses. They had wandered over Tower Bridge after cocktails, a curry and an hour or so at a lap dancing club. Cocaine as well as alcohol fuelled their mood. All were former public school boys, the nation's brightest and best. Wealth creators.

"I'm sorry lads but I'm closing up," Michael Robertson said, apologetically.

"We just want one last drink," the self-appointed spokesman for the group said. He spoke in the form of an order rather than request. The former rower stood over six feet tall. His jaw was chiselled and even Hugh Grant would have envied his head of floppy brown hair.

"I'm sorry, we have to close," the landlord reiterated, this time with as much firmness as politeness in his voice.

"C'mon Rupert, let's just go. The place is a fucking dive, fit for plebs, anyway," his compactly-built companion remarked. Justin Dalton lightly clasped his friend on the elbow as he spoke but he was shrugged off. Rupert Spence did not understand, or appreciate, the concept of "no". The gilded youth, whose parents had never refused him anything, was used to getting his own way, especially in the case of procuring women. He had once been accused of raping a woman after a night out in *Boujis*. The case didn't even go to court though, as it was his word against a hairdresser's from Balham. His father had provided the best legal team money could buy. The Spence family were even tempted to sue the girl for vexatious litigation.

"No, I want to stay and be served here."

"Just give us one drink and we'll get out of your hair. It's Christmas. We've got plenty of money. It looks like you could use a few extra quid, from the state of this place," the third young trader in the group, Hector Baring, said. He eyes devoured the bottle of Jägermeister behind the bar. He fingered the small plastic bag of cocaine in his pocket again, paranoid that someone might have stolen it.

The landlord stared with trepidation at the three young men and then at Devlin. His mouth was agape but no words issued forth. He was tempted to call the police but he feared that doing so would stoke rather than put out any fires. He knew from experience that if he served the drunken and belligerent youths one drink then they would ask for one more – and one more after that. They had the devil in them – or just too many units of alcohol.

"You've been asked to leave," Devlin said, evenly, as he got up from his stool next to the bar and walked towards the three men. The landlord edged around the bar and locked the till. Devlin's arms hung down by his side, like a gunslinger ready to draw. But, like a town sheriff, Devlin preferred to end things peaceably. "I can give you the number for a local cab firm if you like."

As much as one might have imagined the former soldier being similar to a coiled spring he appeared tired, or even bored, by proceedings. His brow was creased, as hard as corrugated iron. He scrutinised the trio, making a risk assessment of the situation. He'd had a fair few drinks but a para who was unable to fight drunk was no para at all. All three could pack a punch – but Devlin had no intention of allowing any of them to land a punch. Their unofficial leader, Rupert, looked like he had some conditioning. Perhaps he boxercised or practised a martial art – or more likely he took Zumba classes, Devlin fancied. Ultimately they were amateurs and he was a professional.

"And who the fuck are you?" Rupert asked, raising his voice – incredulous and insulting. The derivatives trader equated volume with authority.

"I'm nobody," Devlin replied.

"Why don't you mind your own business old man and sit back down. Or fuck off altogether," Justin Dalton advised, walking towards Devlin and puffing out his barrel chest.

The former soldier smiled to himself. It was the first time that anyone had ever called him "old".

Perhaps I'm not long for this world after all.

"What do you think you're going to do? Throw us out?" Rupert said, part laughing and part snorting in derision.

"There's three of us and one of you. Do you have a death wish?"

Devlin could smell the curry and lager on the young man's breath. He recoiled more from the trader's liberal use of cologne though. The stench was nearly as pronounced as his arrogance and sense of entitlement, the soldier considered. He had encountered more than one Rupert during his time in the army.

"Something like that. You can always call up a few more friends to be on your side if you want to make it a fairer fight."

Devlin stared at the young man with thinly veiled contempt. Goading him. If the would-be alpha male threw the first punch then Devlin could claim self-defence, if the police got involved. Violence doesn't solve everything, but it does resolve some situations.

Man is born to trouble as the sparks fly upwards.

Devlin subtly altered his stance, so his feet were apart, in order to be better prepared to attack or retreat backwards to avoid any initial blow. His opponent would probably look to swing his arm in a right hook. He would have plenty of time to move inside and strike first, if that was the case. Instead, however, Rupert Spence merely tried to force Devlin backwards, out of his space, by shoving him in the shoulder. The former paratrooper stood statue-like. He sighed, in relief, that finally he was justified in drawing blood – and wiping the self-satisfied grin off his antagonist's face.

Devlin whipped his forearm around so that his elbow smashed into the young man's fine, aquiline nose. The sound was somewhere in between a crunch and a crack. Rupert Spence was immediately disorientated. His vision was blurred and his natural reaction was to bring his hands up to his wounded face. He would have lost his feet but Devlin held him up by the lapels of his coat, so that he could whip his right forearm around again and break his nose a second time. Elbows, knees and foreheads were far more useful in a fight than making a fist and throwing a movie-style punch. All too often Devlin had seen men break their hands. The harder they hit the worse it was for them. Amateurs. Blood and cartilage glistened, as the bridge of Rupert's nose opened up. This time the city trader fell to the floor, groaning.

Hector Baring let out a curse and squared up to Devlin. He raised his hands, like a boxer, but couldn't then decide whether to attack or back off. There was nothing he had learned on his business course which applied to his situation. Devlin experienced no such moment of indecision. His arm shot out like a ballista bolt and the hard base of his palm connected with the young man's throat, just beneath his chin. Hector made a slight choking noise. Fear gripped him and the gargling sound he was making turned into a whimper. Hector Baring wished he could be back at the club, with the Estonian dancer whispering sweet nothings and flicking her tongue out, swirling it around his ear. The young man performed his own version of a table dance however as he stumbled backwards and fell in between the gap of one of the pub's booths.

Justin Dalton's eyes bulged in rage. The fearless fly-half lowered his square head, thick neck and rounded shoulders and charged Devlin as if he were a bull. But Devlin moved with the swiftness of a matador. Devlin grabbed the top of the back of the chair nearest too him and swung it round, smashing it against the shins of his powerfully built assailant. The chair broke, falling apart like Lego, but it did its job. Dalton fell to the floor, snarling in pain. He slowly rolled over on his back, to witness a stoical looking Devlin standing over him. The impassive soldier stamped on his opponent's groin – twice. Dalton writhed in agony, twice, before turning his head and retching, ruining the carpet even more.

Devlin grabbed Rupert Spence by his hair and half-dragged him out of the door. The soldier ordered his two friends to follow him. Devlin gave the three men directions to the nearest main road, in order to flag down a taxi. The defeated young men, our brightest and best, were too ashamed and too hurt to fully take in what the brutal stranger said however.

Devlin went back into the pub. The landlord's mouth was agape. He recalled something the former soldier once said to him: "Train hard, fight easy." Robertson was taken aback by his friend's ferocity and efficiency in dealing with the youths. At no point had Devlin appeared to lose control of himself during the fight.

"I'm sorry about the chair. I'll be happy to pay for it."

"No, laddie, it's fine. Thank you," the landlord uttered, his voice somewhat croaky. He needed a drink.

Devlin's brow was still furrowed, in annoyance rather than sorrow. His "work self" had crossed over into the domain of his personal life.

"Please don't tell anyone about what just occurred, especially Emma," Devlin said, with a pained expression on his face.

"Don't worry, I won't," Michael Robertson promised, out of loyalty to his regular or, perhaps more so, out of fear.

Later that evening, as Devlin lay in bed, he wondered if he had performed one of his small acts of kindness by ejecting the unpleasant trio from the pub (God knows what might have happened if he hadn't been there) or had he committed an act of violence — a sin — which he would need to atone for by another thousand acts of kindness? Had he turned his moral switch on or off?

9.

Morning.

A sterile sun hung in the air, its watery light seeping in between dreary clouds. The view of the back garden was an island of calm compared to the throng of reporters and photographers at the front of the house. Virginia Pound sat in her Victoria Plum kitchen and stared at a photograph of her husband. The photo was of him and their eldest daughter, Beatrice. She was dressed in her graduation gown. It had been a special day for the whole family. Yet still he smiled in the same fake way whenever a camera was in front of him. The same expression on his face could be found in a thousand photographs of him with his constituents. When Virginia had first met Martin Pound, whilst campaigning for a seat on his local council, she had been impressed by his energy and conviction. She fell for him, they got engaged and she proudly composed the copy for some of his campaign literature. He was handsome, eloquent and genuinely wanted to make a difference. Martin Pound was a caring Conservative, a catch. Her friends envied her. She sacrificed a burgeoning career in journalism to play the loyal wife and devoted mother. If only *he* had been so loyal and devoted, she mused. The higher he climbed politically the more of his principles fell by the wayside. In the end he never even tried to reach a compromise with his beliefs. Compromise turned into capitulation. His first affair was with a constituent and his second was with an intern. Virginia lost track of his infidelities after that. She lost track of the money he squandered through bad investments and gambling as well. But still she played the loving wife (having no other role open to her). Virginia hosted dinner parties, pounded the pavement in painful heels on the campaign trail and was a patron of a number of charities which meant little or nothing to her. She was "Mrs Martin Pound". Most of her days were spent shopping and being a domestic goddess. In the evenings she helped her children with their homework and then worked her way through a season of Desperate Housewives and a bottle of mid-priced Rioja. Few of her friends envied her life now. She loved her children dearly, but they were growing up fast and would eventually fly the nest. Virginia Pound wasn't celebrating that her husband was dead – but she realised that she now had the opportunity for a second chance in life.

Virginia looked good – and not even just for her age. Friends said that she looked like Sophie Raworth. She thanked God, and her genes, each month that her long blonde hair was still free from any streaks of grey. A tan from her recent trip to Cyprus had given her complexion a healthy glow and concealed some of the wrinkles lining her forehead and eyes (perhaps she would have Botox, when the life assurance payment came through). Spin classes helped maintain a naturally elegant figure. She still turned the heads of plenty of men her age – but she would now turn the heads of younger men, she vowed to herself. She had taken a younger lover, her daughter's tennis coach, out of revenge for her husband's first affair many years ago. She would take another.

Virginia sat by the kitchen table with a cup of coffee and a half-eaten bran muffin in front of her. The news was on the television and her laptop was open. Worried that it might seem inappropriate for a widow to be out shopping so soon after her husband's death, Virginia had bought a number of new outfits online, in which to appear in front of the cameras. She wanted to look glamorous, yet solemn, like a female news anchor. Thankfully her local salon would send someone around to the house do her hair and nails.

The ex-*Daily Express* journalist had spent the morning going through articles relating to her husband's death. She needed to know the facts – and fiction – that were being disseminated. The court of public opinion was the highest in the land, for good or ill.

Virginia had also called her lawyer again. She needed to know how she should manage the evidence in her possession, which could expose or compromise a number of people (lobbyists, fellow politicians, property developers etc). She had yet to trawl through all of the documents and emails on the memory stick but her husband had saved everything. Among other things there was a series of emails exposing how a windfarm company had paid her husband to promote the "green" argument for sustaining the massive subsidies and tax exemptions the industry received. She wondered how, such were the frequent payments her husband gleaned for "consultancy" work, he could still be mired in so much debt. But the gambling debts, payment to escorts and keeping his mistresses in clover added up. *Why couldn't he just have kept on screwing his interns? Then we wouldn't be in this financial mess.*

Virginia needed specialist legal advice on how much evidence she was obliged to pass on to the police, and how much she could hold onto, to sell to newspapers or utilise to secure a book deal. She wanted to take advantage of the situation, strike while the iron was hot before she became yesterday's news. Virginia also made a call that morning to Phillip Simmonds, a publicist-cum-media agent. Simmonds had been described as a "young Max Clifford" — but in a good way, if it was humanly possible. Simmonds briefly offered his condolences before running through his terms of business. He agreed with his new client that she should put her story out there immediately (although she should make sure to sell that story to the highest bidder, but Simmonds would happily handle that, for a twenty-five percent commission). Virginia Pound was a wronged woman, a victim of a violent crime and a politician's wife. There were numerous angles to play, he argued enthusiastically. Simmonds promised to make some calls. Virginia argued that she did not want to use any short-term exposure to leverage just one big pay-off however. She wanted the agent to use the tragedy to organise a regular column for her in the *The Times*, *Evening Standard* or *Grazia*. She had been a good, punchy journalist over a decade ago. She could be the same again, or more. The wife and mother had more life experience and could write upon a variety of topics. Her ultimate ambition was to appear as a semi-regular guest on *Loose Women*. Her friends would envy her again then. She would explain to her children how she needed to work more and couldn't spend so much time looking after them. But she would hire a nanny. They would understand, Virginia reasoned. She was doing this for them, to provide for their future, after all.

*

The Parker brothers sat in the back of the blue Porsche Cayenne as it gunned its way towards the centre of town. Byron had just explained to his bleary-eyed sibling that it seemed the politician's wife was indeed in possession of information on a memory stick about some of Pound's business dealings. Byron's contact in the police couldn't be sure about the nature of the information however — or if it incriminated the brothers.

George Parker held his large bald head in his hands — he resembled Marlon Brando's Kurtz in *Apocalypse Now* — and let out a groan. "Fuckin' Pound. We should have tortured the sly bastard to silence him before we had him killed. I'm not having his stupid bitch wife be responsible for me doing time. If it's even just a rumour that this memory stick exists — and our names could be on it — then that's enough to sign her death warrant. We should act quickly too, just in case the police decide to put some protection on her. We don't know what other enemies Pound made. Plenty it seems. We'll kill the wife and retrieve the memory stick. We might even be able to make a few quid out of the memory stick ourselves. She's a looker — and I'd prefer to put something else in her mouth other than a gun barrel — but needs must. We should at least try and sort it so that her kids have no chance of witnessing anything though," Gentleman George stated, in deference to his late father's code of conduct that young children should never be harmed in the name of business.

As George Parker spoke, his voice more guttural than usual, his brother raised an eyebrow and looked askance at the carpeted footwell of the vehicle. It was littered with cigarette butts, fast food packaging, some suspect-looking pills and a small transparent envelope of cocaine. Byron not only disapproved of the mess because of the chance of police pulling them over; he also disliked the fact that his brother's young children used the car. He didn't want his nephew and niece growing up with their father's habits — and IQ.

"I agree," Byron replied, resigned to events. It was a shame to have the wife pay for her husband's indiscretions – but it was also a necessity. The choice between whether he or Virginia Pound suffered was no choice at all. "I've also had an idea as to how we might kill two birds with one stone. I can contract the job out to Porter again. I will try and get the name of his operative out of him when I do so. Once the job is finished I'll suggest that we pay him in cash. When we meet we'll dispose of him. And then catch up with his associate." The asset of Porter had now become a liability for the accountant-criminal. Byron Parker was confident of finding another fixer who could second him for the Garrick.

"If the prick doesn't give up the name of his man I'll get it out of him."

There was a gleam in his brother's eye and verve in his tone which Byron found unattractive. He recalled the last time George had cause to be violent towards a woman. One of their call girls had been on the take. "Women – and their divorce lawyers – have been torturing me for years. I was due some payback," the brutal, priapic enforcer had grimly joked to Jason and Leighton afterwards.

"I'll make the call to Porter and set things in motion."

"Good. Fingers crossed we won't have to pay the prick any more money before we off 'im. Any other things we need to discuss?" George Parker asked, his mind half-distracted by a ripe looking twenty year old walking along the pavement in stripper heels and a figure hugging dress. She reminded him of a friend of his eldest daughter who he wanted to fuck.

"We've sold the three properties on the new development at Greenwich. We should net half million. A Canadian pension fund has bought the apartments. They may well rent them out, once finished, but they may just leave them empty and sell when the price is right."

George Parker pursed his lips, almost in a kiss, and nodded in appreciation. The thought of making money turned him on as much as the blonde in the stripper heels.

"Gorgeous. Fucking gorgeous."

"One bit of bad news is that we might need to find another manager for The Blue Note. Bobby's wife wants to have him move to Australia, so she can be with her sister. Bobby does a good job at the club. It'll be a loss."

"Australia? It can't be that fuckin' great there. All the bloody Aussies want to come over here. Want me to give Bobby, or his wife, a slap and tell them to stay?"

Byron mulled over the option of his brother intervening — as it would prove an inconvenience finding the right new manager and revenues at the club would dip. But he decided against it. They needed to start running their empire like businessmen rather than thugs, he told himself.

"No, Bobby can go. He's been loyal and hardworking, as much as it seems he's under the thumb of his wife. Our loss can be Australia's gain."

Their driver, Jason, braked suddenly. He spat out a curse at a cyclist and then apologised to his employers.

"Don't worry. The cyclist cunt jumped the light. He's probably late for a meeting with some tofu. Prick!" George Parker exclaimed. He planned to open the window and knock the skinny faggot off his overpriced bike should the car catch up with him.

Byron Parker rolled his eyes and pressed his lips together in mild frustration, preventing him from swearing and sounding like his brother, as the sudden jolt made him misspell a word in the email he was composing to his stockbroker. The traffic was beginning to snarl up, as they headed down Charing Cross Road, towards Shaftesbury Avenue and the Century

Club where they were due to have a meeting with the actor, Connor Earle. Connor had been described as a "poor man's Ray Winstone and even poorer man's Michael Caine". Earle was an old school friend of the brothers and had set up a meeting with them in order to discuss a business opportunity. He wanted George and Byron to invest in a gangster movie he was intending to produce. He would give them a credit as producers and the investment could be written off against tax. Byron would tell the actor that he would consider the offer (with every intention of not investing a penny). However, it was worth having a short meeting with the scrounging actor. Earle was friends with a number of the cast of EastEnders and other people in the media. He could push more product out to them.

They can kill even more of the few brain cells they have left between their ears.

Byron craved a coffee, the drug of his choice. He noticed how his brother was increasingly fidgety – and sniffed repeatedly. He was craving something other than coffee. Byron failed to mention the plastic envelope of coke beneath the heel of his left shoe. Instead he gazed out of the window and watched the world go by. A stream of shoppers, tourists, workers and others — most with their heads buried in the screens of their smartphones — snaked up and down the streets. Byron noticed a fair few elderly businessmen turn off to head towards Soho. More than one might be heading to a brothel that he owned.

London was a din of iniquity.

Everyone was a sinner or customer.

Business is good.

10.

Oliver Porter answered Byron Parker's phone call and told him that he would be happy to take on the additional contract. He also agreed to his fee being paid in cash after the job was completed.

"I'll be paying even less tax on the money than if it went into my Cayman's account. My associate may not be keen on joining us when we meet but I'll speak to him. I just wouldn't want to make any promises. Also, let me take you out to dinner in January. Come to the Garrick and I can introduce you to some people who will support your membership bid."

Byron Parker offered up a laugh in response to Porter's joke about tax and accepted his invitation to dinner — all the time believing that he was talking to a dead man. But for all intents and purposes it was business as usual.

Porter pressed the button and ended the call. Lying came as easily as breathing to the two men. But in truth most people, most of the time, lie to themselves or others. It was the human thing do so.

Never work with children, animals or gangsters.

The fixer exhaled, puffing out his cheeks, and slumped down on the bench where he was sitting. Porter became the most world-weary person in view. For once he hoped that he would be proved wrong in his calculations — in his pessimism — but the Parker brothers intended to betray and murder him. He felt deflated but through an act of habit his body and mind became taut again. The blood returned to his face, as if he were a fresh-faced officer again receiving his first important order. As troubling as the news was that the Parker brothers wished to kill him he was consoled by the argument that they had no idea that he had every intention of killing them.

Porter sat on a bench in St James' Park and waited for Devlin. A number of shopping bags sat next to him from the likes of Hamleys, Boodles and Hatchards. Peace offerings for his wife and children. Porter had promised them he would be at home for the next three weeks —— and he had broken his word. He pictured again how his wife had pursed her lips in response to hearing the news. "I hope it's a matter of life and death," she had said, after taking a breath, with little humour in her voice. Yet she walked out of the room. There were no protests or histrionics. There was no point in trying to question him on his reasons for travelling back to the capital.

The silence had been deafening as his wife drove him to the train station that morning. Most of their silences were comfortable but this one wasn't. But she had still kissed him goodbye and lovingly said "take care". Marriages survive by leaving some things unsaid, rather than said, Porter philosophically thought to himself.

The cold wind chilled Porter's scalp, cutting across it like a razor blade made of ice. The sensation prompted Porter to remember the advert, for hair transplants, he had glanced at in *The Spectator* the previous week. The procedure had worked wonders for Wayne Rooney, the ad pronounced. For a second or two the balding Porter was tempted to check out the company online. But he smiled to himself rather than tapped the name into the browser on his phone. What would be the point of the act of vanity? Would he be doing it to attract a mistress which he had no intention of procuring? And Victoria would love him in the same way, regardless of the state of his hairline. As Porter thought of his wife though he was gripped by a sense of terror, rather than fondness. A shrapnel of despair lodged itself into his breast as he imagined George and Byron Parker driving through the gates of his house. Porter pictured his wife and children and realised that he had everything to lose. The former soldier didn't want to admit it to anyone, least of all himself, but he was scared. The even cadence of his heart and breathing became discordant, as if someone had swapped all the white keys with the black on a piano. His expression, for a brief moment, became contorted. *A secret life can only remain secret for so long. The truth will always out.* The dark, vile, polluted world of his work life cast a shadow over the veritable paradise of his life at home.

Devlin walked towards his associate, his expression seemingly frozen in the gelid air. The two men had often met at the park. The bench was reasonably secluded and one only needed to turn one's head slightly to catch a view of Buckingham Palace. The two patriotic soldiers had served the crown rather than self-serving politicians. Their hearts swelled in their chests that little bit more at seeing the Union Jack rippling in the breeze on top of the palace.

If Porter wanted him to do another job then Devlin would hear him out, but he would probably turn him down. He didn't need the money and he felt perpetually tired (but still a good night's sleep proved elusive). He certainly wouldn't work on Christmas Day. In a small nod towards some remnants of religion and faith Devlin believed that the twenty-fifth should be given up to God in some way. It would feel too wrong to take someone's life on Christmas Day.

"You're looking well, Michael," Porter remarked, in a spirit of politeness more than honesty, as he shook his old friend's hand. But Devlin immediately recognised that something was wrong. His palm was moist and the lustre in his eye, which could shine in the face of an abhorrent world, was missing.

Devlin was tempted to reply that his liver had been getting plenty of exercise this month. But he decided against it. He remained silent, hoping that it would prove a prompt for Porter to get down to business quickly.

"I have some good news and bad news. The bad news is that the Parker brothers want to kill me. They're only human, some might say. You may have seen the news. Virginia Pound made a statement, implying that she has evidence to suggest that her husband wasn't just the victim of street crime. The brothers are worried that they could be exposed. They consider me — and you — to be loose ends they need to tie up. What is the world coming to when you can't even trust a pair of vicious gangsters?"

Devlin listened on impassively, although he could not help but notice the anxiety which crept into Porter's voice, ousting out his normal jocose disposition.

"And the good news?" Devlin asked, his voice low and neutral.

"The good news is that the Parker brothers think I'm unaware of their intentions — and that I'm not willing and able to kill them first. I'll be doing the world a favour by wiping away their blight. George Parker is little more than an animal. He should have been put down, or at least neutered, years ago. And Byron Parker's sole virtue is that he isn't his brother. When their lights go out the world will be a brighter place. There are poppy growing warlords in Helmand with more scruples that those cretins. I'm worried for my family more than me. They should not have to pay for my sins. I need you to do the deed. You're the best man I've got. I'll pay whatever sum you want. You could make enough to retire. The contract will be for both of them — and it won't be a case of two for the price of one. Seven grams of lead, times two, will solve our problems. The good news is that they spend plenty of time together. Although they will also have bodyguards. I am having an associate hack Scotland Yard for their file. I can provide you with some more intelligence this evening. I am usually the person who fixes things, who is owed a favour. But I now need to ask for one. And I need you to let me know now, either way, whether you can do it. I only have a small window of opportunity. There will be no hard feelings if you want to turn the job down."

Despite the cold a few beads of sweat had formed on Porter's temples. Devlin had never seen the former Guards officer scared or vulnerable before. Porter resented himself for having to nigh on beg someone else to solve problems of his own making. But needs must.

Devlin stared out across the park. Bone dry, withered leaves scraped along the asphalt path. A hotdog vender warmed his hands from the steam coming off his cart. Shoppers walked through the park briskly, looking to get home or out of the cold. Lovers walked hand in hand, more slowly. The gentle clip-clop of horses could be heard in the background.

They don't quite sound like the Four Horseman of the Apocalypse.

Devlin briefly thought how he could disappear. He would be leaving behind next to nothing and he had next to nothing to take with him. The Parker brothers would have more chance of finding Lord Lucan. Porter had dug his own grave. The fixer could fix things himself. He could ask another shooter on his books or, if things became truly desperate, he owned more than one gun himself. But...

I know what I have to do. You wouldn't think much of me if I abandoned a friend in his hour of need. Even if I fail I'll succeed. Because I could be seeing you again soon.

"I'll do it. And you won't have to pay me. Think of it as my Christmas present to you," Devlin said, his brain already ruminating on the possible location of the hit. Killing had not quite become as easy as breathing for the assassin, but the list was growing longer in regards to things which seemed more difficult.

Porter breathed out and his expression softened in gratitude and relief. He closed his eyes and clasped his friend's forearm, offering up a silent prayer of thanks. He Porter made a silent promise — which time might erase the sovereignty of — that he would not be fix any more contracts involving innocent or good men.

I'm saved.

"You're making me feel somewhat deficient. I've only bought you some cufflinks in return. I'd like to invite you over for Christmas though, if you don't have any other plans. I'm sure that you have spent far too many Christmas Days on your own, over the past five years. If your culinary skills are as good as mine then Christmas dinner will be thoroughly unpleasant. I've just ordered a goose that could feed a brigade. I'd welcome a drinking companion, who has no desire to watch Strictly Come Dancing. You could travel down on the twenty fourth and attend midnight mass with us, at our local church, if you want. Or perhaps we should spend time in the confessional — although if the two of us were to confess our sins we might still be there on Boxing Day, or Shrove Tuesday even. You will turn the heads of a few of the young, available women — and ones that are married — in the village too. What do you say?"

The clip-clop of horses grew louder as a brace of attractive horsewomen approached, dressed in riding breeches and scarlet jackets. One looked like Kate Beckinsale and the other resembled a young Julie Christie. Sometimes Devlin's promise to Holly and God was hard to keep.

Devlin was going to reply that he couldn't be sure he'd be free on Christmas Day, as he might well be dead or serving at Her Majesty's pleasure. But he didn't.

"Let me get back to you soon, when I know my plans," he said, committed to being non-committal.

"That's fine. Nice fillies," Porter exclaimed, as the horsewomen rode by.

Devlin wryly smiled to himself. He knew his friend was complimenting the shiny-coated mares rather than the two comely riders. Devlin had never known Porter to even look at another woman in the time he had known him, let alone have an affair. As much as he sometimes reminded Devlin of a modern day Harry Lime he was a good husband and father.

He's worth saving. I'm just not sure I am.

11.

Fields, buildings and skeletal trees passed by in a blur —
and not just because Porter had consumed a bottle of Chianti
at the Athenaeum after meeting Devlin. He was now on the
train home, being gently rocked from side to side as if he
were in the cradle again. Yet he sat in his First Class seat
uncomfortably. Any man who communes with his conscience
or thinks about death shouldn't feel at peace. For a moment
or two the fixer felt dizzy, nauseous, by the fate which hung
across his shoulders like a milkmaid's yoke. Life was a blur.
All he wanted to do was get home to his family, curl up on
the sofa with his wife and experience the light in his
children's eyes when they opened their presents. Contentment
is so much better than happiness.

He pitied Devlin. He would go home to a black hole, where
his wife and unborn children were, at best, spectres. Five
years ago Porter had invited his operative over for Christmas
out of a fear that the recent widower might put try to put a
bullet through his skull and, as much as Devlin was an
admirer of Joseph Conrad, the assassin wouldn't miss unlike
the melancholy novelist. Five years. So little and so much had
changed, for both of them. One could be forgiven for thinking
that the soldier's grief was unnatural or unmanly. Porter once
mentioned to Devlin how Holly would have wanted him to
get on with his life, find someone else. Devlin vaguely
nodded in agreement but Porter's words fell on deaf ears.
Fathoming the soldier's grief, or love, for his late wife was as
difficult as getting blood out of a stone.

Porter had recently woken from a dream, having dozed off shortly after the train left the station. The dream was thoroughly restrained, English and mundane — up to a point. He and his family stood in the passageway by the door, waiting for Devlin to arrive on Christmas day. His wife was wearing her favourite lilac dress. Porter spoke of the soldier's heroic acts in Afghanistan. He told his children that for every classic novel they had read Devlin had read ten — or twenty — more. "He is Meursault, Sharpe and Homer's Hector all rolled into one," Porter remarked in the dream. He also wanted to tell his wife that Devlin had been their guardian — or avenging — angel who had saved them all. But some things must still be kept secret, even in the realm of dreams. And so they waited for him to arrive. And waited. It began to snow heavily outside. The goose sat on the table, and loomed even larger for the fact that Devlin might not eat his share. His children began to complain that they were hungry. His youngest son shivered. "He'll turn up," Porter assured his family more than once. "He's a good man, the best man I know." There was, finally, a knock on the door. The snow stopped falling, his son ceased to shiver. All would be well. But instead of the stoical features of his friend Porter was met by a gnashing George Parker when he opened the door. His demonic eyes were ablaze with violence and cocaine. Stalactites of drool hung down from his mouth, like fangs. He was carrying a meat cleaver. Byron Parker stood behind his brother, fastidiously filing his nails. A picture of cold insouciance. All was lost. Porter woke up with a jolt, just as the meat clever buried itself into his sternum.

Devlin.

The name was tantamount to a prayer. He was the best man that he knew, Porter realised, but that might have had something to do with the company he kept. Devlin was worth a thousand members of the Bullingdon Club.

As Porter watched a man in ill-fitting blue overalls fill up a vending machine at Slough train station he vowed that he would change his ways if Devlin succeeded. Porter had told himself over the years that he was making a difference in the world by accepting certain contracts. But he knew that the only difference he was making was to his bank account. Porter shuddered — and loathed himself — thinking of the similarities he shared with the reptilian Byron Parker.

For years Porter had told himself that he needed to make money, through honest means or otherwise, to provide for his family. The ends justified the means. But he had enjoyed his work too much.

The wheels beneath him screeched along the track as the train left the station. His ears were soon assaulted, however, by a far more unwelcome sound — that of conversation. Three young women, with outfits as loud as their voices, had come into his First Class carriage. One of them put her muddy, Nike-emblazoned feet on the seat opposite to them. Another chewed gum and tapped so incessantly on her phone that Porter wondered how her fingers had not been worn down to mere stumps. He prayed for a ticket inspector to deliver him and point them in the direction of their correct carriage. Porter turned his head to take in the increasingly green scenery but still had to suffer the sound of them. He winced every time they laughed or yelped. He wanted the earth to swallow him — or preferably them — up as they each went through who they'd like to see enter "the jungle" for some ghastly TV programme which pitted vulgar celebrities against each other. When one of the trio of slatterns commenced to talk about the new photos they had uploaded onto something called "Instagram" Porter wryly implored God to return him to his dream.

***

"He sees you when you're sleeping
He knows when you're awake
He knows if you've been bad or good
So be good for goodness sake."

Devlin listened to Bruce Springsteen and a number of other artists with Christmas songs. Cigarette smoke filled the room. Devin was tempted to try and root out Holly's old iPod. She had a couple of playlists devoted to carols, hymns and Christmas hits, which she had played throughout the year. "It's good to feel Christmassy on other days of the year. Although I'm not sure how many people feel Christmassy on any day of the year," his wife had once remarked, her voice tinged with ruefulness rather than anger.

Devlin finished off writing an email to his accountant, listing some instructions for if anything should happen to him. He had also emailed his lawyer. His foster parents would receive the bulk of his estate when he died. He regretted not seeing them. But there wasn't time. He wanted to say goodbye to them, thank them, but without them getting an inkling that he might be seeing them for the last time. He felt guilty — and his money would not wholly compensate for the time he should have spent with them over the years. But there were lots of things — too many things — Devlin had cause to feel guilty about. They were strewn out along his life like beads upon a rosary.

As soon as he got home Porter forwarded on all intelligence he had on the Parker brothers. Scotland Yard were, ironically, an accomplice to murder — such was the wealth of information in the files that the hacker had stolen. The brothers had been subject to police surveillance on more than once occasion, and thankfully their routine seldom changed. Devlin had lots to plan in just one night. The location and timing of the hit would be key. Most of their day was spent travelling around central London. The amount of cameras — and people — littering the streets ruled out a hit in the likes of Shoreditch or Soho. Devlin had enough weighing on his conscience without shooting innocent bystanders. If nothing else it would be unprofessional and inefficient to injure someone in a crossfire. He was also wary of entering their houses to carry out the job. Not only did both men have families but he couldn't be sure who else could be armed and frequenting the sites. Porter was right in that he needed to find a moment to hit both men together. Given that the brothers would be accompanied by their two bodyguards that would mean four hits at one time. Normally Devlin would avoid such a scenario. There were too many variables. The odds were greater on getting away clean. All would be armed, except for perhaps Byron Parker (so plan things as if he would be armed). Fail to prepare, prepare to fail, the soldier in him stolidly remarked.

Aware that he might have to carry out the job the following day, Devlin sipped his whisky. What with not knowing if he would see Christmas in the flat he had opened the bottle of McClelland's. His ashtray was full by the time he decided on his plan of attack.

At the end of each day, at approximately 6pm, Byron Parker was dropped off at his house in Chislehurst, before the car then took his elder brother to his nearby home. The property was gated and there would be a small but significant window of opportunity. The police report was sufficiently detailed enough to note the type of gate and security system and, after some research over the internet, Devlin worked out the timings. Fortunately there was a small park at the location where Devlin could wait and view the car from afar as it came down the street the house was situated on. The report also noted that their vehicle was not bullet-proofed – and that there was an absence of CCTV cameras at the entrance to the drive.

Devlin spent the next hour committing a map of the surrounding area, where the hit would take place, to memory. He needed an element of good fortune for the street to be empty when he approached the car but otherwise the plan was sound.

The wind howled outside. A few revellers could be heard, singing and wending their way through the square below. The soldier cleaned and oiled his gun, a SIG-Sauer P226, before picking out a book for some late night reading. Devlin thought to himself it may well be the last book he would ever read. He wanted it to be special — and needed it to be relatively short in order to finish it in time. He thought about reading some Chekhov or Camus but he picked out a well-thumbed copy of *The Great Gatsby* to take to bed with him. The novel had been the first book he and Holly had read together as a couple.

12.

Although he could not find the time to travel to his foster parent's care home Devlin ordered a cab the following morning to take him to Garrett Lane cemetery. Before the taxi arrived he popped into the florists. Out of habit and superstition Devlin wanted to pick up another fresh bouquet of lilies. And he also wanted to see Emma. There was a small hole inside him that only she could fill. Her loveliness was a balm. He owed Emma an explanation, a thank you or a goodbye. Devlin rehearsed a few sentences beforehand as he was putting on his grey suit. But some sentences — or sentiments — which seem fine when voiced by the soul are too naïve or brittle to live in the outside world. It's sometimes best that they remain stuck in the throat. When he entered the shop to discover Emma was absent (her part-time assistant, Molly, was looking after things) Devlin felt the butterflies in his stomach expire. He felt the chill December wind on his face and a presentiment that he would never see his good Catholic girl once more. God had somehow cheated him out of saying goodbye to another loved one. Because today might be his last day on earth.

But what of heaven? And hell? As he stood before his wife's grave Devlin believed that he could endure the latter, knowing that Holly was experiencing the former. But he had faith he would see her again, otherwise his life would have been for nothing. During his youth and time as a soldier Devlin considered God to be a cruel or indifferent deity, an abusive or absent father. Most of the time Devlin could laugh along at the joke of life, but in his heart of hearts Devlin knew that God embodied love and forgiveness.

Devlin raised a corner of his mouth, in a gesture towards the tiniest of grins, when he remembered his favourite Churchill quote: *"If you're going through hell, keep going."*

The widower again pulled up any weeds around the grave and also removed a few stray cigarette butts. He bowed his head in remembrance whilst turning his wedding ring, as if screwing something in or out. With each turn his soul seemed to stretch out even more, like he was being tortured upon the rack by the Inquisition.

Devlin turned his stony face up towards the sky. Anyone observing the solitary figure before the grave might have thought he was imploring God. But Devlin had communed enough with God for three lifetimes. In truth he was merely assessing the weather. The forecast was, thankfully, for clear skies later. The temperature would be mild for the time of the year. His heart could afford to be numb but his hands and fingers couldn't be. It would be another fine night for killing.

Many men, from killers to martyrs, often dream of fame after death — as if fame could be equated to eternal life. They imagine the news reports, church services, tweets or obituary pages. But when Devlin thought of his death he didn't want to be mourned, celebrated or even remembered.

I just want to see you again.

***

Oliver Porter's office was one of the most secure and attractively furnished "sheds" in the country. A back massager was seated on top of a black leather Eames lounge chair. Other pieces of furniture were made from the finest mahogany and English oak, including a bookcase containing a complete set of Loeb classics. The "home from home", as

Porter sometimes described the out building, was also filled with items from foreign countries he had visited: rugs from Iraq and Afghanistan covered the floor; his coasters were from the famous Armenian pottery shop in Jerusalem; a Browning pistol, which had once belonged to Eisenhower, was mounted in a glass case; and an antique Russian icon of the Holy Mother hung next to the door. Occasionally, after imbibing a few drinks, Porter imagined that the figure in the artwork was staring at him disapprovingly. She was a mother scolding her naughty child. But at other times she appeared to be full of grace rather than condemnation. The office also contained a fridge, safe, Bausch and Lomb stereo and other essentials and luxuries. Accomplished copies of Grimshaw's *Reflections on the Thames* and Goya's portrait of the Duke of Wellington adorned one of the windows. The fixer promised himself that, one day, he would purchase a genuine Grimshaw landscape.

Wagner played in the background — but at a barely audible level. The television was on — but on mute. A steady stream of emails began to pile up on the laptop screen. Many involved invitations to lunch or Christmas drinks. But, unless he was summoned by the Queen or Palmerston, he would politely decline them all.

Porter sat at his desk with his fully charged mobile phone in front of him. Devlin had sent him a message saying that he was intending to carry out the job today. More than anyone else he knew Porter believed that Devlin would try and make good on his word. Yet, as much faith as he had in the former paratrooper, Porter also believed in having a plan B. Money and passports sat on the desk, next to his laptop and bronze busts of David Hume and Talleyrand. Should Devlin fail to carry out the hit properly Porter was ready to whisk his family away on a surprise holiday. He would also pay for a brace of other operatives to carry out hits on the Parker brothers. Money was no object. George and Byron Parker had to die.

But the hit would be difficult, even for a seasoned professional such as Devlin. He had little preparation time. The intelligence was good but still deficient. Four targets quadrupled the risk. When Porter briefed Devlin however he instructed the assassin to prioritise taking out the brothers: "Cut off the head and the snake will die."

Porter briefly ruminated on the scenario of Devlin succeeding in killing his enemies but being apprehended by the police. He knew the soldier could be trusted not to betray him. The police couldn't threaten or bribe him. How can you condemn someone who has already condemned himself? No man is an island but the soldier came close. Michael Devlin would be able to endure a prison sentence, so long as he had enough books to read, Porter half-jokingly mused. He was a man who could be bound in a nutshell and consider himself a king of infinite space.

The fixer poured himself another small measure of Laphroaig and thought once more about how thoroughly unpleasant the world was. The single malt shone like honey in the midday sun. He recalled a line from Graham Greene, which Devlin had once quoted to him whilst raising his glass in a toast:

"*Whisky – the medicine of despair.*"

***

Devlin felt a small twinge of guilt as he came down into the foyer of his apartment building. It was time to go to work. The smart reception area to the building was an amalgamation of polished oak and marble. He nodded to

Derek, the friendly and efficient Pakistani concierge, and realised that he should have got him a Christmas present or end of year tip.

It might now be too late.

The thought was soon swotted away. As Devlin was leaving Emma came into the building, carrying various bags of shopping. Her cheeks were a little flushed. She was wearing a woollen jumper with a colourful Christmas design on it that one of her customers had knitted for her. Devlin noticed Emma was wearing a touch more lipstick than usual. It made her smile wider and more luscious, although perhaps she was also smiling more for seeing him.

Devlin was wearing a padded blue Barbour coat over his grey suit. He was also now wearing his black Sig Sauer P226 beneath his suit jacket, in a shoulder holster. The suppressor sat in his right coat pocket. A copy of *The Great Gatsby* hung out of the left. The pistol was powerful, compact and reliable. People had let him down over the years but the Sig Sauer never did. Devlin had been given the weapon as a present by a US special forces operative in Helmand, after the two men had spent a long, boozy night talking about guns, Hemingway and Ulysses S. Grant. The pistol was the chief tool of his trade and had never let him down. Devlin fancied that, should he ever be stranded on a desert island, it would be the third item he would take with him, alongside a copy of the Bible and the complete works of Shakespeare.

When Emma had first seen Devlin there was a flintiness to his expression. But when he saw her the scowl immediately fell from his face. Wistfulness now shaped his countenance. Emma simultaneously thought how much she liked him and also how much she didn't know him. So much of Michael was below the surface.

"Molly mentioned that you came into the shop this morning. Sorry I missed you. I'm glad I caught you now though. I wanted to say goodbye and happy Christmas. My plans have changed and I'm heading back to Somerset today," Emma said, wishing that she was wearing something more flattering than her festive jumper.

For a moment or two Devlin stood silently before her, entranced. The last time he had felt so nervous had been when he had asked Holly to marry him. He had faith she would say yes but dreaded she would say no. He had clutched the engagement ring's small box so hard that it dug into his hand. But he barely felt any pain. When she said yes his heart had leapt up to the heavens.

The gun weighed heavy on Devlin's shoulder. He wanted a drink. He forced a smile and fingered his wedding ring.

"I'm glad I've caught you too. There's something I wanted to speak to you about."

After missing Emma that morning Devlin had promised himself that, if he saw the florist again, he would offer up his last confession to her. If she knew about his vow to God and Holly then she might understand why he couldn't give himself to her. If she knew what he did for a living then she might be repulsed by him and go to the police — punish him for his crimes. He admired her. He maybe even loved her, as a friend. But love cannot endure the real world for too long. The air that we breathe seems to poison it. Love may even be a complete myth. The existence of love can only be taken on faith.

Devlin shuffled his feet slightly as if he wanted to set himself — or prepare to run away. Emma was one of the kindest souls he had ever known. He suddenly thought how she reminded him of Tolstoy's Natasha Rostova. But was he

Andrei or Pierre? He thought, for a splinter of a second, how she could forgive and understand him. Love him. If she consoled him then he might not want to ever leave. But work — duty — called.

"What is it?" Emma said, her voice imbued with more concern than curiosity. She lightly placed her fingertips on his forearm.

"It's nothing. It can wait until January. Sorry, I've got to go. Have a nice Christmas too, Emma."

Devlin quickly kissed her on the cheek and briskly walked out the door. Although he had brushed his lips against her cheek Emma still felt the tingle of when he had kissed her on the lips, all those months ago. She had noticed the copy of *The Great Gatsby* in Devlin's pocket. She wanted to quote from the novel, to let him know that he was special and meant something to her.

"You're worth the whole damn bunch put together."

But the moment was gone. Some things are not meant to be.

13.

As Devlin wended his way through London in the back of the taxi some of the sights prompted memories (of childhood, drinking holes and courting Holly). Some were good and some were bad. He was unsure whether he would miss the capital or not.

Devlin got out of the cab around a mile from his intended destination. He walked with his head hung down as if he were playing a game of avoiding the cracks on the pavement. Finally he came to the small park, which overlooked the entrance to George Parker's house in Chislehurst. The property was valued at eight million pounds, but anyone buying the house, with any semblance of taste, would have wanted to substantially redecorate it.

Thankfully the park bench that offered the best view of the road leading up to Parker's home was free. Devlin pulled his scarf up to partially cover his face and sat down and read. Night had fallen like a veil, but there was ample street lighting. The shortest day of the year was fast approaching though, for Devlin, time dragged on. A few dog walkers and locals ghosted past yet no one seemed to take notice of him. There was nothing to notice. Devlin calculated the time it would take him to get up and un-assumedly walk towards the house. He believed he could do it in the time it would take the car to reach the gates (given the number of speed humps strewn across the street that the vehicle would have go over, slowly). The only potential variable which could ruin his plan would be the appearance of a passer-by. But so far the road and park were proving to be deathly quiet.

Usually, before a job, Devlin was too focused on the task to suffer any anxiety. But something out of kilter churned in his stomach. He had no qualms about ending the lives of the Parker brothers. Yet still the killer felt uneasy, like the time when he took his first confession. The priest didn't frighten him but the thought of God seeing all did. The boys Devlin knew who were older briefed him on what he should confess to — or rather make-up. He didn't confess anything of importance to the priest that day but that night Devlin confessed to God. Guilt eclipsed any notion of absolution or redemption. Sin was real. No matter how much Nietzsche he read, God wasn't dead.

In between rehearsing the hit in his mind Devlin felt like a condemned man, due to climb the scaffold. He wryly smiled to himself as Chopin's funeral march played in his inner ear, as a soundtrack to his thoughts.

The readiness is all.

***

Byron Parker rolled his eyes. He had just finished talking to Connor Earle on the phone. Although Byron had been careful not to promise the actor anything Earle was behaving like the money was already in the bank. He talked enthusiastically about approaching Craig Fairbrass' agent. Maybe they could even convince Vinny Jones and Tamer Hassan to be in the movie. "They'll add class and bums on seats. I swear on my son's life, we're going to make a million each on this," Earle declared, high on hope — or a more chemical-based drug.

Byron also rolled his eyes on noticing the new tattoo on the back of Jason's neck, as the stolidly built bodyguard drove them home. As well as a strange Celtic symbol brandishing his large bicep — which various football players and popstars had a tattoo of too, believing the mark to be a source of virility or power — Jason had the word "Respect", in a Cyrillic font, written across the back of his neck.

Byron looked across and askance at his elder brother, sitting to the left of him in the metallic blue Porsche Cayenne. George Parker was asleep, although his mouth was still half open. The enforcer had had a long day — taking drugs, eating a long lunch and breaking the jaw of a gay Bulgarian pimp. Gentleman George boasted how he'd had a long night too, having taken one of his daughter's friends out to a club.

"I showed her a good time. I showed her an even better time afterwards, eh? I promised her a part in Connor's movie. Perhaps we should invest in the film after all."

Byron Parker did his best to tune out his brother's conversation and snoring. Despite not liking his elder sibling he was bound to love him. Together they were greater than the sum of their parts — an alloy, forged in the fires of brutality and efficiency. Each administered to the parts of their empire they were proficient at.

Byron continued to work his way through a few emails on his smartphone. He was keen to take care of all urgent business before Christmas. One piece of business was his desire to buy a number of flats in Elephant & Castle. Although the area was depressed at the moment he believed that, given its proximity to both the City and West End, any property he bought couldn't fail to appreciate in value. We need to think long-term, Byron Parker posited — as though he were Goebbels, believing in his own propaganda of building a thousand year Reich.

Byron took off his glasses and, extracting a small, pristine white cloth, cleaned the lenses. For a few seconds everything was a blur and he squinted like a child but then the world came sharply back into focus.

The car travelled over the first speed bump, at the top of the road leading to his brother's mock Tudor mansion. George Parker stirred, a bear waking up from sleeping through the winter. He rubbed his nose and sniffed, hoping to shake lose any vestiges of coke from his nostrils.

* * *

Devlin calmly stood up and slid the paperback book into his coat pocket. He had now nearly finished the novel, having read up to the part where George Wilson was about to shoot the eponymous hero. As he left the entrance to the park the assassin quickly retrieved his weapon and attached the suppressor. All the time the Porsche continued to draw closer, occasionally slowing to negotiate a speed bump. Devlin could make out that there were four people in the car.

Four targets. Thirteen rounds.

The road was deserted. Devlin was a gunfighter entering a one horse town. His gait was smooth but as he grew closer to the gates his footsteps grew heavier as if he were traveling to a funeral.

The Porsche braked before the large, black steel gates (which resembled two Rolls Royce Silver Shadow grills next to each other). Leighton — the Parker brothers' other bodyguard — retrieved the remote control from the glove compartment. Devlin timed his walk perfectly and stopped by the driver's side of the vehicle. George Parker briefly scrutinized the pedestrian but judged him to be a nobody. Byron Parker's gaze fixated on the small scar above Devlin's eye.

Devlin raised his arm, mechanically and purposefully. His features were relaxed, free from enmity. His moral switch was off — or on, given his targets. The assassin took out the driver first. Two shots zipped through the window, entered the side of Jason's right breast and scythed through his heart and lungs. He was dead before he knew it. Although the sounds of the suppressed shot and thud as the bullets hit their mark were not music to Devlin's ears there was still something familiar, natural and pleasing about the noise. It meant that someone had been killed and he was still alive.

Byron Parker's hand reached out and clasped his brother's knee, but the rest of his body froze in terror. His last thoughts were for his wife and children. It looked like he might die of fright. But instead Byron Parker died from two nine millimetre parabellum piercing his chest. Blood began to stain his white shirt immediately, as if someone had already placed two red roses on the dead body.

The bodyguard in the passenger seat pulled out a Glock 18. Leighton fired off a curse rather than a round however as he forgot to switch the safety off. The sight of his dead friend in the driver's seat also gave him pause. But Devlin paused not. The first bullet entered the bodyguard's sternum, the second blew away half his neck. Gore splashed against the window behind him. The tintinnabulation of awful dance music could still be heard pouring out from his headphones but Leighton was no longer listening.

A faint smell of blood and cordite filled the air.

One target. Seven rounds.

In order to gain a workable line of sight for his final victim the assassin moved a couple of steps towards the passenger end of the Porsche. But it was Devlin's turn to pause as he found himself staring down the barrel of a chrome-finished Browning pistol. George Parker was just in the process of turning the safety off. As enraged as the gangster was he was also, largely, keeping his head. This wasn't his first gunfight and he didn't want it to be his last. A ringed finger curled around the Browning Hi-Power's trigger.

Devlin refrained from firing his own weapon. Time moved quickly and slowly. Death will compel a man to commune with God. Devlin was resigned to his fate. He would allow George Parker to shoot first. If he died, he died. But should his opponent fire and miss then Devlin believed it would be a sign from God — and Holly — that they wanted him to live. He would be allowed to turn the page. He needed a new covenant to live by. It was absurd but true.

Devlin lowered his gun slightly as George Parker raised his. The gangster couldn't miss. His snarl morphed into a triumphant smirk. Blood from the black bodyguard's neck freckled his face. George licked his lips, enjoying the taste as much as cocaine. But just as he was about to fire his weapon his brother's body slumped forward, onto his arm, and ruined his aim. Perhaps it was an act of God. Perhaps, in his dying moments, Byron Parker deliberately leaned forward. He and his brother had been inseparable for so long, Byron didn't want to go to heaven — or hell — alone. Byron wouldn't want to see his brother survive him and inherit their criminal empire.

"Holly," the widower said softly – but yearningly.

Devlin uttered the word like a prayer. If his final thought in this world was for his wife then she would be the first thing he would see in the next. *Have faith*. Devlin heard the sound of the gun. His eyes were closed. He was expectant more than fearful. He prepared himself to be consumed by darkness or light. But damnation or deliverance failed to arrive. The gangster's bullet struck the inside of the car door.

Whether God had spoken to him or not a survival or killer instinct kicked in again, fitting like a key to a lock. Just as George Parker was about to take his second shot Devlin swiftly moved his own gun into position and emptied the magazine into his target. The Sig Sauer became an extension of his arm, the dark part of his soul. The semi-automatic was a marriage of precision and power — a marriage immune from divorce. Sometimes a gun will fire a man, given its weight and the force of its recoil. But Devlin was in full control of his actions when he shot George Parker. Parker deserved to die.

The contract killer removed the suppressor, holstered his gun, breathed out and surveyed the scene. The street was still deserted. As much as adrenalin coursed through his body he felt a sense of peace wash over his heart.

Devlin pulled out a small Turkish flag from his pocket and tossed it into the back of the vehicle. The flag was a calling card for an increasingly ambitious Turkish crime syndicate who were looking to expand their powerbase in the capital. It wouldn't do any harm for the remnants of the Parker family and the police to focus their response to the shooting on the Turks.

The temperature dropped but the soldier didn't feel cold. The stars seemed dull, as if the angels had failed to polish them for a while, but they still shone in the velvety firmament. Michal Devlin lit a cigarette, walked back through the park and hailed down a black cab to take him back to Rotherhithe.

Job done.

14.

Oliver Porter looked positively Churchill-like. He puffed on his cigar with one hand and nursed a brandy in the other as he sat, slumped, in his gazebo, having recently finished his Christmas dinner. It had been a long, calorific day. His family had exhausted him, but in a good way. A heater hummed in the background, glowing like the embers of dusk. A gust of wind blew through two silver birch trees, which flanked the elegant, oak gazebo.

Michael Devlin sat next to him, his Christmas party hat still comically askew on his head. He sipped upon a Bushmills and breathed in the cigar smoke in compensation for only now smoking one cigarette an hour. Devlin had travelled down to visit Porter and his family on Christmas Eve. A few drinks on arrival had emboldened him to attend midnight mass. He felt slightly nervous entering the church. Perhaps he had too many memories of dull, overlong sermons in the cold on uncomfortable pews. Sometimes things can get too Catholic. Or he was scared that God and Holly would be present - and grief and despair would take hold of him, trap his heart in a vice. But his fears were unfounded. There was mulled wine, a warm atmosphere and plenty of hymns and carols. Porter introduced his friend to more than one young woman, a slightly older divorcee. Devlin even found himself singing at one point.

Christmas Day had been enjoyable. Porter and his family were welcoming and fun. He occasionally held court as he told some (sanitised) war stories. Occasionally the widower experienced shooting pains, as if he were suffering pangs of angina or gout, as Devlin thought of how in another world he could be have been spending Christmas with Holly and their family in a similarly beautiful house in the country. But that was another world…

"I understand your decision to take a break from things for a while although I hope you don't disappear for too long," Porter remarked, as he swirled the remainder of his brandy around in his glass. The fixer was worried about his friend's state of mind - as well as his own business. There were plenty more politicians who needed a bullet in the head, he darkly or amusedly thought to himself. "Call it what you will – a bonus or sabbatical pay – but I've taken the liberty of depositing some money into your account. Treat yourself. Meet someone. Marriage might compel you to come back to work sooner, as you'll want to get out of the house. Even more so, though divorce will compel you to come back to work, as you'll need the money."

"I'm not sure what my plans are for tomorrow yet, let alone the next six months or so. Man plans, God laughs," Devlin replied, not committing himself to returning to work either way. Death had stalked him enough - or he had stalked death - for more than one lifetime. "You'll be pleased to hear that I've met someone though."

Devlin smiled as he thought of Emma. His expression softened – and not just because of the drink.

"Really? I'm intrigued. Tell me more, if you don't mind me asking."

"She's a good Catholic girl, for my sins …"

Devlin planned to ask Emma out on a real date. He wanted to be back in London with her. Back in the land of the living.

Darkness Visible

Thomas Waugh

"The past isn't dead. It isn't even past ."
William Faulkner.

"If you have a soul you can't be satisfied ."
Graham Greene.

1.

Helmand. 2006.

The sweltering, saffron sun threw beams of light along the narrow streets of the ramshackle Afghan village. Michael Devlin moved forward, his gun raised, flanked by two other members of his squad from 3 Para: John Birch and Christopher Connelly.

The two-dozen strong patrol, riding in a convoy of Snatch Land Rovers, had been heading back to their forward base when a voice came over the radio. There had been reports of shots fired from a nearby settlement. The squad needed to check the area. As the radio went silent again an air of trepidation and frustration inserted itself, like a noxious gas, into the vehicles. The soldiers knew that routine patrols could prove anything but routine.

"Fuck," John Birch, a flame-haired squaddie from Ashford in Kent exclaimed, banging the butt of his rifle on the floor. "God knows what we'll be heading into now. Military intelligence. What a fucking oxymoron. We could be driving into an ambush, with half the Taliban in the region waiting to greet us. Or it could just be some dippy teen has got his hands on a Kalashnikov for the first time - and he's fired off a few rounds. And there I was looking forward to "steak night" back at the base. Those greedy bastards already there will probably wolf all the good cuts down before we get back. I'll be left with a piece of meat tougher than an old shoe. It'll still taste better than my girlfriend's cooking though, I expect," the squaddie joked, grinning at anyone who was listening.

Devlin noticed that when his friend smiled his face became rounder, almost cherubim-like.

Christopher Connelly forced a smile in reply. The gangly nineteen-year-old was only six months into his first tour. He had partly joined the army to learn a trade. Jobs and training were in short supply in his hometown of Northampton. His plan was to keep his head down, follow orders and become an apprentice mechanic. Once he was trained up he would leave the army and go into partnership with his uncle to buy a small garage. They'd even picked out a potential site for the business, underneath the arches near his parents' house. Connelly took a sip and then several gulps of water from his canteen. He was looking forward to getting back to the base too, having arranged with his fiancé to chat over the internet. He also wanted to write another letter to his parents, assuring them that all was well.

Whilst a number of soldiers rolled their eyes or cursed in response to their new orders Michael Devlin's expression remained unchanged, save for a slight narrowing of his already pillbox-like eyes. Devlin's countenance, varnished by the sun, was lean and hard. Some might have viewed the paratrooper and considered that life had worn him down. Others would have judged that everything was just water off a duck's back for the philosophical, or fatalistic, soldier. Whilst other squaddies played video games or chatted on Facebook, Devlin could often be found with his head in a book. He enjoyed a drink as much as the next man (or perhaps even more so), but during periods of sobriety he often kept himself to himself. But although few would claim to have known Devlin, or to have warmed to him, everyone welcomed his presence on a patrol. He had more verified kills than any other soldier in the battalion. On more than one occasion he had taken the fight to the enemy and pulled the squad out of a hole. Devlin was good at his job. Killing.

Yet it had been more than a fortnight since the soldier had engaged the enemy in a firefight. Devlin was beginning to feel a dull ache in his stomach, or yearning to kill – as if he were a drunk who had gone too long without a drink.

The purring engines now growled into life, as the Land Rover gunned towards the target. Birch sensed the tension in the roasting vehicle and told a joke. More than one para closed his eyes and put on earphones, like a boxer closing himself off to the world before a fight.

The village shimmered in the distance, like a mirage. The commanding officer was Major James Hyde and the men duly congregated around him as they climbed out the vehicles on the outskirts of the settlement. The soldiers had visited the village a few months back, providing security for a bunch of DFID workers. All Oxbridge educated - entitled, frightened, nowhere near as clever as they thought they were and zealously good intentioned. But the road to hell, or Kabul, was paved with good intentions.

The village had seemed like a ghost town during their last visit. Most of the Afghans retreated into their houses when the soldiers arrived. The wiser heads among the villagers knew all too well that the British and Americans in Helmand would be but fleeting visitors to their country. Merely passing through. Once the war ended the Taliban would crawl out from under their rocks like cockroaches, or scorpions, and carry out reprisals against any collaborators.

Hyde issued his orders calmly and clearly. Four generations of military command ran through him, like writing through a stick of rock. His men were to watch for IEDS and sniper positions. They would sweep through the village in groups of three. Normal rules of engagement applied. The soldiers nodded, checked their weapons once more and spat out any gum. Safeties were off. Helmets were re-positioned and tightened. They were ready. A sense of professionalism began to oust a sense of trepidation. As people in the army often said and thought, *we are where we are.*

A thick, familiar film of sand and dust covered everything: buildings, windows, clothes and skin. Birch had recently found himself having a drink with a foreign correspondent, who called the phenomenon "the patina of Afghanistan." The para scrunched up his face, in confusion and contempt, and called it "sand and dust." After several bouts of virtue signalling, claiming that the "ordinary people of Afghanistan were some of the nicest and most peaceful souls on earth," the correspondent finally invited the soldier to speak, rather than just listen. Birch shrugged his shoulders, gulped down the remainder of his beer, and remarked that "the only thing more hostile than the environment here are the people, ordinary or otherwise."

The sun stung rather than massaged the back of Devlin's neck as he moved stealthily forward. A few dirty grey clouds, dull next to the cornflower blue sky, crawled along, as slowly as a hearse. Devlin wasn't sure whether he could consider himself Catholic or not anymore, but he yearned for a God-sent plague to purge the land of wickedness. Of the Taliban and their ilk, who derived a sick pleasure in stoning homosexuals to death, mutilating female genitalia and slicing the lips and noses off those they judged to be friends of the infidels.

Goodness is just an idea. But evil exists in this world, as sure as the sun is in the sky.

As well as checking his fields of fire Devlin kept a watch on Connelly. The young man was jittery. British patrols had been ambushed in similar situations before. Sweat wended its way down his stubble-filled jaw. His head darted everywhere - searching for the enemy - but too fast and frantically to survey the scene properly. Devlin made sure the recent recruit's finger was off the trigger, lest he discharged his weapon by accident.

Birch uttered a curse underneath his breath, as another blister burst on the sole of his right foot.

Devlin noticed movement in a ground floor window to his left but it was just a child, staring wide-eyed at the strange looking soldiers. He was an island of innocence in an ocean of turpitude. His parents soon appeared at the window and ushered the boy away, avoiding the paratrooper's adamantine gaze.

Something was amiss. It was quiet. Too quiet. Devlin fancied that the squad were akin to a bunch of teenagers walking around a haunted house. Sooner or later something would happen. One of them would be attacked. Bullets could come out from nowhere – and everywhere – in Helmand.

Devlin held up his hand, signalling for Birch and Connolly to halt, when he spotted an old man standing in an alley. A wizened, leathery face was framed by a wispy grey beard and wiry black hair. A solitary front tooth hung down in his mouth. Birch and Connelly remained in the main street whilst Devlin approached the gnomic figure in the alleyway.

Off-white sheets of linen fluttered over them, strung out on a washing line between two houses. A long-tailed rat scurried towards an inviting pile of refuge. The paratrooper made a motion with his rifle for the Afghan to show and raise his hands. Rather than make a gesture of surrender however, the villager raised his twig-like arm and stretched out his bony forefinger.

"Bad men," he ominously croaked, jabbing his finger in the direction of the end of the street Birch and Connelly were stood on.

Connelly died instantly. The first bullet, whip-cracking through the air, tore half his face off. Further shots ensued. Some struck the plaster-covered buildings on either side of the street. Some spat out from the semi-automatic machine pistol and kicked-up tufts of dust. But a couple also hit the paratrooper in the legs, flooring Birch.

Devlin's radio crackled into life but he ignored it. Instead he sped towards the mouth of the alley and poked his head around the corner and quickly assessed the situation.

Connelly was beyond help. At the end of the street Devlin observed the gun-wielding Afghani. He was no older than thirty. Rather than wearing the traditional garb of the Taliban his enemy was dressed in a pea-green polo shirt, cream trousers and expensive loafers. His black beard was neatly trimmed. Glossy black curls hung down, parting in the middle of his forehead. His build was slight, serpentine. His bloodshot eyes were stapled wide with violence and narcotics. Yet his enemy was not so out of control that he wasn't conscious of the need to retreat. Soon other soldiers would descend upon his position. The well-dressed Afghani barked out an order for two of his confederates to hold their position whilst he ran in the direction of his vehicle, a silver Mercedes G-Class Jeep (modified to be bullet and blast proof).

On the opposite side of the street Birch writhed in agony, his face contorted with shock and terror. Bits of bone, as white as mistletoe berries, glinted out from cherry-red flesh from where the bullets had shredded open both his legs. He stared at Devlin and asked – moaned – for help. Birch heard the two men, armed with Kalashnikovs, cock their weapons at the top of the street. He was an easy target.

But the enemy had a new target, as Devlin came out from the alley and into view. The young Afghani on the right, baring his yellow teeth in malice and savagery, opened fire on the British soldier. But the rifle fired him, rather than he fired the rifle. The Kalashnikov wriggled in his hands like a freshly caught eel. A few bullets struck the ground and then he over compensated and shot way above his target's head. Before the Afghani could adjust his aim however, Devlin let out a short burst of controlled fire – and scythed down both men. On seeing the first round strike the younger man's abdomen Devlin turned his rifle on the weasel-faced gunman next to him and poured four bullets into him. Centre mass.

Devlin bellowed out for a medic to attend to Birch but then lost no time in pursuing his quarry. When he reached the end of the street however he saw the Mercedes heading off in a cloud of dust. The soldier crouched down, buried the butt of his rifle into his shoulder and fired at the vehicle. As talented a marksman as Devlin was though, the rounds pinged harmlessly off the reinforced chassis and bullet-proofed tinted glass.

The usually stoical paratrooper let out a curse and kicked the ground. He then took a breath however and began to march back to where Birch was receiving medical attention. As he did so he passed the Afghani teenager, who he had shot in the stomach. He was still alive. The adolescent, doubled-over in pain, his clothes soaking up the blood, gazed up at the British soldier imploringly. He was keener to see a doctor, as opposed to seventy-two virgins, Devlin considered.

He shot the youth once in the chest and then once in the face.

Witness testimonies concerning the incident reported that the enemy was reaching for his gun. Many unofficially judged Devlin had shot the Afghani to put him out of his misery. It was a mercy killing. But Devlin executed the whey-faced adolescent because he wanted to. It felt good. Right. He was uprooting one more weed, so hopefully something better could grow in its place. Devlin even heard a voice inside his head, divine or otherwise, as he pulled the trigger.

Kill him.

*

"Promise me, no matter what happens, that you'll find and kill the bastard who attacked us. Give me your word of honour," Bitch rasped, as he clutched Devlin's hand in the evac-chopper, as they made their way back to base. His breathing grew shallow. His usually ruddy complexion grew pale. "If I somehow get through this I'll butcher him too, for young Connelly."

"I give you my word," Devlin solemnly replied, as he bowed his head whilst making his vow to his friend – and to God.

"That fucker wasn't Taliban. I bet he's linked to one of those poppy growing bastards. Not that I want to condemn the morphine trade too much right now," the soldier joked, as he glanced at the drip by the side of him and forced a feeble grin.

Devlin forced a smile too, after leaning over his friend to catch his words above the noise of the thrumming helicopter. The bright, arid landscape below scorched his eyes as he stared out the window.

Devlin nodded, agreeing with Birch about the prospective identity of the Afghani who had wounded his friend and murdered Connelly. Their suspicions were confirmed two days later. Devlin was called into a meeting with Colonel Charles Tyerman, shortly after hearing the news that the surgeons were unable to save his friend's legs. Birch would be wheelchair bound for the remainder of his life. He had also just spoken to Christopher Connelly's father over the telephone.

"Christopher often spoke about you. I know how much he looked-up to you and how much you kept an eye on him. You're a good man," Peter Connelly expressed, his voice as brittle as egg shells. Devlin could also hear Mary Connelly sobbing in the background.

I didn't keep an eye on him enough though. And I'm not sure how good a man I am.

Fury, guilt and sorrow entwined around Devlin's intestines, like barbed wire.

"At ease, Michael. Please, take a seat," Charles Tyerman remarked. The request sounded more like an order.

A blade of light cut through the room. Motes of dust danced in the air. A fan hummed in the corner and blessedly kissed Devlin's sweat-glazed forehead. He quickly surveyed the office. Photos of Tyerman's wife and children sat either side of his desk. Maps and satellite imagery hung on the wall, as well as a large poster which read, *"Don't be the best you can be. Just be better than 1 & 2 Para."*

Tyerman's compact frame betrayed time spent in the special forces. His hair was streaked with grey, his aspect steely and unflinching. Tyerman valued efficiency over flair, competence over courage. He seldom asked someone under his command to do something which he had not already done during his own career. He valued the lives of his men and always made sure the base's bar and library were well stocked. When he spoke to the Connellys about their brave son he passed on his private phone number and email and said that they were welcome to get in touch at any time. And meant it.

The Colonel was better at giving orders than following them – and as much faith as he had in the men under his command, he cultivated a thinly veiled contempt for his paymasters. Tyerman believed in having a Plan A and Plan B. But the British government, whether embodied in a junior civil servant or the Prime Minister, didn't have a plan. Didn't have a clue. The veteran officer didn't suffer fools gladly, as much as he was always glad to see fools suffer.

Tyerman noticed Devlin glance at the balled-up piece of paper littering the left side of his desk. The Colonel made a fist with one hand and cupped it in the other. He smiled or sneered – breathed or snorted – and spoke:

"That there is a printout of an email from an overpaid, underwhelming mandarin who works at the Ministry of Defence. He has promised that the right equipment and more helicopters are on their way. He quotes that the Prime Minister will be as good as his word. Which is what worries me. Politicians. They should all be strung up at Traitor's Gate. John Reid, a sack of shit in a cheap suit if ever there was one, declared that we could complete our mission here without having to fire a single shot."

Tyerman shook his head in disbelief and disdain. His hands now formed themselves into two fists.

"But I have not called you in to talk politics, Michael. I have called you in to depress you in a different way. The good news however, if we can deem it as such, is that we

know who our gunman is. Rameen Jamal. He is the son of
Hakim Jamal, a local drug lord. Rameen is fond of driving to
certain villages in the province and, along with his coked-up
associates, raping young women. Some as young as twelve.
As you know we found several girls in the settlement who
had been sexually assaulted. Thankfully we disturbed the
bastards before they could have their way with all the women
they picked out to abuse. We know he's guilty and Hakim
knows he's guilty. But we will be unable to bring him to
prosecution, for any of his crimes. Not only is Hakim close to
Karzai but he is also an ally of ourselves and the Americans.
He sided with us rather than the Taliban so we turn a blind
eye to his poppy farming – and his son is similarly
untouchable. This is not to say that the snake won't stab us in
the back at some point. The result is that - officially - Rameen
wasn't even at the village. He has several witnesses who will
testify that he was home, at prayer. But unofficially, if you
see that bastard in your sights, take the shot. God knows, I'll
do the same. You're an outstanding soldier, Devlin. Not
because you follow orders or keep your kit in good order. No,
I consider you an outstanding soldier because you're good at
killing. If I gave you and another ten men a knife or gun and
ordered you to go into the woods together – I'd have every
confidence that you would be the last man standing. Out of
all the soldiers under my command you intrigue, or scare, me
the most. I still can't work you out. I pulled your file again
this morning. Although you were an orphan it seems you
were eventually placed with a good foster family, who
brought you up well. You do not have a criminal record but I
know you've been in more than one scrap over the years. I
noticed on one form that you marked you were a Catholic -
but then you crossed it out and put Atheist. You never

attended university but I warrant that there is no one better read in the regiment. I remember I once saw you in the library, reading a copy of *A Gun for Sale*. I asked you what you liked about Greene's books and you replied that you sympathised with his characters. That good men can do bad things and bad men are still capable of a shot at redemption. But I am still unsure which kind of character you are, or will be. You do not seem to want to progress in your career in the army, as much as you're capable of doing so. You're not interested in medals or citations. In another lifetime, you might have been a Templar Knight. You seem to be on a personal crusade. You signed-up after nine-eleven, because you wanted to help defeat the Taliban. But maybe you signed-up to defeat – or find – something in yourself. The truth is that I don't know. You may not know either. But as much as you intrigue and unnerve me I have no desire to change you - just in case I somehow, in fixing the man, break the soldier in you. Every time you take the life of an enemy you are saving one or more of our own. So, my advice to you is keep on keeping on."

Tyerman paused to both retrieve a cigarette and scrutinize the soldier opposite him. He was interested to see how Devlin would react to his assertions. Would he disagree with his character assessment? But the officer had more chance of getting blood out of a stone. For the most part Tyerman's words passed through him like a phantom. More than seeming defiant or introverted Devlin appeared indifferent, Tyerman later thought. But the meeting had not been a complete waste of time, the squaddie judged. Far from it. Because Devlin now knew the name of the man he had to kill, to keep his promise to Birch.

2.

Unfortunately, Rameen Jamal didn't ever come into Michael Devlin's sights again. And by the end of the year he finished his tour and left the army. He had given his all – but it wasn't enough. Tyerman called him into his office again to persuade the soldier to change his mind. But he had more chance of changing the seasons. Devlin went back home to London. He drank and read heavily whilst scratching out a living. Soldiering had given him a sense of purpose and belonging. Or the illusion of such. But working as a glorified security guard for a merchant bank didn't quite provide the same levels of engagement.

Yet Devlin eventually found all the purpose and belonging he needed when he met Holly. She was something – someone – special. Good natured and good humoured. Her smile was never vapid, her promises never hollow. There are some women who can prove the existence of God to a man, just by the way they laugh or commit small acts of kindness. Devlin became more like the person he wanted to be when he was with Holly. Good natured and good humoured. He didn't so much find himself, as she found him. Devlin became a husband and was eight months away from being a father. But instead Devlin became a widower, when Holly died from a hit-and-run accident. They never apprehended the driver and for a time the image of Rameen Jamal was replaced by the faceless figure of Holly's killer. Happiness is a mayfly.

The hard, cold soldier grew harder and colder. Grief ate away at him like a cancer, but one which the patient didn't want to remove. He bought bottles of her perfume and sprayed them around the house – and re-sprayed the letters she had written to him when they first started dating. He listened to her favourite songs, as if she were still in the room and could enjoy them – like a ghost, haunting him. He re-played old messages she had left on his phone, just to hear her voice. The former paratrooper walked the streets, his head bowed down as if he were always going to or coming from a funeral. He talked to God, if only to curse him or deny his existence. Devlin was burdened with the knowledge that everyone in the world was a sinner. Including himself. The widower couldn't decide, drunk or sober, whether he was too strong – or too weak – to commit suicide.

He was saved, if saved can be deemed the appropriate term, by Oliver Porter. An ex-Guards officer, Porter worked as a fixer (or "facilitator") for corporations, the security services and criminal underworld. Devlin was invited to become a contract killer – a gun for sale - and took to the profession like a duck to water. He was as reliable and methodical in his work as a surgeon. Clinical. The profession was well-paid and Devlin bought a luxury apartment close to Tower Bridge. He regularly visited his foster parents again and started to drink in a local pub, which furnished him with more than enough society for his needs.

Devlin spent several years drinking, reading and killing. Until six months ago, when Devlin started dating Emma, a florist who lived in his building. He told Porter he was retiring. She made him want to return to the land of the living, turn the page. Their first date was in January and come February – on Valentine's Day – Devlin asked Emma to move in with him. He did so by attaching a key to his apartment to Violet, her black and white mongrel dog.

"I don't want to waste any more time than I have to, waiting to be with you," he lovingly declared, as Violet sat between the happy couple and licked them both affectionately, approving of the union. Later that evening Devlin remembered how he once considered, after Holly died, that the remainder of his life couldn't help but be a waste of time. He would be fated to spend his life just loitering on the planet, until he died. Until he saw Holly again.

Devlin considered that he would ask Emma to marry him, before the start of the summer. Then, at the beginning of June, he planned to ask her by the end of the summer. On more than one occasion he walked into jewellers and enquired about certain engagement rings he thought she might like. And he even paid a deposit on one, with a band subtly designed in the shape of a rose – her favourite flower. But every rose has its thorn. Devlin's doubts ran deep, like a bottomless well. He felt like he was still married to Holly - like a devout catholic unable to countenance divorce. He thought about Holly every day and wished he could be with her, in this world or the next. In some ways, he was having an illicit affair with his dead wife, as Devlin found himself lying to Emma about the amount of times he was visiting Holly's grave. There would be three of them in any marriage. Every day he felt like he was being unfaithful to at least one of them.

*

The dead of night. Devlin stood in his living room and stared at the message on his phone. He didn't recognise the number. But he knew who the text was from.

He's in the country. We need to meet .

The evening was balmy and starless. Clouds mottled the sky, like a bruise. Devlin had been careful not to wake Emma. She slept so peacefully, thoughtfully, as if she were praying. Violet yawned and padded her way across the wooden floor. She sat at his feet, her ears pricked to attention, cocking her head slightly. She raised her paw to his shin a couple of times, either to snap her gloomy looking master out of his reverie or, more likely, to prompt him to give her a biscuit from out of the cupboard which she often wistfully glanced up at.

Devlin could ignore the message or refuse to meet. Refuse to do what Birch would ask him to do. Beg him to do. Devlin had made a new life for himself.

But we are where we are.

The professional killer couldn't escape his past. Or he didn't want to.

3.

Just one more. That was all he needed. Devlin was tempted to pop into a newsagent to buy a pack of cigarettes. He nostalgically remembered how, when he first started to smoke as a teenager, shops would sell cigarettes individually. Especially to children. Devlin had quit smoking earlier on in the year, at the same time as Emma moved in with him. She didn't ask him to stop. He just did, out of consideration for her. He also wanted to prove something to himself, as well as to Emma.

But he still missed the acrid, fragrant, moreish taste in his mouth. He missed the sensation of the cellophane being peeled off a fresh packet and the comfortable feeling of a cigarette resting between his fingers. He missed the sight of a silken tendril of smoke streaming up from an ashtray. Writhing. Dancing. Devlin kept his word however and hadn't touched a cigarette since the morning Emma had moved in.

He made his way south, along Tower Bridge Road. A cool breeze tempered the heat of the midday June sun. He was due to meet Birch at the *Huntsman & Hounds* pub, just off East Street. Devlin was wearing jeans, a loose fitting purple t-shirt and white Reeboks. He blended in and looked anonymous.

He arrived at the pub early. He wanted to have a drink first and collect his final thoughts before Birch arrived. Devlin's nearest local was *The Admiral Nelson* but he felt it was too close to home, to discuss what they needed to discuss. He often drank in the Huntsman when he wanted a quiet drink, without fear of Emma walking in on him. Michael Robertson,

109

the landlord of the Nelson, had also treated him differently (with either a wariness or awe), after Devlin violently ejected a few drunken city traders from the pub six months ago.

The Huntsman had recently re-opened and been refurbished. The owners had sensibly retained the smoked glass windows and the old wooden bar, gleaming with varnish and a thousand spilled drinks which had seeped into the grain over the years. Sepia-tinged photographs of Walworth Road and East Street Market, populated by flat-cap wearing costermongers, decorated the walls. The old brickwork and some of the original fittings remained exposed and gave the venue character. A mahogany bookcase sat in one corner. Patrons would leave and take books. When Devlin was last there, the previous week, he dropped off a copy of Conrad's *Lord Jim* and picked up *Call for the Dead*, by John le Carre. A worn, toffee brown sofa sat in the opposite corner, somewhat out of place. The rumour was that the owner had picked it up second-hand from a seedy strip club in Shoreditch. A couple of the regulars were tempted to run a black light over it, to confirm their suspicions. But they then thought better of it. Ignorance was bliss, they concluded. Thankfully the pub was devoid of televisions and overly intrusive music.

Devlin nodded to Terry Gilby, the amiable landlord of the pub. Terry replied with a smile and, most importantly, a pint. Far more than a local politician, priest or social worker, Terry listened with patience and sympathy to his customers' problems. And far more than any politician, priest or social worker, Terry was also able to fix their problems, albeit temporarily, with a drink.

Devlin greeted a couple of regulars, who he knew from previous visits to the pub, and bought a round.

"I'm just due to have a meeting but I'll join you for a couple later," Devlin said, downing half his refreshing pint in a few gulps. The beer temporarily quenched his desire for a cigarette.

I'll need a real drink by then. To forget about myself. And what I'll have to do.

Birch entered. Devlin offered up a smile for his friend, hoping that it was imbued with pleasure at seeing him rather than pity. Birch gruffly exclaimed that he could manage, as he awkwardly manoeuvred his wheelchair up the step and through the door of the pub. Devlin surveyed his friend. His face was gaunt, his cheeks hollowed out like a couple of old stone castle embrasures. When, or if, Birch grinned now his expression would no longer possess a cherubic quality. The sanguine had become the choleric. The stumps of his legs, as well as his torso, were withered. His skin was no longer tanned, but rather tinged with jaundice. His eyes were glassy and red-rimmed. Birch wore a stained polo shirt and black tracksuit bottoms, pock-marked with various cigarette burns. Faded tattoos – of Gillingham FC's club badge and 3 Para's insignia – brandished his hairy forearms.

Devlin insisted on getting his friend a drink – a pint of bitter with a large whisky chaser – and the two men found a table in the corner. As they positioned themselves however a couple of other people entered the pub and sat on an adjacent table, limiting the scope of what they could discuss.

"Have you seen anyone from the regiment recently?" Devlin asked, hoping that Birch still had a network of companionship and support. It would help expunge the guilt he felt at having not kept in touch with his friend.

Birch shrugged his sloping shoulders in reply. Devlin remembered how his shoulders used to once stand to attention at right angles. His bull-neck had turned into turkey wattle.

"I went to some benefit thing about a month back," Birch remarked, his voice rough with cigarettes and bitterness. "At least the drink was free. Hyde was there. He's got a job with some big American company. He's put on plenty of weight. Perhaps it's to help him fit in better over there. I also bumped into Cheeseman. He's just got married. She's young enough to be his daughter, the lucky bastard. I met her. Blonde, as you'd expect. Her two best assets are there for the world to see – and I'm not talking about her brains or personality. She'll doubtless cheat on him at some point – but not before he cheats on her... Tyerman was there too. He asked after you, said that he'd hoped you'd be at the party. He wants you to get in touch with him. I think he wants to offer you a job. All he could offer me was the number of some counsellor. But all they do is ask questions. None of them have any answers to anything. God knows how many of them have asked me about my childhood. I tell them that my mother and father didn't shoot me in the legs and ruin my fucking life. For the money the government pays these quacks for each session they may as well buy me a bottle of Talisker. I'd feel better then," the ex-soldier remarked, half-joking, before downing the dregs of his whisky. He refrained from telling his friend that Tyerman smoothed things over later at the party, when Birch drunkenly groped a waitress and the manager of the venue wanted to throw him out.

Although Devlin frequently sent cheques to various charities associated with the regiment he had long given up attending the gatherings and events they arranged. He wanted to put the war and his life as a soldier behind him. Afghanistan had been a fool's errand in many ways. The army baulked at calling it a defeat. But the British and Americans had poked a hornet's nest – and got stung. The once Great Game, in the nineteenth century, turned into a campaign of Whac-A-Mole. The army would seemingly knock-down the Taliban in one location, only for it to pop up in another position a week later. The allies also had one hand tied behind their backs in the form of nervous, stingy and incompetent administrations who refused to let the likes of Tyerman and General Petraeus take the fight to the enemy. Many of the schools that the army had helped to set up and provide security for were now being disbanded. Half the Afghan army resembled the Keystone Cops, whilst the remainder would switch their allegiance to the enemy as quickly as night turns into day, or as soon as the bribe went into a pocket. For both the Taliban – and poppy growers – it was business as usual. They had won the war.

Birch began to drum his nicotine-stained fingers on the table, as he impatiently waited for the couple in earshot to finish their drinks and leave. Although their backs were turned to him he still gave them looks like daggers when they laughed, or when they debated getting another drink in. He puffed out his cheeks in relief when they declined to do so however. As soon as the pair were heading towards the door Birch leaned towards Devlin, his eyes as wide as a zealot, and urgently spoke:

"I've found the bastard. He's here in London - staying at The Ritz. I've got his name on Google Alert and something popped up last week. Apparently, he's part of an Afghan trade delegation."

Devlin calmly nodded his head in reply, whilst twisting his wedding ring around his finger. Emma said she was fine with him still wearing the gold band Holly gave him. She could be so understanding and lovely at times that it hurt. Through a gap in the smoked glass he saw a shabbily dressed man limping across the street, his jaw and eye heavily bruised. Yet Devlin strangely envied the forlorn figure. As he was smoking.

"I know. I went online and did some research, after I received your message. He will be well guarded. The hotel will be filled, wall-to-wall, with cameras. It's doubtful we'll be able to get our hands on his schedule to select an optimum venue and time. Usually a job like this needs weeks of planning," Devlin said, doubt and caution seasoning his tone, as he felt his phone vibrate in his pocket. He wryly smiled to himself, on the inside, as in the past Oliver Porter used to send him texts this time of day, proposing that they meet to talk about a job. Yet the text on Devlin's phone now was merely a message, informing him that his new flat-pack bookcases were due to be delivered to his apartment tomorrow morning.

"Are you trying to back out or to talk yourself out of it? Because you won't be able to change my mind. I've waited years for this. I've thought about killing the bastard since that first night in the hospital, when the fucker took my legs and life away. When you made your promise. When you gave your word of honour." Spittle came out of his mouth and flecked the table.

Devlin furrowed his brow, either reliving the sorrow of the attack in the village or regretting the vow he made. A man can't outrun his shadow, or escape his past.

"I'll keep my word," he replied, either defiantly or defensively.

"This is not all about me. This is also about getting justice for Christopher. The only way we can. You know I'd do it

114

myself, if I could. If I wasn't in this," Birch asserted, his face contorted in frustration and enmity, as he banged the sides of his wheelchair. Terry – and the regulars – briefly turned around but then buried their heads back into their pints. Devlin had also positioned himself so that he blocked any view of the raw rage and resentment smouldering in Birch's features.

Murdering Rameen wouldn't bring Christopher back, Devlin thought – rather than saying it out loud.

"I know," he remarked, nodding his head in agreement. Devlin remembered how trigger-happy Birch had been back in Helmand. He didn't lack for courage, albeit some might have questioned his ability to shoot accurately.

"You must have taken on more difficult jobs, at shorter notice," Birch whispered.

Although Devlin couldn't be wholly sure whether he regretted making his promise to kill Rameen Jamal, he was beginning to regret his decision to tell his friend about his former profession. He had done so when Birch had been at a low ebb. Devlin wanted to show to his friend that he trusted him – and that he could easily afford to give him the envelope of money he left on the crippled soldier's bedside table. Birch reacted by saying, half-jokingly at best, that he wished he had enough money to hire Devlin and fly him to Kabul, to kill Jamal there. Birch also enjoyed hearing about some of the jobs. Most of the targets deserved to die. Murdering corrupt politicians, pension stealing businessmen and debt-ridden B-list celebrities wouldn't cure the world of all its evils, Birch thought. But it was a start.

"I've taken on more difficult jobs. We just need to be careful. I have to think about Emma though. I've retired and forged a new life for myself."

Should Porter have offered him a similar contract then Devlin would have walked away, with no regrets. There were too many unknowns. There was no time to properly reconnoitre the target and location. 'Normal life' may have dulled the steel it took to pull the trigger too.

I could be rusty...Train hard, fight easy. Fail to prepare, fail to prepare.

"But I'll do it," Devlin added, with more resignation than determination. A promise is a promise.

The past lingered, like the taste of cigarettes.

4.

The two men had a couple more drinks, but mainly sat in silence. Brooding, for different reasons. More than most, soldiers keep their own council. Just before Birch left, Devlin reached into his pocket and pulled out a half-inch thick brown envelope.

"Are you okay for money?"

Birch shrugged his sloping shoulders again, unwilling to admit how desperate he was. He still, just about, had his pride. But he took the money.

For the next couple of hours Devlin had a drink with Terry and a stream of regulars, who drifted in and out of pub.

Drink lubricated the atmosphere. No one virtue signalled. No one talked about the latest reality television show. People just laughed and joked with others – and about themselves. The afternoon sun glinted off a brass plaque, which hung over the bar: "*When you have lost your Inns then drown your empty selves, for you would have lost the last of England.*" *Hillaire Belloc.*" Devlin didn't quite know if he was being himself or forgetting about himself. But the laughter and jokes were as welcome as a cigarette. Perhaps even more so.

Devlin squinted and turned his face away from the blast of light and warm air that hit him on leaving the pub. He sent a message to Emma to say he would be home soon – and that he would take her out for dinner that evening. He also sent a message to Oliver Porter, asking for a meeting as soon as possible. He would call in a favour from his former employer. Devlin needed to get away with murder, again.

*

Porter was couched in a new black, leather Eames chair in his office, at home, when he received the message from Devlin. He raised his eyebrow in mild surprise and, such was the curiosity or concern he felt, put his glass of Sancerre back on his desk rather than to his lips. Distinguished flecks of silvery-grey coloured his slicked-back hair. He wore a Brooks Brothers cream linen summer suit, along with a tailored pale blue shirt from Harvie & Hudson. Polished gold cufflinks and a vintage Patek Phillipe watch adorned his wrists. As a hangover from his time as a Guards officer Porter was clean shaven. Sometimes he even shaved twice a day. He liked the way his wife cupped her slender hands around his face. It was both sweet and sensual. Porter's face was also tanned, from a recent family holiday to Florida. He broke a promise he made to himself that he would never set foot inside Disney World, "the high temple of vulgarity. Filled with plebs." And the place proved even more awful than he imagined, both in terms of the cuisine and overly sentimental people. "For every selfie they upload, God should take a day off their life," he had remarked, in earnest, to his wife – shaking his head in disappointment as much as disparagement just before he took a bite of a greasy beef burger (whilst closing his eyes and picturing himself back in *Boisdale*).

Porter now maintained a study inside the house instead of working in a specially constructed outbuilding at the end of the garden in his home, situated in a village just outside of Windsor. Porter had largely retired from his job as a fixer. He certainly refrained from taking on any contracts that operatives such as Devlin fulfilled. Having become a target of the Parker brothers six months ago, Porter decided to take stock of his life, while he still could. With the help of Devlin, he retired the gangsters - permanently. Porter only took on consultancy work now and acted as a facilitator for putting relevant people in contact with one another. He didn't miss the long hours, or threats to his life. Instead of reading intelligence reports - or emails from oleaginous representatives of thuggish Russian oligarchs - the latest thriller by Michael Dobbs sat open on his antique walnut desk (which the dealer claimed had once belonged to Ford Madox Ford). A portrait of his great-grandfather, a ruddy-faced bushy-moustached cavalry officer from the Great War, gazed out imperiously across the room. A thick column of smoke, from a King of Denmark cigar, vaunted upwards.

Porter spent most of his time at home nowadays, instead of attending meetings in Geneva or at the Garrick Club. He went shopping with his wife, Victoria, or spent idle afternoons fly-fishing on the Kennett. He drove his children to school and picked them up. He was teaching his youngest son how to play the piano and bought his eldest son an air rifle, which they used to shoot at foxes from the drawing room window. "Ideally, I'd like a socialist or Gerry Adams to come into our sights," he had wistfully remarked to the boy. On the advice of Devlin, Porter bought a dog and regularly walked the handsome looking – but admittedly slightly dotty – Dalmatian, which the ex-soldier had affectionately named Marlborough. As a result of the extra exercise provided by Marlborough Porter had lost some, albeit not all, of his paunch. He smoked and drank a little less – and duly looked and felt healthier. Life was good.

The smell of his wife's rosemary lamb filled his nostrils. The faint sound of her singing from the kitchen gently poured into his ears. Since spending more time at home he realised how much – and how well – Victoria sang. The children were away and they would have the house to themselves tonight. They would curl up on the sofa and listen to Wagner or, more likely to please his wife, some caterwauler called Celine Dion. Should they time their mood and energy levels right they might even make love, he fancied.

Porter read the text message from Devlin. He wanted to meet. Over the past few months the fixer had ignored similar messages, or politely declined to meet, other former associates. He was out of the game – and had no desire to be tempted back into it. Devlin was surely out of the game too. He wished his ex- employee well. Porter had met Emma, back in late January. She was pretty, witty and decent. A nice catholic girl. And she was good for him. A part of Porter had to acknowledge however how much Devlin's retirement was a waste of talent. When securing a client, Porter would often advertise Devlin as being "a natural born killer." He was methodical – engaged and yet detached. Devlin didn't necessarily enjoy killing. But he was good at it – and could live with himself, as easily as the politicians he knew could live with lying. Some of the kills Devlin had carried out over the years had been made to look like accidents. But some needed to be violent – and make a statement. Porter recalled how a client had once asked for a target to be taken out by a knife, instead of a gun. It had something to do with the target having killed the client's father with a machete, during the Rwandan genocide. Devlin had worked to the brief – and Porter sold the knife on to the contractor, for him to display in a glass case in his government-funded house in Sierra Leone. Poetic justice costs more than mere common or garden revenge.

Porter would meet with Devlin. He owed him a debt of honour. Porter had dug them both into a hole - (a coffin-shaped hole) - with the Parker brothers six months ago, but Devlin had dug them out of it. Victoria and his children were safe because of him. Because of Devlin, Porter had been able to give himself a second chance. He just hoped that Devlin was giving himself a second chance too. The fixer sent a message back to say he could meet Devlin tomorrow. He would book a table out on the summer terrace of the Savile Club. Porter thought how he could do some shopping along Jermyn Street beforehand.

Perhaps he is getting married and wants to invite me to the wedding.

*

Devlin continued to walk home, his head bowed down. For some reason, he was gripped by a strange sense of superstition (whether it was a hangover from being catholic or a soldier) and he avoided stepping on any cracks in the pavement. Devlin remembered how he had played the same game before his first kill for Porter. Mossad had commissioned the hit. The target had been an obese computer hacker, one Ralph Herron, from Camden. Mossad wanted Herron executed for having released government files on the internet which put several of their agents and troops in harm's way. That the hacker's heroes included Julian Assange and Bono didn't endear Devlin to the target either. He tracked Herron down, shot him in his damp flat and retrieved the relevant files. Few would mourn the man - save for a handful of warped lefties who read his blog about Palestine, the escorts he booked and the owners of local takeaway shops he ordered food from.

Devlin was tired. His bruise-coloured eyelids weighed as heavy as the burden on his shoulders. The heat sapped his strength, or enthusiasm for life, too. He stopped, waiting for a gap in the traffic on a busy road. Devlin glanced across the street to witness a rat-faced teenager throw an empty Coke can at a bird on the pavement. He then heard the thumping sound of a loud car stereo to his right. The driver had his windows open, sharing the too-many-beats-per-minute with the world. Devlin was tempted to teach the man a lesson. He was wearing a shell-suit. A tattoo, which Devlin couldn't quite make the details out of but knew it looked ugly, was splayed across his neck. Zombie-like he bobbed his head to the rhythm of the music, either stoned or wishing to appear - in his mind - cool. A baby in a pram started to wail as it passed by the garishly coloured vehicle. An elderly lady winced, almost in pain, as the polluting noise assaulted what was left of her eardrums. Devlin imagined going up to the driver. He would politely ask him to turn the music down. No doubt he would refuse – and have a few other choice words for the pedestrian. Devlin pictured himself grabbing the man by the back of the head and smashing his face, twice, into his steering wheel. And he would have deserved it, either for his original sin or for wearing a shell suit, Devlin darkly and dryly mused.

But Devlin just walked on. A police siren could be heard in the background. People bumped into one another and offered up half-hearted apologies, or not, as they remained glued to their smart phones. Devlin thought again about buying a house in the countryside, in a village which had a nice local pub and a florist's, that he could buy for Emma. He could endure the poor air quality of the capital. It was merely everything else that seemed to choke the life out of him. Devlin felt like he was the only one who knew he was diseased, or that he was the only one immune to modern life. London was diverse yet dull, liberal yet self-obsessed. As an eighteen-year-old Devlin had adopted a Manichean view of the world. There was as much good as evil on the planet. But the soldier had seen too much, or thought too much. Cruelty outweighed compassion, vanity eclipsed valour. If only more people read The Pilgrim's Progress. They used to.

But, instead of the Slough of Despond, London had turned into a giant Hollywood film lot – replete with greed, egos, tawdry affairs, vacuity and backstabbing. But London told itself it was the dream factory, full of philanthropy, internationalism, creativity and moral certitude. Nothing was more precious than a sixteenth minute of fame. People judged themselves to be all powerful moguls or directors but, in truth, they were just someone else's sceneshifter. Everyone was an actor or actress, spouting out clichés. They just didn't all know it.

Devlin's head throbbed, either from the drink or despair. Emma was thankfully still at work when he got back to the apartment. He didn't want her to see him like this. Images of Christopher Connolly, Birch and a bestial-eyed Rameen branded themselves in his thoughts but eventually Devlin buried his head in a pillow and fell asleep. Dead to the world.

5.

Sequin-like stars adorned the velvety night sky. The dark jade river rippled and shimmered. Occasionally, when there was a lull in the hubbub of the restaurant, The Pont de la Tour, Devlin could hear the distant sound of the Thames splash against the bank. True to his word he arranged to take Emma out to dinner, after he had slept and then taken a cold shower. He hadn't once craved a cigarette since she returned to the apartment.

Emma gazed out the windows and took in some of the affluent, attractive couples walking by. Holding hands. Being – or projecting being – in love. Blissfully happy – or blissfully ignorant. Perhaps there wasn't such a world of difference between the two, she fleetingly fancied. Women tossed their heads back and laughed. Men ran their hands through product-filled hair and covertly glanced at other women. Emma took comfort from the thought that she wouldn't want to swap Michael with any of the younger, gayer peacocks on show. Her other boyfriends had read Men's Health magazine and carried the baggage of unfulfilling careers in the finance sector. Devlin read Tolstoy and had once carried a gun. He was a generous lover. She never tired of him running his fingers along her spine – making her entire body tingle. She would arch her back in sinuous pleasure and stretch out her toes in reply, willingly surrendering to his strong yet tender touch. And Emma believed that she loved him better than any of her sorority outwardly loved their partners. But Emma's satisfied air was tinged, tempered, with the thought that she still didn't know Devlin as much as the other women knew the men they were with. There were gaps, like missing notes in a symphony. How could she help him if she couldn't first diagnose what the problem was?

Emma smiled at him – nigh on toothily grinning. Her freckles were in bloom. She was wearing a silk, floral print mini-dress he had bought her just before Easter, just before he had taken her away to Florence for a romantic weekend. They had also gone on holiday together to Gambia and Holland – for the Tulip festival in May. Every trip had been wonderful, although on every trip she wondered if he might propose to her. It wasn't just the good Catholic girl in her that wanted to get married and have children. Although it was perhaps the good Catholic girl in her that wouldn't commit to children before marriage. Emma's red hair glowed in the candlelight. The crucifix glinted too, resting on her chest, above the plunging neckline of her dress. Emma was a Catholic, but thankfully no nun. Her sapphire earrings, which Violet had also acted as a courier for on the day after Valentine's, sparkled - but came a distant second to the light in her eyes. Devlin thought how, whilst he believed most people were guilty of some form of sin when encountering them, Emma believed everyone was worthy of forgiveness. Both stances seemed equally Catholic. He often wondered if she would forgive him, should he confess to his sins. To his crimes. But no. He couldn't risk losing her.

People were often attracted to each other out of a strain of narcissism, he considered. They saw something similar in their partners and duly loved them for it. But Devlin was attracted to Emma for traits which were absent from his own history and character. Her clemency. Her unaffected kindness. It came naturally, that Emma's first thought was for others – whilst what came naturally to Devlin was violence. Emma remembered everyone's birthday and listened to the concerns of friends and strangers alike. She regularly drove an elderly widow, who lived in their apartment block, to her hospital appointments. And she was compassionate and thoughtful not because she could then tweet about her actions and receive "likes", as if the world were watching and scoring her like a talent contest on TV. No. Emma was good-hearted because she believed God was watching her. And Devlin admired her for it.

He smiled at her. She noticed how, more than most, he looked younger when he smiled. His jawline softened. The taut muscles in his cheeks and around his eyes relaxed. Devlin was wearing a navy-blue blazer she had bought him for his birthday. Desire gleamed in his aspect, replacing the tiredness from his afternoon spent drinking. Emma's grin became a little abashed when she remembered the last time they were at the restaurant. It was the evening of Devlin's birthday. A few days beforehand Emma had accidentally come across a picture, of Holly, in a draw. The former model was stunning. Envy prickled her skin and innards. The feeling, justified or not, that she was Devlin's second choice – a booby prize – compared to being married to Holly struck her, like a gavel on a block, again. And again. As uncharitable or unchristian as it felt Emma grew to resent Holly, her beauty, (which, annoyingly, was natural rather than manufactured). Initially, when they started dating, Emma wanted to convey to Devlin that she had no desire to replace Holly or have him forget about his first wife. She never mentioned that she didn't like him wearing his wedding ring still (if only because it caused confusion with some people). She knew how he regularly visited her grave and, in some senses, still talked to his wife. More than he spoke to his girlfriend. But things had changed. If asked she wouldn't be able to nail the reason down, but Holly was akin to the 'other woman', casting a shadow over her relationship and future happiness. She was a rival. The enemy. Emma had caught a glance of Devlin's phone the week before his birthday, whilst he was listening to music, and the screen read 'Holly's Playlist'. And so, during their meal in the restaurant, Emma had enticed Devlin into the restroom, locked the door, and had sex with him. She needed him to forget about her. Emma needed him to prove how much he wanted her too.

The comely waitress placed Devlin's entrée of scallops on the table but his eyes still feasted on Emma. His nose also drunk in the perfume she was wearing. Not just because he too recalled their previous visit to the restaurant, or rather it's restroom. There was no one else on the planet he wanted to be with right now. But Devlin feared that, should he tell Emma how he felt, she would immediately question if there was someone else, in Heaven as opposed to on Earth, he would rather be with.

"So how was your friend today?" Emma asked, as she took another sip of wine.

"He's in a bad way, unfortunately. It's hard to adjust to civilian life, let alone being injured. He's still reliving the conflict, or wants to re-fight the same enemy. You can either leave a piece of yourself back in Afghanistan or bring a piece of the war back with you," Devlin replied, hoping that his candour about Birch would in some way compensate for his own guardedness.

"You so seldom speak about your time in the army," Emma countered, her voice tip-toeing but deliberate.

Did he speak about it with her?

"There's not much to tell. I spent most of my days getting sunburnt and reading Flashman novels," Devlin replied, feeling that he was being, at least, half-truthful. "My duties mainly involved babysitting aid workers and civil servants. I remember one senior wonk from DFID. He lasted all of three days in Helmand. He claimed he was suffering from diarrhoea and needed to go back home. But when he heard any gun go off we suspected that he started shitting himself for a different reason."

Emma laughed. It was one of the nicest sounds in the world. She didn't, however, want to let him off the hook in terms of deploying humour to deflect attention away from how army life – and then civilian life – changed him.

"How much do you think Helmand changed you?"

"I'm not sure," Devlin remarked, truthfully. Reading Dostoyevsky and Nietzsche had, perhaps, a greater effect on his thinking than any time spent in the army. The great changes in his life had come from when he first met Holly – and then when she died. He recalled a quotation from Nietzsche: "*That which does not kill us, makes you stronger.*" But Devlin wasn't now so sure. Had meeting Emma changed him? Time would tell, he sometimes thought. At other times, he believed she had – and changed him for the better. But she wasn't Holly.

"You should try and talk about your time in the army more," Emma said, concerned. "It doesn't need to be with me. Are you due to see any other old friends soon from the regiment?"

Devlin was going to argue that he didn't need counselling, like Birch – and that his time in Helmand didn't define him. He was also going to posit, testily, that he didn't need to go to confession. But he refrained from saying anything. Devlin didn't want to fight.

"No. But John mentioned that my former CO is keen on getting in touch – to offer me a job. He runs a company which organises personal security. I'm enjoying my retirement too much however. Which reminds me, I'll be having lunch with Oliver tomorrow. We're having a catch-up and he's got some investment opportunities he wants to discuss."

Devlin didn't enjoy lying. But he had to admit that he was quite good at it.

"You should meet up with this CO still. You might be able to persuade him to give John some work."

"That's a good thought."

It was – and he would duly contact Tyerman. But as Devlin worked his way through a carafe of wine and waited for his main course his thoughts turned to Rameen and The *Ritz*. The streets would be busy around the hotel and he could easily disappear into the crowd. But he would not be able to conceal himself from the numerous security cameras in the lobby and each individual floor, even if he could disguise himself as an employee.

6.

Emma mentioned that she needed to get home to call her Mum, but she didn't want Devlin to rush in finishing his coffee.

"You may want to take your time. I'm sure you'd rather not overhear a conversation about how much I'm not disappointing my mother, but how I could do so much better if only I listened to her advice."

"I'll catch you up. Say hello to your Mum for me. And that of course I agree with her, in that her daughter can do better than me."

"Don't tempt me. Besides, she thinks you're the one thing in my life that doesn't need changing. Mum called you a "gentleman." And Daddy called you "a real man" when he first met you. I think he envied the fact the you carried a gun. Sometimes he wants to carry one too. Especially when he's home alone with Mum."

"Can't I be both? Probably not," Devlin drily replied.

When he got up to kiss her goodbye he pulled her close, gave her more than just a peck on the cheek and ran his fingers down her spine, along the zip at the back of the dress, which he would pull down when he got back to the apartment.

When Devlin left the restaurant, he decided to take the more scenic route home and walked along the riverbank. The route also didn't pass any shops which sold cigarettes. He wanted to be good. Devlin sat down on a bench, which he often stopped at when taking Violet out for a walk each morning. He liked the openness and serenity of the river. Warm lights – red, white and amber – glowed from the buildings on the opposite bank. He put his earphones on and listened to a few songs on his smart phone. Holly's Playlist. He had found the playlist whilst going through her iPod, a few days after her death. She had mentioned, long before that, how she had a special collection of songs which she listened to – that reminded her of Devlin and how she felt about him.

"You'll always be a part of me
I'm part of you indefinitely
Boy don't you know you can't escape me
Oh daring 'cause you'll always be my baby."

A sleek party boat, blaring out Abba, motored past and a gaggle of women, from a hen party in full swing, waved at Devlin and blew him kisses. He half-smiled but wasn't tempted to reply in kind.

"I ain't gonna cry no
And I won't beg you to stay
If you're determined to leave boy
I will not stand in your way
But inevitably
You'll be back again
'Cause you know in your heart babe
Our love will never end…"

Devlin closed his eyes and let the cool breeze fan his face. He placed his hand by the side of him and imagined Holly taking hold of it. He remembered how she used to squeeze his hands at parties when she rightly felt that he was getting stressed. Any anger or anxiety would then dissipate, scatter life blossom from a tree. She would grin – humorously and beautifully - and Devlin would be reminded to laugh at himself – as well as any vexing guests standing in front of him.

Just say the word and I'll stay retired. Just say anything. Please. Let me know you're there…

Devlin couldn't really tell how long he sat on the wooden bench but eventually he got to his feet, with a slight sigh, and continued to make his way home. He turned in from the riverbank and walked down a narrow cobblestoned alleyway which led him towards his apartment block. As he switched off his music and put his headphones into his jacket pocket he heard a voice in front of him.

"Excuse me mate, but have you got the time?"

The man, in his mid-thirties, was wearing a Burberry jacket, jeans and loafers. He was lean-faced and red-eyed.

Devlin glanced at his Breitling watch and replied that it was coming up to eleven o'clock.

"Thanks, mate," the fellow Londoner remarked and walked on. As soon as he was behind Devlin however the man, Sean Grady, turned and nodded to his two confederates, who had appeared at the end of the alley, just ahead of Devlin.

The first figure, Dougie Cochrane, was heavy-set with a shaven head. When he puffed out his barrel chest – and pot belly – his Ben Sherman shirt rose-up and exposed his hairy navel area. His nose was flat and round, like a snout. Devlin casually noticed the tattoo of a bird on his right hand, signifying that the man had spent time in prison. A tattoo of a couple of tears on his cheek signified that he had murdered two people, at least. The wiry, fidgety figure next to him was Steve Farrell. His face was marked with a stud in his nose, a bar in his cheek and a gold chain hung between two piercings in his left ear. The pale-faced Farrell, who was spending most of the summertime laid out in bed monged-out on skunk or high on heroin, bit his nails and tapped his right foot. His beady eyes flitted between Devlin and Grady, as if awaiting instruction. Devlin couldn't quite decide if the adolescent, even higher on coke than his two friends, was anxious from fear or champing at the bit to commit an act of violence.

"We'll take your watch, wallet and phone. We'll take that wedding ring too. And if you say you can't take it off we'll cut it off," Grady remarked, pulling out a slim flick-knife. There was a glint of sadistic pleasure in his voice and sinister aspect. The drug dealer, who called himself a "Bermondsey Boy" but was born and bred in Eltham, had stabbed and assaulted people ever since his teens. He enjoyed it. And violence worked. He profited from it. Although Grady had no need for extra funds, the take from the mugging would pay for their night out. It had almost become a ritual as well for the trio to turn over a well-heeled innocent stranger whilst high, before or after an evening out at a strip club over the river.

"Big Dougie" had heard his friend say similar things during their sport before but he still sniggered as if it was the first time he'd heard it. He cupped his large left hand in his right one and cracked a couple of knuckles, hoping to intimidate Devlin. His victim was dressed smartly. He no doubt was well spoken and had a good job, Cochrane judged - just like the lawyers and detectives who conspired together to send him down for manslaughter.

The likes of him owe the likes of me. This is just payback.

Devlin slowly and subtly moved so his back was towards the wall. He was happy for them to think that they had cornered him – but his intention was to position his assailants so that no one could attack him from behind.

"You can make it easy for us or hard for you. This isn't the first time we've done this, as you can probably guess. Do you know how much trouble you're in right now?" Grady remarked, baring his teeth in a cruel grin and holding up the blade of the knife. Twisting it, at his victim's eye-level.

Devlin's features tightened, congealing like cement. His body became taut, yet his heartbeat only quickened a little and his tone was measured. Sincere.

"I do. But do you? I'm going to count to five. If you're still here after that then you can hold yourselves responsible for my actions. It'll be easy for me to be hard on you. Walk away now, or lose the ability to walk. One."

Cochrane furrowed his bovine brow in confoundment or indignation. Grady shook his head, in disbelief. His victims had tried to run before, cry for mercy, womanishly scream for help, or even vainly attempted to fight their way out of trouble on one or two occasions. But no one had ever threatened the robber band before. Grady considered the man was just posturing however. His words were bluster – a bluff.

He needs to be taught a lesson.

Grady figured that the well-dressed man before him probably ran his own business and wasn't used to anyone challenging him. Bermondsey had been gentrified by whole swathes of middle-class tossers. People who preferred lattes to beer. Easy prey.

Farrell grinned, nervously or otherwise, revealing a couple of banana-coloured crooked front teeth.

"And what do you think you're going to do after you get to five?" the vicious drug addict remarked, thrusting his chin forward – and then spitting a gobbet of pea-green phlegm on the floor, close to Devlin's foot. A sociologist might try and make excuses for the goblin-like Farrell. They could have

134

blamed his background – an absent father and alcoholic mother. Or they could explain how the Tories were responsible for selling off the playing fields in his area, when he was a boy. But Devlin wasn't a sociologist. He had merely concluded a long time ago that some people were just unpleasant.

"I'm first going to rip that chain out of your ear. Depending on whether your friend here falls on his front or back I'm going to sheath his toy knife in his thigh or arse. And as for this tattooed ape here, I'm going to gouge out his eyes. Two."

Cochrane's entire face was now screwed up in malice. He seethed rather than breathed. Grady ceased shaking his head. Farrell's bemusement morphed into wariness. All three men offered each other astonished glances. Perhaps they were waiting for someone to take the lead and say something. But they never got the chance. There was no "three".

Devlin felt he was justified in lying about counting to five. He swung his leg and buried his foot into Cochrane's groin. The big man's thuggish countenance was now creased in agony. A shocked Grady was the next to fall as Devlin moved forward and whipped his elbow around. The blow cracked the drug dealer's right cheekbone. A disorientated Grady stumbled, lost his footing on the cobblestones and fell on his front. Devlin thought of how easily Emma could have been attacked, instead of him – just before he picked up the knife and plunged the blade through his jeans and into his left buttock. There needed to be more retribution in the world, divine or otherwise. There was something amiss with Devlin's moral compass, which he was aware of, compared to most other people. The discrepancy was no greater than the difference between true north and grid north. But it was significant. Grady squealed and then whimpered, prostrate on the ground, grasping the air in an attempt to pull out the knife. The drug-addled Farrell seemed paralysed, unable even to make the decision of fight or flight, as he stared wide-eyed at what was occurring. Devlin hesitated not. He moved swiftly and with purpose, as if playing speed chess. He grabbed his attacker – or victim – by his scrawny neck and slammed him against the wall. Devlin then put a hand over Farrell's mouth as he yanked the gold chain out of his ear. Farrell's face contorted in terror and pain. Blood splattered against the ground. Devlin moved his mouth closer towards the adolescent's good ear.

"If you scream, when I remove my hand, I'm going to cut off your other ear. Do you understand?"

Farrell nodded in reply. His pallid features grew even paler. When Devlin stepped away the mugger duly sobbed, rather than screamed, as he put a trembling hand up to his wounded ear.

Cochrane dry-heaved. Drool fell from his twisted lips. Just as he began to regain his breath, from being winded by Devlin's initial attack, he raised his head – only to be struck by a left-right-left combination. Devlin - who had taught himself to box and been conditioned through milling when first joining the paras – hit his opponent hard enough to draw blood and knock him to the ground. But not so hard as to injure his own hands in the process.

Once floored Devlin pressed his knee on the large thug's chest, put one hand over his mouth and gouged out his left eye. Out of a sop to mercy Devlin desisted from blinding the animal in the other eye. He did however jump up and bring his foot down on Cochrane's right ankle, shattering it against the cobblestones. Blood-curdling screams blew through the alley like the mistral. Throughout the attack the contract killer's movements had been fluid, clinical. Devlin didn't enjoy violence. But he had to admit that he was quite good at it. He had seen worse. Done worse.

"If I see any of you again, or hear a report that you have attacked anyone else, I'll kill you."

They had no reason to think he wouldn't keep his word. Cochrane groaned – blood trickling like tears from his gruesome looking eye socket. Grady murmured a curse – and whimpered. He winced too, upon finally summoning up the courage and coordination to remove the flick-knife from his buttock. Farrell remained limpet-like against the wall. His ear still smarted, to say the least. He closed his eyes and prayed that Devlin wouldn't come back to him, as he had assaulted Cochrane twice.

The trio resisted not when their attacker rifled through their pockets and retrieved their phones and wallets. Devlin would note their names, in case he saw their faces in the area and needed to track them down. He would then toss the wallets and phones in the Thames. What money he recovered he would place in Emma's *Christian Aid* box, which sat on her shop counter near the till. He would do so when she wasn't looking. At the end of the month, when she emptied it, she would get a pleasant surprise. He wanted her to still believe in charitable acts and that people were fundamentally good.

The robber band would have to somehow reach a hospital. But they would not report the incident to the police. The police were still the enemy and – ironically or not – they still had their pride. As much as they would demand vengeance too they also had no real desire to cross paths with the well-trained psychopath again.

As Devlin was exiting the alley he caught the sight of a curtain move. A boy peered out his bedroom window – and

Devlin was reminded of the young Afghan who had stared at him in the village, just before the fateful attack. He felt a twinge – of regret, duty, conscience or bloodlust.

*

Like an actor waiting in the wings, about to go on stage, Devlin took a deep breath before turning the door handle and entering the apartment. The adrenalin he recently felt had subsided. He had taken his jacket off beforehand, having noticed a cutlass-shaped crimson stain on the lapel. He would take it to be dry-cleaned near the *Huntsman & Hounds*, lest their local drycleaner mention the stain to Emma, when she popped in there. Devlin didn't enjoy leading a double-life. But he had to admit he was quite good at it.

He walked into the living room and poured out a large whisky. Emma had opened the balcony door and the breeze fanned his face. A framed print of Holbein's *The Ambassadors* dominated the main wall. Holly had bought it for him. They had discussed the painting on their first date together. To put her own stamp on their home Emma had furnished the walls with several pictures from her previous flat: Brueghel's '*Winter Landscape Bird Trap*' and Beuckelaer's '*Christ Carrying the Cross*'. She had also gifted him a large print of Jacob van Ruisdael's '*Wheat Fields*'. His and her bookcases flanked a leather sofa. His included various works of military history, philosophy, novels by Greene, Dostoyevsky, Camus, Conrad, Balzac and others. *Hers* were filled with a collection of Jane Austen hardbacks, historical romance novels and literary biographies. They often read from each other's shelves however. She wanted to understand him more and he thought she had good taste. A large Persian rug – a gift from Porter – lay next to a rustic oak coffee table. When it arrived at the apartment he was tempted to check the item for listening devices.

Emma came in from the kitchen. Devlin liked the way her heels clicked on the wooden floor. A film of sweat glistened on her brow, neck and shins. There seemed little difference between the smoothness of her skin and the silk dress. He wanted her more than the whisky – or a cigarette. He always made sure he never thought of Holly when he was making love to Emma, albeit he sometimes pictured her before or afterwards.

"How was your Mum?"

"Well, she was complaining that my father was spending too much time at the golf course – and then getting under her feet when home. She mentioned that her neighbour has just bought a "loud and unsightly" foreign sports car. She advised me to grow my hair longer and that I should have "underlings" work at the shop so that I can spend more time networking and courting corporate clients. Whatever that means. As for the rest of the country it's apparently going to rack and ruin. In short, my mother is fine and feeling herself," Emma said, smiling demurely as she sided up to Devlin and took a sip of his whisky. She failed to report however that her mother had asked her, again, when Devlin was going to propose.

Violet soon followed Emma into the room, having finished a late-night marrowbone treat. The friendly, adorable mongrel wagged her tail and leapt up at Devlin when she saw him. He could never be unhappy in her company.

7.

The air was awash with citrus sunshine. A few wisps of cloud were scattered, rose petal-like, across a burning blue sky. London was either on the cusp of a heatwave or already experiencing one. Devlin appeared uncomfortable in a jacket and tie and pulled at the neck of his shirt as he walked out onto the first-floor terrace of the Savile Club. Devlin had pressed his shirt with extra vigour that morning, as if he were back in the regiment. He had also polished his shoes as if he were due to step out onto parade in them. He didn't usually mind if his shirts were a little crumpled, or if his shoes went unpolished. It was a reminder that he was now free of the army and could breathe out in terms of the unpleasantness of Northern Ireland, Iraq and Afghanistan. And he was free from following orders.

Oliver Porter was already sitting at a table to the rear of the terrace. Whether as a host or guest he liked to be punctual. There is a rule at various London clubs, whether officially stated or not, that members should refrain from shaking hands. It implied that one was doing business at the club, instead of spending one's time recreationally. The bonds of friendship were far stronger than any ties to a club for Porter however, and he wilfully ignored the rules to shake Devlin's hand when greeting him. He duly noticed how irritated his guest seemed in his tightly buttoned-up shirt.

"You're welcome to loosen a button, Michael. I won't tell anyone. I get paid for keeping secrets – but I'm happy to keep this one for gratis," Porter amiably exclaimed. Devlin glanced at the table and noted that his friend had already worked his way through half a bottle of burgundy. He half-smiled, nodded in reply and unfastened his top button.

With no more than a wink, a pencil-skirted waitress briskly attended to their table so Devlin could order a drink. Maria had served Porter on more than one occasion. She now knew when to approach the charming (but never forward) club member and, more importantly, when he didn't want to be disturbed. She also knew that, whether he was having a three-course meal or just a coffee, she would receive a crisp fifty pound note as a tip - (which Porter made sure went to the sweet-natured waitress, instead of going to the establishment).

"You're looking well," Devlin remarked, after ordering a large vodka and tonic. And he meant it. Porter always looked well, like a well-preserved piece of waxed, oak furniture. He couldn't help but notice how much weight his friend had lost since he had last seen him a few months back. Where once Porter had been jowly his countenance was now lean. His skin, stretched across his face, made him look slightly reptilian. But perhaps he was being unkind in thinking such a thought, Devlin considered. So much and so little can change in a few months. Devlin internally winced, thinking how much it must have cost Porter to buy an entire new wardrobe.

"It's the new and improved me," Porter replied, briefly looking down at his stomach – or lack of one. "Retirement suits me better than I thought. Victoria has been Stasi-like in keeping watch over me, in terms of what I eat and drink. But I've also been good myself. It felt somewhat strange at first – and I'm still not wholly enamoured with my new regime – but the aim is to continue to be good."

Devlin couldn't quite tell if Porter was referring to his diet, or moral health, after he finished speaking. Perhaps he meant both.

"Retirement suits us both, it seems," the former contract killer asserted, with less enthusiasm than his friend.

"And how's Emma? I hope you've been smart enough not to let her slip through your fingers. I liked her – and not just because she kindly laughed at all my bad jokes. Ill-dressed feminists will of course shrilly despise me for saying so and accuse me of being patronising – but women are our better halves. What was it Kingsley Amis once wrote? "Women are really much nicer than men: No wonder we like them.""

"She's fine. We're good," Devlin replied, slightly uneasily, as he recalled how, after making love to her the previous night, he thought of Holly. He had also drunk a large measure of brandy, in attempt to wash away the craving his mouth had for a cigarette. Devlin sat up in bed in the middle of the night and stared fixedly at the wardrobe on the opposite side of the room, wanting to scratch the itch of holding his gun in his hand and cleaning it – and experiencing the kick of the recoil again. But Emma lay asleep next to him, her head resting on his chest.

"I'm pleased to hear it. I thought you might have asked to meet to tell me the news that you're getting married."

Porter noted that Devlin was still wearing his wedding ring from his first marriage. He should have taken it off years ago. There were occasions when Porter judged that his friend, like Hamlet, displayed a degree of "unmanly grief" in his attachment to Holly. He worshipped her memory as if he were the last devotee to an ancient religion.

The words almost stuck in Devlin's throat, partly because he couldn't ever recall the last time he had put them together in a sentence:

"No, I'm not getting married again. I wanted to see you to ask for your help."

Devlin proceeded to tell his friend about the attack in the village and its aftermath. His voice was devoid of emotion, as if he were delivering a routine sitrep - which is not to say that his heart wasn't full of ire and pity as he spoke. Devlin also declared his intent to murder Rameen before he returned to Afghanistan.

"He's staying at The Ritz. I could use the help of your hacker to find out what you can about his itinerary – and what protection he has. I will also need him to get into the system and turn the cameras off... I'll be willing of course to pay the going rate for any services you provide."

Devlin only knew the name of Porter's hacker by the name of "Mariner". Mariner had access to foreign and domestic government databases. As well as providing a wealth of intelligence for Porter, Mariner had also helped Devlin during a hit a couple of years ago, when he shut down the security and camera systems of a boutique hotel in Marseille. Devlin suspected that the famous hotel would be a difficult hack, but not an impossible one, for Mariner.

Porter listened to his friend and only occasionally interjected to clarify a point or two. He gently nodded his head, furrowed his brow and steepled his fingers – as if he were Sherlock Holmes deciding whether to take on a case or not.

A sterile, or diseased, silence hung in the air after Devlin said what he needed to say. Porter took a deep breath and puffed out his cheeks on exhaling, all the time craving a cigar. He rubbed his hand across his forehead, either in despair or to wipe away the film of sweat on his skin. Ironically, he judged Devlin was being absurd or conceited in believing that he owed this Birch fellow, or the dead young squaddie, a debt of honour. Yet Porter would not deny help to his former associate – because he owed him a debt of honour. He would however attempt to talk Devlin out of a decision which could ruin his friend's life – and potentially his own too.

"It's only proper that I should tell you what I tell other people who come to me in a similar vein. If there is any other way to gain restitution, or solve the problem, then do so. There is an attractive finality to death but our sins have a way of coming back to haunt us. Whether through the agency of God, some cosmic fate or more mortal means, it is all too often the case that we must atone for our actions. As much as I may be able to lower the risk, a risk still exists nonetheless. Before you make your final decision, you should think of Emma, of your foster parents and what will happen to you – and them – should you be captured and prosecuted. If you fail, then Rameen or his father Hakim might succeed in the role of avenging angel. This John Birch could also be charged with conspiracy to commit murder. Even if Mariner proves successful in temporarily disabling the security there are still too many variables involved in the job. We do not know the quantity and quality of the security personnel. What if you encounter a hotel staff member in the hallway, after coming back out of Rameen's room? What about if the room is full of escorts or innocent civilians? I'm all for reducing the number of British civil servants we have, but there are kinder ways of doing it. And what if you are caught on a tourist's mobile phone when walking through the foyer? You're breaking your own rule of making a leap into the unknown. God knows what you will face when you pull out your gun and step into the suite. If I had come to you with this job, to complete in such a small timeframe, you would have doubtless said "thank you but no thank you." You used to think you had nothing to lose. But you don't anymore," Porter argued, resisting the temptation to tell Devlin that his own safety could be at risk if something went awry. He selfishly wanted his retirement to last. "You mentioned you owe it to your friend to go after Jamal – but if he was any sort of friend he wouldn't ask you to jeopardise everything… Your war is over. Let the past remain in the past. Killing him won't make your friend walk again or bring that poor boy back to life… As you know, when you first retired, I was keen to have you come back and work for me. But then, I must confess, I admired you for giving yourself a second chance. You got out. Why do you want back in?"

"I made a promise to someone," Devlin replied, his voice a mosaic of regret, resignation and dogged determination.

"*Mine honour is my life; both grow in one; take honour from me and my life is done.*"

"The world won't fall apart if you break your word, Michael. I have recently been reading about William Marshal, the medieval knight. Chivalry was always more of an idea than a reality. England's greatest knight broke his word more times than a cabinet minister. I am of course worried that, whether you are aware of it or not, you are getting back into the game for a different, darker reason. Have you ever heard the name George Scarrow?"

Devlin shook his head, half noticing the portraits of Edmund Burke and David Hume which hung behind Porter.

"Scarrow was, like you, a soldier. He first served in the paras and then the SBS. He was pensioned off early when a bullet injured his shoulder and he couldn't be fit for active service in any regiment. Scarrow was smart, brave and not a little insane when his blood was up. Soldiering had been his life and no sooner did he leave the army than he signed up as a mercenary. He worked in personal protection in Afghanistan, he worked the oil tankers in Somalia and did a few jobs for myself. The work paid well and he told me – and himself – that he had to keep working to pay for two divorces and school fees for his children. But after one or two drinks Scarrow would tell you the real reasons why he couldn't retire and adjust to civilian life. He told me that he missed the adrenalin rush of being a soldier. There was no other drug like it – and trust me he experimented with a few. If he didn't have a mission or cause, then there was a gaping hole in life. He knew how absurd he sounded when he said it too – but he had been a soldier for so long he didn't know how to be anything else. He thought he wasn't good for anything else. As Thomas Paine once wrote, "Habit makes more converts than reason." And so George kept working. He drank like a fish and smoked like a chimney. His reflexes slowed and he grew careless on jobs. The spirit may be willing but the flesh is all too often weak. George contracted cancer and passed away around half a dozen years ago. Old soldiers do die, as well as fade away. There must have been no more than ten people at his funeral to mourn and celebrate his life. Even his ex-wives and children were absent. I visited George in hospital and one of the last things he said to me was that I shouldn't ever go chasing past glories – because you can never catch up with them. I would rather you didn't follow George's path. Give yourself something to live for, rather than die for. Civilian life isn't all that bad, so long as you don't spend too much time in the company of other civilians," Porter asserted. He felt a shard of shame at lying to his friend – as he had made-up George Scarrow and his emblematic life story – but things needed to be said, he judged.

"It'll be just one last job. But I'll understand if you can't help me, Oliver."

"But you'll proceed even without my help?"

Devlin nodded his head. Porter sighed - and then sent Mariner a text message to say he needed to meet with the hacker after lunch.

***

Emma shook the charity tin on the counter at the florists and smiled, as she heard the rustle of several notes inside. Sunlight poured through the window like honey and a symphony of scents sewed themselves into the air, like fine silks embroidering a tapestry. The shop looked beautiful. Takings were up for the week, again. But something was wrong. Emma shifted on her stool, uncomfortable, like a princess with a pea beneath her mattress, as she recalled her prosecco-fuelled conversation with her friend Samantha at lunchtime:

"You should stop having sex with him until he proposes. Or give him the best sex of his life, in order to prompt him to pop the question," Samantha half-joked, as she offered a demure look to their Italian waiter. Although recently married, the bored housewife was not averse to having some fun while her sales executive husband was away on business ("I know that he cheats on me when he's in Paris, so why shouldn't I cheat on him occasionally?").

Emma had laughed at her friend's comment, but bittersweetly. She was ready to commit to him. She loved him. And marriage would deepen, sanctify, their love. There are some Catholics who like to collect sacraments like service medals. And the sooner she married the sooner she could have children.

"Or, I've got an even better idea," Samantha remarked, her eyes narrowing in a spirit of gleeful, tipsy deviousness. "I can let you have the keys to our apartment in Paris. If he doesn't propose to you during a romantic weekend in the city of lovers, then he never will. And it'll be his loss."

Emma tapped her foot on her stool in excitement – and nervousness – as she considered the plan. With every tap, she vacillated between hope and dread, painting scenarios of him proposing – or her leaving. Emma also thought of all her friends who had married (and some were now divorced) – calculating how long they had dated their partners before they had gotten engaged.

If only he'd take off his wedding ring. Show me a sign.

8.

Good weather only lasts for so long. Around dusk the clouds congregated together like a pitchfork-carrying mob and soon afterwards the heavens opened. The storm hissed and spat like a mongoose. Violet lay curled-up on the sofa and, her brow furrowed, gazed out the window, gloomily wondering if the drear and violent weather would ever end. She lay in between Devlin and Emma. A selection of country songs, by Hank Williams, Glen Campbell and the Dixie Chicks, played in the background. As Devlin had often remarked over the years, to anyone who would listen, country music was one of the best things America had ever given the world.

"Now, you're looking at a man that's getting kinda mad
I had a lot a luck but it's all been bad
No matter how I struggle and strive
I'll never get out of this world alive…"

"It sounds like a plan," Devlin said, after half-listening to Emma talk about arranging a trip to Paris. "Can we finalise things next week though?"

Devlin was distracted, like a man on a train worried about missing his flight at the airport. Emma noticed how he had been on the same page of the book he'd been reading for over ten minutes. The oppressive humidity only fanned the flames of their frustrations. He needed space and quiet, to think about the job. He needed to research various pieces of information on his laptop, but dared not for fear of Emma glancing at the screen and quizzing him. He wanted to think about Rameen, stoke the furnace of vengeance in his heart. He wanted to work his way through the bottle of Grey Goose vodka in the freezer, instead of just having a couple of glasses. He wanted to take out his weapon and lay its constituent parts on the kitchen table and clean it – smell the gun oil on his fingers. He wanted a cigarette and to listen to more Hank Williams, with the volume turned-up. He wanted his privacy and home back for the night, with only the dog and the ghost of Holly for company.

"Galveston, oh , Galveston
I still hear your sea waves crashing
While I watch the cannons flashing.
I clean my gun, and dream of Galveston.
I still see her standing by the water,
Standing there looking out to sea.
And is she waiting there for me,
On the beach where we used to run?"

"It'd be nice to set a date now, just to give Samantha notice and to make sure the apartment will be available when we want to go," Emma replied, trying to impress upon him the importance of the trip. She breathed or sighed at witnessing him twist his wedding ring. Emma wanted to leave for Paris as soon as possible, to know whether he wanted to marry her. To know if he loved her. She was wearing a pair of white, linen trousers - which clung to her shapely legs – and a purple, satin blouse. Emma fingered her crucifix as she spoke. She often did so when praying, or agitated.

"I've just got a few things on over the coming week. For one thing, I'm meeting my old CO tomorrow about a possible job - for me and, more importantly, John. I don't want to arrange a trip and put Samantha to any trouble, only to cancel any plans a couple of days later."

"I done my honky tonkin' round and had a lot of fun

But somehow I can't understand how one and one makes one

I like to cuddle near you and listen to you lie

But get that marryin' out of your head I'll be a bachelor till I die…"

The shushing sound of the rain did nothing to quieten the nagging voices in their heads. There was tetchiness in both their tones. She knew he was hiding something from her, as usual. He knew she was being unreasonable. But things would just simmer rather than come to the boil. Emma recalled how, when talking to Samantha earlier, she had revealed that they never really argued about anything.

"Perhaps we should argue more. It might be a good thing. It'll make us more like a normal couple," Emma wryly asserted.

"And it'll be a good dress rehearsal for married life," Samantha added, humourlessly, as she thought of her rich – but fantastically dull and selfish – husband. The former school teacher but now housewife couldn't remember the last time they had been in each other's company for more than two days, without having a full-blown row. "In the next year, I'm going to need to get pregnant or get a good divorce lawyer," she confessed to Emma after ordering a large gin and tonic, to help wash the prosecco down.

Whether due to the thunder outside or turbulent atmosphere in the apartment Violet let out a whimper and nuzzled Devlin. He responded by rubbing her belly affectionately.

"It's alright. It'll soon all be over. All will be well."

A storm can only last for so long.

"It's been two long years now

Since the top of the world came crashing down

151

And I'm getting it back on the road now
But I'm taking the long way
Taking the long way around ..."

***

Oliver Porter wrinkled his nose at the slight inconvenience of the storm. He would have to wait to take Marlborough out for his evening walk. The consultant sat at his desk, cradling a glass of brandy in his hand, it's stem between his fingers as he lovingly swirled the golden liquid around before letting the elixir warm and stimulate his throat. An air purifier hummed in the corner and generated a cooling breeze. Porter closed his eyes and let the air fan him whilst he scrunched-up his toes on the thick claret carpet in his office, before turning his attention to the computer screen.

Mariner had sent an encrypted email to say he had compiled a file on Jamal, which he would courier over to the Savile tomorrow afternoon. The hacker also confirmed that he could disable the relevant security systems and cameras at the hotel, although Devlin would only have a window of twenty minutes before a series of protocols kicked in and the staff – and police – would be alerted. Mariner also mentioned he would enclose a special key card in the folder, which Devlin could use to open the door of the relevant suite at the hotel.

Porter pursed his lips and rolled his eyes when he opened his associate's invoice. The fixer had once defined happiness as having more money in one's bank account at the end of the month compared to the start of it. But just this once Porter would ignore his own Macawber-like philosophy to re-pay his debt to Devlin. He had little doubt that the honourable – or daft – soldier would have kept his promise to try to assassinate the Afghan without him. At least, by giving him as much assistance as he could, Porter would narrow Devlin's odds in succeeding. There was more than a slither of selfishness in Porter's supposedly selfless offer however. If apprehended then it was possible that previous hits could be pinned on Devlin – and traced back to him (not that Porter believed, for one second, that Devlin would ever give him up to the authorities to lessen his sentence). But, for once perhaps, Porter's motivation wasn't wholly borne from self-interest.

You did warn yourself years ago, Oliver, about making friends in this business. And now you're paying for it.

Devlin was different. He was the only operative Porter had invited to his home and introduced to his wife and children. Most killers, almost by definition, were psychopaths. The army occasionally attracted them – or created them. Porter had little difficulty in spotting and recruiting associates when he began to grow his business. Contract killers often lacked empathy and a regard for conventional morality. Something was missing in their brain chemistry, or had been added. Some told themselves that they killed for money – but in truth most were sadists. Violence – and killing – could be tantamount to a drug. *Cruelty may be more addictive – and ubiquitous – than nicotine.* Yet Devlin was different. He neither lacked empathy nor a moral code. If he was a depressive, he was stoical rather than manic. If he was a drunk he was a sober, or even happy, drunk. More than anyone else Porter had encountered, Devlin killed out of a sense of righteousness. His targets were the corrupt and the cruel. He was meticulous in his planning to avoid anyone innocent being in the line of fire. But righteousness can be as addictive – and cancerous – as nicotine. The soldier's righteousness – and sense of honour – could now be his undoing. And who is truly righteous? Priests and Bob Geldof? Or anyone who forwards on a tweet by Michelle Obama? If none but the righteous deserved to live, Porter considered, then the planet would be deserted.

Devlin argued that this would be his final job. But he sounded about as convincing as a barfly who had just declared that he had taken his last drink. Maybe he was fated to never find peace. He was, like Coriolanus drenched in blood, drenched in too much sorrow and sin. He missed his wife too much. The widowed lovebird doesn't sing. Porter had been worried in the past that, wearied with taking other lives, Devlin would one day ultimately take his own. At first Porter was concerned that he would lose an asset. But now he was concerned that he would lose a friend.

9.

Maria directed Devlin to where Porter was sitting, in a quiet corner of the club. A large Glenmorangie on a coaster was also waiting for him at the table. Porter finished off his gin and tonic and requested another. He couldn't help but notice how the bags under Devlin's eyes were more pronounced. His hair, despite being relatively cut short, was uncharacteristically unkempt – and his shirt hadn't been crisply ironed, compared to the day before. *He's fraying.* Perhaps he's having doubts and second thoughts about the job. But it was in hope more than expectation that Porter thought Devlin would alter his course – even if he knew he was about to sail off the edge of the world.

Deep-throated laughter sounded from an adjacent room, where a party of people – consisting of politicians, senior civil servants, journalists and political lobbyists – were having lunch. More than one guest had spotted Porter as he entered the club. At first, he was accosted by the political hack Simon Wendle, the son of Sir Anthony Wendle, the former Labour cabinet minister and MP for Sunderland. Ampleforth, and living in the shadow of a brilliant but emotionally retarded father, had damaged him. Tony Benn had once said that Simon Wendle would go far. In Benn's defence, it wasn't the only thing the diarist got wrong in his life. The journalist and political commentator sat by the phone each morning, waiting for an editor at The Guardian or a producer at Sky News to call him. He could have a fervent opinion on anything, for a modest fee. Wendle had taken to spending his afternoons at the Savile of late, in order to supplicate the great and the good who were also members of the Garrick, to nominate him for membership of the more prestigious club. Wendle sawed the air with his hands, like a bad actor, when he spoke – or rather pontificated. He sounded like Brian Sewell, sucking on a lemon. And looked like Ben Bradshaw, after a pub crawl. His palms glistened with sweat or oil from his slicked-back hair, Porter observed. The fixer smiled politely and duly pretended to be interested in his morsels of outdated gossip and latest newspaper column. Like a wasp noticing a brighter bloom however, Wendle excused himself from Porter's company when he observed a close friend of Paul Dacre enter the club. His last words were to promise to have lunch with Porter soon. "Why don't we go to the Garrick? You are still a member, aren't you?"

Before Porter had time to draw breath, or sigh, he was approached by Walter Leach, the new Tory MP for Welwyn Hatfield. Half a dozen years ago, unbeknownst to Leach, Porter had been asked by a cabal from the 1922 committee to dissuade him from running as a Conservative candidate in a key by-election. Employing an intermediary Porter forced Leach to withdraw from the race by blackmailing him with knowledge of the businessman's tax affairs. Ironically, two years later, Porter was asked to work on Leach's campaign when he ran for parliament in a marginal seat in Somerset. This time Porter leaked news of a Labour candidate's extra-marital gay affair to the press. "Red Ted Beds Young Black Fred in Garden Shed," isn't a headline that's easy to come back from in Frome. And he didn't.

And so Walter Leach entered office. Porter had recently read a profile of the MP:

"He's like Michael Fabricant, but with slightly tidier hair…
or a slightly more honest Grant Schapps… crossed with a
slightly more intelligent Nikki Morgan and less self-serving
Michael Gove. Indeed, Walter Leach may have been created
in a lab to produce the best, or worst, Tory politician known
to man."

As much as Leach had recently preached how he was
working night and day to save his local hospital from closure
– as well as working every hour to secure the best Brexit
possible – the member of parliament for Welwyn Hatfield
was far more concerned about how much his wife would take
from him in the divorce settlement.

"I would greatly appreciate your advice at some point
Oliver. My lawyers are proving to be far too scrupulous. I
need to know how best to hide my assets, else she'll fleece
me of everything. She just wants to leave me with the flat in
London, which I haven't had time to properly flip yet. I also
don't want her to use the money set aside for my boy's
education to go towards paying for a new pair of tits and a
ghastly Audi TT. She may be playing the victim in the press.
But if you watch carefully enough, when she wipes away the
tears, you'll see the bitch has claws instead of fingers."

Porter offered Leach a vague promise that they would
discuss things in more detail soon but then excused himself:

"I apologise, Walter, but I need to meet someone
downstairs. I'm late and he may already be here."

"Oh, sorry. Is it urgent or can you spare a few more
minutes?"

"You might say it's a matter of life or death. But it
concerns something even more important than that. Lots of
money," Porter said, whilst rubbing his hands together,

grinning sumptuously and forcing a coin-like glint into his eye.

Leach replied by chortling and nodding his head in approval.

"Well let me know if I can do anything in the House to help proceedings." He then disappeared into the direction of the bar, to expense another drink.

Porter walked off in the opposite direction, wryly or woefully thinking to himself how the Savile used to be home to the likes of Charles Darwin and Kipling. But nowadays the club was populated by lawyers, hedge fund managers and media consultants. They hung around the place like harpies or gargoyles, perched on gothic cathedrals.

God help us.

Porter passed the memory stick and hotel key card to Devlin.

"No doubt you'll scrutinize the information later but I thought I might give you some of the highlights now. Your friend Rameen worked his way up, or down, from rapist to politician. Several years ago, his father gave the Karzai government a substantial bribe so his son could serve as a trade delegate and diplomat. Suffice to say he uses his diplomatic pouch to transport a variety of opiates around the world, as opposed to any official papers. He has also used his diplomatic status to grant him immunity against rape, criminal damage various and traffic violations. MI5 put him under surveillance at the beginning of the week. So far, our esteemed Afghani trade delegate has assaulted two escorts from the comfort of his hotel suite. They were paid off however and told to keep their mouths shut, although that will prove easy for one poor girl it seems as he broke her jaw. He usually wakes just after midday and goes shopping. He's spent more time in Harrods's this week than a footballer's wife. He has attended one or two scheduled meetings with trade representatives but "the devout Muslim" – as he's been described on his government's website - has been either drunk or high when he's done so."

Devlin's jaw became squarer as he compressed his teeth together. Determination, rather than moral outrage, shaped his features. He tapped his fingers on the table in front of him, restless and eager to pull the trigger on the target. He wanted to feel the recoil of his gun again. The sensation would jolt through his arm and maybe jumpstart something in his heart.

"What does the file say about his security detail?"

"He has come over with two trained security personnel. They will be armed. When they are with him in the hotel suite though they may well be getting high. Our government has generously provided him with some additional security, albeit the file states that they only accompany their charge when he is scheduled to leave the hotel. As you will notice though the intelligence isn't altogether up-to-date. What with being painfully under resourced, MI5 have moved the surveillance team to another person of interest."

"Do we know why he's in London? Is there any intelligence that suggests links to terrorism?"

"I'll come to that in a moment. Ostensibly our honoured guest is in town to negotiate a trade deal, with an Anglo-American pharmaceutical conglomerate, for his father's opium crop. Most of the crop will of course still be set aside for less law-abiding cartels. In return DFID, as a sweetener to seal the deal, will be re-directing a large part of its Afghan aid budget into Hakim Jamal's bank account. Oh, what a tangled web we weave, the British government should say to itself. But, alas, all too often it doesn't. But in regards to Rameen he is too much of a liability to be invited into the inner circles of terrorist networks. He is about as likely to tie-up a terrorist attack as he is his shoelaces. The real target on Five's watch list this week was his fellow trade delegate, one Faisal Ahmadi. There is intelligence from MI6 on the file I've just given you. As a teenager, he fought in the ranks of the mujahedeen against the Russians, working with the CIA to distribute Stinger missiles to jihadists throughout his province. It seems Ahmadi is as forgiving as a Christian however, as he now works alongside his former enemy to provide intelligence about the US to the Russians. Ahmadi is known for his predilections of sitting in on torture sessions and grooming boys. But he doesn't drink and is duly called a "dedicated Muslim" on his government's website. As well as serving as Hakim Jamal's right-hand man, Ahmadi is also responsible for running a network of people smugglers. Partly he does so for money. He's only human, as well as being monster, after all. Let us not gild the lily and deem them political refugees. Smugglers are principally transporting economic migrants across Europe. Young Muslim men. And for every hundred economic migrants Ahmadi's associates smuggles into London, Paris and Brussels, he is also smuggling half a dozen agents of Islamic State into the West. During the course of this week he has had meetings with a handful of Imams, who are known to work as recruiters for Isis. Although they may preach a message of peace to their flocks in the Midlands, they also take the wolves aside and encourage them to bare their teeth. Under the guise of charitable donations Ahmadi provides funds for the Imans to expand their operations and out-reach programmes through mosques. He has links as well to the Saudis and, using his diplomatic status, serves as a mule – delivering money and instructions to special interest groups in the UK who lobby for the introduction of Sharia law in designated parts of the country. The hotel will need to change the carpet after the stain Jamal leaves, so you won't be inconveniencing The Ritz too much if you retire Ahmadi as well. Indeed, you'll be doing the world a veritable favour. I suspect the security services might even give you a medal, rather than prison sentence, if they apprehend you."

Porter glanced at up a frowsty looking portrait of Palmerston hanging on the opposite wall, looking down on them. He imagined the portrait coming to life, with the statesman offering Devlin an encouraging pat on the shoulder and conspiratorial wink.

"I'll be sure to introduce myself to the dedicated Muslim," Devlin replied, evenly. He had already determined that he would take down any of Rameen's personal security in the suite, when he met with his target.

"You will need to do so soon. The pair are due to fly back to Kabul before the beginning of next week. Have you set a time for the job yet?"

"Tomorrow night."

The words cut through the air and came to a dead stop like a guillotine. Although there was a finality to his tone Porter still wanted to give Devlin – and himself – a way out.

"You still have time to change your mind. Nature will take care of the snake sooner or later. He'll either kill himself through an overdose, or upset the wrong person. I am sure that your friend, Birch, wouldn't think less of you if you didn't keep your promise. A promise you made, in extraordinary circumstances, over a decade ago."

"He would. And so would I."

Maria interrupted the sterile silence. Porter ordered a couple more drinks. By mutual, unspoken, agreement the two men chose not to talk about the job. Instead the pair discussed the recent Test Match at Lords and asked about the latest history books they had read. Porter had just worked his way through Robert Tombs' *The English and Their History*. "He makes a salient point on nigh on every page... The book should be put on every syllabus in the country. Which is why it won't be." In reply Devlin mentioned how he had re-read Ronald Syme's *The Roman Revolution*. Porter remembered studying the text during his time at Magdalen. Augustus Caesar had brought peace and stability to Rome not because of his willingness to compromise and forgive – but rather because he defeated all his enemies. There were no pieces left on the board to justify playing the game anymore. When asked about deciding the fate of Julius Caesar's murderers the young Octavius had answered, flatly, "They must die". No doubt that chapter resonated with Devlin, Porter mused.

The sun throbbed, as if it were in pain, as the two friends stood upon the steps of the club, on Brook St.

"Just get in touch if you need anything. Let's have another drink when it's all over. I've got a bottle of Dalmore I've been saving for a special occasion. We need to celebrate our retirement. Again."

"I'm grateful for your help, Oliver. I owe you," Devlin remarked, with a splinter of emotion in his throat.

"Nonsense. You don't owe me, or anyone else. They'll be no need for you to say "give a cock to Alcibiades," Devlin warmly replied, making reference to Socrates' last words – to indicate that all his debts, real and metaphysical, had been paid.

Devlin nodded and offered up a fleeting, wry half-smile. The quote prompted him to remember his favourite line from Plato:

"*Be kind, because everyone out there is facing a hard battle.*"

Devlin still valued Plato's words and the idea of kindness. But he didn't want to dwell too much on them at present. He had murder on his mind.

There was little left to say. Porter squeezed Devlin's forearm in a fraternal, or even paternal, gesture. His muscles tensed up at first, but then relaxed – like someone surrendering to a needful embrace.

Porter squinted in the light but his expression remained pinched – pained – for a different reason. He lingered on the steps as Devlin walked away, his head lowered – fishing through his pockets for his headphones, to listen to music. The cynical fixer was not usually prone to sentiment or superstition but he was momentarily gripped by a dreadful presentiment. That something would go awry with the job. A few atoms in Porter's heart wanted to chase after Devlin. Grab him by the lapels of his jacket. Shake some sense into him. Tell him he was insane or being more conceited than a poet. He wanted to come out with a poignant, or hackneyed phrase, to cause him to think twice: "Love is not a disease but a cure." Emma could save Devlin, in the same way Victoria saved him. But it wasn't Porter's way to raise his voice, make a scene or lose his composure. Sangfroid. Englishness needed to be preserved. Porter didn't want to raise any eyebrows, although he realised that he didn't give a damn about the good and the great of the Savile Club compared to Devlin. Besides, Porter was ninety-nine percent sure that there wasn't anything he could have said or done to alter Devlin's course. He may as well try and change the past.

We are where we are.

10.

Devlin walked briskly down New Bond St, weaving his way through the throng of shoppers, his forehead pleated in thought. He kept his head bowered down, not wishing to look anyone in the eye. He purposely didn't listen to any songs on "Holly's Playlist." He always felt uncomfortable thinking about her when planning a job.

A statuesque blonde, with the hint of a Russian accent, asked him for a light, as she tucked a ringlet of hair behind her ear. She smiled invitingly. A cream, lace-hemmed summer dress swayed above sun-burnished thighs and Christian Louboutin heels. Maybe she was an escort. Maybe she liked the way he looked. Maybe she could see into his soul and shared his love of Chekhov. Or maybe she just wanted a light. She was attractive. But not beautiful. Holly was beautiful. Devlin politely let the woman down, albeit he was tempted to ask for a cigarette in return.

He walked on.

"When you think that you've lost everything
You find out you can always lose a little more
I'm just goin' down the road feeling bad
Tryin' to get to heaven before they close the door."

His phone vibrated with a message from Birch, asking for an update. It wasn't the first message of its kind he had received in the past few days – and it wouldn't be the last. Devlin felt like he had a Jiminy Cricket-type figure on his shoulder, although Birch couldn't have exactly been considered the voice of his conscience.

*

Devlin met Tyerman in the bar of the Cavalry & Guard's Club, on Piccadilly. Tyerman got up from his Chesterfield chair and strode across the room to greet his former squaddie. He shook his hand – vigorously – and looked him squarely in the eye as he told Devlin how good it was to see him again. Despite having left the army five years ago, Charles Tyerman still retained his military gait and bearing. His back was ramrod straight. His chin jutted out like the white cliffs of Dover. His hair was now mostly iron grey, streaked with black. Tyerman's default expression was still as serious – or severe even – as Devlin remembered. Although from the outset he knew that the Colonel's heart was in the right place. He genuinely cared for the welfare of his men, which was more than could be said for his counterparts in Whitehall. As much as he valued discipline his decency shone through as brightly as the brass buttons on his dress uniform. Tyerman gave a lecture to each batch of new recruits who arrived in Helmand. He revealed how, if he hadn't signed-up, he would have been a History teacher. During his monthly newsletter to the regiment he would include quotes from Horace, Gibbon and Ralph Waldo Emerson, among others. As a result, Tyerman was a far more well-rounded and cerebral officer than many of his martinet colleagues. And Devlin respected him for it. He respected him for the conviction in his voice and fervour in his eyes when he said that, should Jamal come into his own sights too, he would kill the man who had taken the life of one of his young soldiers. More than most, Tyerman was a good and honourable man, Devlin conceded.

A trio of jaundiced septuagenarians worked their way through a bottle of Dow's vintage port at the bar, re-living the Falkland's campaign. Their lips and gums were radish-coloured. They croaked more than spoke. Devlin couldn't quite tell if their eyes were glinting, or merely rheumy. The past was all they had, he initially thought. But then corrected himself. How did he know? They could still be married – and maybe they had children and grandchildren. They probably had more interests than himself – and a wider circle of friends. They had probably done something with their lives and made the most of their time.

The past is all I have.

Battle scenes and portraits of hoary, monocle-wearing officers dominated the walls. The smell of furniture polish, port and lavender wafted through the air. Tyerman ordered a couple of drinks and the two men sat by the fireplace. A marble mantelpiece, home to some freshly cut flowers and two antique Regency pistols, sat beneath a large reproduction of Benjamin West's "*The Death of General Wolfe.*"

"You're looking well, Michael," Tyerman said, his voice as clear and hard as ice. He spoke like a House Master from Harrow, one who was efficient as opposed to eccentric.

"So are you, Sir," Devlin replied. The trim figure in front of him appeared younger than his fifty-five years. As ever his face was clean-shaven, smoother than the surface of the varnished, lion-footed coffee table which sat between them. The tan from Helmand had been replaced by one gleaned from time spent at his villa in Cyprus. His new suit was made to measure, his shoes handmade. Devlin had also observed the electronic key to a Mercedes, when Tyerman had extracted his wallet from his pocket to pay for the drinks. He also knew, from what Birch told him, that Tyerman owned a flat in Chiswick for when he was up in London – but his main home, replete with a swimming pool and tennis court, was just outside Winchester.

"Life is good. I can't complain... Unfortunately, John wasn't looking so well, when I saw him last. Time doesn't heal all wounds. I believe in leaving the past in the past. But that's easy for me to say. What happened to him was awful. I have encouraged him to see a specialist counsellor and had charities get in touch to provide financial support but he's getting worse, I fear. Retreating into himself."

"Rather than charity, I think John needs a job. A sense of purpose and belonging again. I appreciate your offer of a position at your company, Sir, but I will only consider it if you're able to take John on too. I'd be happy for you to subsidize my pay – to the point where I'd be paying his salary out of mine."

Tyerman narrowed his gaze a little and surveyed Devlin, as if he were studying a map – assessing the terrain of where an ambush could occur or where he could best counter-attack his opponent. He hadn't been expecting Devlin to come up with such a proposal – but nor did he reject it out of hand after hearing it. He was certainly keen on employing the former soldier. If Devlin turned out to be half the asset he was in Afghanistan for his company, then Tyerman would be willing to give his more troublesome friend a chance to prove his worth too.

"I'll consider it. I would need to think about a suitable position for John. Neither of us would want him to feel that he's a fifth wheel. As you say, he needs a job instead of charity. But before you commit to any role I should explain more about the company and your prospective duties within it."

Tyerman proceeded to tell Devlin about York Security (named after Edward, Duke of York, an antecedent of Tyerman's who had been a friend to Henry V and had died at

Agincourt). After leaving the army Tyerman raised the requisite capital and founded the company four years ago. He hired various officers and squaddies who had served under him in Afghanistan. They were reliable, proficient and loyal. The army's loss was York Security's gain. An old school-friend, who worked as an executive with Coutts & Co, provided the fledgling firm with regular work. Tyerman's brother-in-law was a partner at a major talent agency and fed him clients for the close protection arm of the operation. The company was continuing to grow and needed more personnel.

"It's got to the point where I am having to put in the occasional shift... In terms of the job it's akin to sentry duty. You just need to have eyes in the back of your head – as well as know when to look away when a client is being indiscreet... Some of the business leaders we look after get accosted by anti-capitalism protesters and middle-class students who want to virtue signal on Facebook about the latest trendy cause – but they hit about as hard as the strength of their convictions... We've had an increase in business lately from politicians too. They've realised they can expense personal security – and it makes them seem grand and important to have close protection. They justify it by saying they've had a threatening tweet. They want to play the victim, without having to suffer the unwelcome ordeal of actually dying... It's more likely you'll have to fend off a zealous fan – demanding one of those interminable selfies – than fight off a gun-wielding jihadist but we sometimes do worthwhile work. And it's well remunerated... We have plenty of repeat clients, who may eventually ask for you specifically... As much as you sometimes endeavour to disguise the fact, you're personable and educated Michael... I can arrange a licence for you to carry a weapon in certain circumstances too."

Devlin wryly smiled to himself. If he took the job, he would likely be guarding the type of people he was previously hired to kill.

"You will be asked to undergo some training – and there's some filling out of forms in terms of compliance and insurance – but we would be keen for you to start asap. The question I ask of everyone who's served before – and spent some time as a civilian – is are you willing to follow orders again?" Tyerman remarked. Again, he narrowed his hard, teak eyes and scrutinized Devlin, as if he were a poker player looking for an opponent's tells.

"It'll be good practise, for if I get married again."

Tyerman forced a half-smile, still more convinced about the ex-soldier's abilities than attitude. As much as Tyerman felt a responsibility for the soldiers who had been under his command he could not risk trying to rehabilitate a soldier – Devlin or Birch - at the expense of tarnishing the reputation of his company. Devlin had been an asset in Helmand but, even then, Tyerman couldn't escape the thought that someone who was that proficient at killing surely also enjoyed it. But he never seemed to lose control. Devlin possessed an air of indifference, far more than violence. Or something possessed him. Something different. Something dislocated. Dark. One of the reasons why Tyerman had asked Birch about Devlin was that he had re-read Camus' *The Outsider* that week. There was no specific reason but Meursault reminded Tyerman of his former soldier and he wondered what had happened to him.

"I was sorry to hear that your first wife passed away. It must've been hard for you. Or it must be hard," Tyerman said. His voice softened. The ice melted.

An awkward pause ensued, as Devlin's expression and heart hardened. He never felt compelled to fill such silences by unburdening his grief. Or telling the world how much he loved her. A problem shared was not a problem halved.

Tyerman deftly broke the silence by asking if Devlin wanted another drink. He also excused himself and went to the toilet.

When Tyerman returned, carrying a drink in each hand, he changed tact and asked Devlin about what he had been doing, job wise, since he left the army.

"I worked in the security sector for Major Burleigh's outfit for a while, but I've not worked in earnest for some time. My wife left quite a substantial estate, which I have been able to live comfortably off. But I'm aware that the money I have in the bank won't last forever – and sooner or later I'll need a job again."

Devlin often explained his lack of employment – and apparent wealth – stemming from his wife bequeathing him money. Holly had worked as a model for several years – and then successfully invested her capital in property. In truth Devlin donated the bulk of his wife's estate to charity when she died. During an idle conversation one evening she remarked that, if something should happen to her, Devlin should live-off her savings. He joked however, somewhat tragi-comically in light of future events, that he would be fine for money:

"Don't worry, I'll make a killing some day."

"I'm surprised you've lived such a life of leisure," Tyerman replied, suspecting that somehow something was amiss. "I always considered that your real enemy in life was not the Taliban but boredom. Remember Father Arnold, our chaplain? He told me how you once quoted Kierkegaard to him – that "Boredom was the root of all evil.""

"You shouldn't believe everything a priest tells you," Devlin countered. He had been fond of Father Arnold. He listened to the men rather than preached. His Irish whiskies were as strong as his faith too.

"Well, believe it or not, I once had a bet with him – about you. You were of course somewhat an enigma to us all. Father Arnold believed that you were a good Catholic. You were just too busy to notice. Or you hid it well, as if you were trying to conceal the fact from God too. I said, however, that you had become a reaction to your boyhood self and were a staunch atheist, not just because I was privy to your files. You were far too well read to subscribe such hokum, I argued. A little knowledge will make a man an atheist, to paraphrase a saying."

"But a lot will reconcile him to religion," – Devlin thought to himself, finishing off the quote from Francis Bacon. He also considered that his former CO was fishing for answers – and just playing the evangelical atheist. On a small corner table in his office one could often observe an open Bible, next to where he kept his sidearm.

"If I am a catholic, I fear I'm a lapsed one," Devlin remarked, the tone of his voice tantamount to a shrug.

The price of knowing Michael Devlin was that one never really got to know him.

"Is there any other kind?"

Devlin remembered re-reading The End of the Affair, a year or so after Holly died. The last line resonated with him:

"O God, You've done enough, You've robbed me of enough, I'm too tired and too old to love, leave me alone forever."

The two men talked some more. Tyerman asked where Devlin was living. Devlin mentioned Emma. He shrugged when asked if he had plans to get married. They also gossiped about what others from the regiment were up to, before Tyerman glanced at his watch and realised he was running late for another meeting.

"Well, we both have things to consider. I will email you with more information and think about how we can utilise John. I should warn you however that I'll be flying off to Cyprus early tomorrow morning for a holiday with the family. I'll be needing close protection should my wife catch me working too much while we're away. But I am keen for you to join the firm, Michael. I don't just want to offer you a job either. I would like you to have a career with us. Sooner rather than later my wife will demand that I retire – and I want to be able to leave the business in the hands of talented and committed people... As much as I am a ghost from the past I also want to represent the future. This is a chance for you to turn the page and start afresh."

Devlin decided he would accept the job offer, providing Tyerman took on Birch too. He could always resign after a few months. By then, he hoped, Birch would have secured his job on his own merits. He could afford to sacrifice three months. It was the least he could do for Birth. Small acts of kindness can add up. But given his sins, Devlin was still mired in debt. How many times must a man post a cheque to a charity, buy a round of drinks or hold the door open for a stranger, to balance the books against killing a man?

Atonement is still a world away.

11.

Muggy. Suffocating. Clouds like cancer growths on x-ray films. The night felt like a nauseous drunk, but the sick would stay in its gullet.

Emma was wearing a white, cotton shirt with mother-of-pearl buttons. With jeans. She looked good in jeans. Holly looked better. But she still looked good. Good, but not great. Emma fanned herself with a magazine and blew air out the side of her mouth to cool her cheek, as she sat in the corner of the living room. She craved a cold shower to startle her skin – and mood – into life. She thought how Devlin used to join her in the shower. She loved the way he would kneel before her and kiss the inside of her thighs as rivulets of water coursed over every contour, freckle and goose-bump. He would dab kisses on her stomach, collar bone, breasts and neck – as if her body was a dot-to-dot picture. Sometimes she would shudder or tingle in brilliant pleasure. He taught her how parts of her body were all connected. Complete. His fingertips and mouth were soft, considerate and deliberate. An internal smile twisted itself into an internal sneer however, as Emma torturously thought that *she* had taught him how to make love. She had been a top model. She had doubtlessly slept her way to the top.

The prickling heat - and thoughts of Holly - irritated her. She hoped a shower would wash away her stresses. Emma half-watched the television whilst covertly glancing across at Devlin. He had the same far-away look in his eye which she had noticed on first seeing him, drinking in the *The Admiral Nelson*. Aloof or lost.

At least he had agreed to go to Paris the day after tomorrow. Emma suspected he had said yes to keep her silent, as opposed to keep her happy. But they had set a date. He had promised – and she couldn't remember the last time he had gone back on his word.

He looked past or through the television – showing the latest adaptation of Pride & Prejudice, which Emma had already sat through a dozen times. Devlin was thinking about what he should wear. Not for Paris. But for the job. He would dress smartly, to blend in with the well-heeled hotel guests. A summer jacket would conceal his shoulder holster and gun. A baseball cap would give the impression that he was an American tourist. The cap would also shield his face from any cameras on the street. He memorised the relevant floor plans and the route he would take up to Rameen's suite.

Anyone possessing a weapon in the Afghan's room would be a fair target. Guilty by association. *Kill or be killed*. Should Devlin confront any unarmed innocents in the room he would promptly lock them in the bathroom without their phone. He would also threaten them. If they gave his description to the authorities, then there would be consequences. The policy had worked before.

Should Devlin somehow suffer an injury he would call a number Porter had furnished him with. He would be provided with transport and medical care. Devlin had never had cause to use the service before but he duly programmed the number into his phone. *Never say never*.

He prayed that any lift he caught up to Rameen's floor would be timely and empty. Devlin was too proud or angry to ask God for anything else however.

Emma got up from the sofa, when the credits to the film began to roll, and said that she was going to take a shower. Devlin seemingly stirred, woke up from being in a world of his own. Was she just telling him – or was she offering an invitation to join her? Even if he had the will and energy to make love, he would deny himself. Like a boxer, the night before a big fight, Devlin never had sex the evening before a job – as much as it might take his mind off things. Once tomorrow was over and done with though he would make things up to Emma. He would make an effort in Paris. He was still physically attracted to her. But that attraction now came and went, like a flickering bulb. But with Holly his desire had always burned bright. But he had something good going with Emma. Good, but not great. But the more time that passed, the less he wanted to marry her.

Am I getting bored with her? Boredom might indeed be the root of all evil.

Emma's goodness and innocence had been part of the initial attraction. But Devlin sometimes experienced a sense of shame for coming into her life. The relationship was built on a lie – or at the very least it had been built upon him not telling her the truth.

If she knew me, she would be rightly repulsed.

Ersatz. Devlin had first come across the term when he was a teenager. He had encountered the word in le Carre's The Spy Who Came in from the Cold – and he duly looked-up the definition. The word struck a chord with the disaffected youth – depressing and enlightening him at the same time. And it still explained, or represented, everything about the world today. Everything was artificial, or an inferior version of how things could be. Only the squalid and sinful seemed genuine. Nothing was real or solid. Except death. *All is vanity under the sun*. Devlin couldn't quite remember if he had been an angry or sad young man, when he had first encountered the term. Perhaps he had been both. The one fuelled the other. His memory could be fuzzy about his teenage years. Before his first kill. The young Michael Devlin was another person. Another role. He was an old school-friend he was fond of but couldn't wholly esteem. Decent but weak. Not that Devlin admired who – or what – he had become.

He had told Emma it was likely he would take the job with Tyerman. He asked her what she thought however – and if she had any strong objections he would re-consider things.

"It could be good for you, going back to work... It's not too dangerous though, I hope," she replied.

More so Devlin brought up the subject of York Security to provide him with a couple of alibis. He mentioned that the company wanted him to go for a medical in the afternoon – and a supervisor had invited him to dinner in the evening to talk about his prospective duties. Devlin intended to visit Holly's grave during the day. And, come midnight, he would be striding through the lobby of *The Ritz*.

Devlin went to bed early that night. Tomorrow would be a long day. When Emma came into the bedroom he pretended to be asleep. For her part, she lay with her back to him, awake for most of the evening. Thinking.

12.

Morning.

Devlin peered out of the window and watched Emma walk across the square below, as if he were a cheating husband eager for the coast to be clear to call his mistress.

He cleared the kitchen table and retrieved the locked box from the bottom of his wardrobe. The converted aluminium camera case contained keepsakes from his time with Holly: photos, with Holly always in bloom and Devlin basking in her light; their marriage certificate; various ticket stubs, from art exhibitions, Chekhov plays and author talks they had attended together; her engagement ring, still brilliantly and painfully gleaming; love letters; a first edition of *Lyrical Ballads*... The box was also home to Devlin's shoulder holster and an ink-black Sig Sauer p226, gleaming in an altogether different way to the engagement ring.

Devlin altered the sizing on the holster. He had put on a bit of weight over the past six months. He had changed, but not that much. *Everything changes and everything stays the same.* He put his jacket on over the holster and was satisfied that the cut still disguised the pistol.

The weapon seemed a little heavier in his hand but it still felt well-balanced and comfortable. As soon as his hand enveloped the grip and his finger touched the trigger he felt that all would be well. Rameen was one step closer to death. The weapon had been as reliable as its user during their jobs together, as if they shared a symbiotic relationship.

Happiness is a warm gun.

He carefully – maybe even lovingly – checked and cleaned the pistol. He rolled each bullet between his thumb and finger before inserting it in the magazine. As a gesture, to cement his decision to retire, Devlin hadn't renewed his membership to the gun club he belonged to – although it was telling that he couldn't bring himself to dispose of the gun at the same time. Perhaps Devlin was too attached to the weapon. Or he always knew he would come out of retirement one day. Kill again.

In terms of killing time, before Devlin had to leave to visit the cemetery, he sat on the sofa and closed his eyes, as calm as a monk, thinking about the task at hand and Rameen. In order to sting his conscience – or the opposite of a conscience – into action, Devlin pictured himself back in the village. He recalled Birch being shot – and Connelly being killed. They fell to the floor, like puppets – their strings cut. Most of the cells in the human body are replaced every seven to ten years. But Devlin's vow had remained, buried deeper than any cell. Ingrained, like his humanity – or inhumanity. His expression was as unyielding as an anvil as Devlin went over his plan again for the evening, committing it to memory like a schoolboy learning his catechism.

When he opened his eyes, Devlin found himself staring at the print of van Ruisdael's "Wheat Fields" on the wall opposite. Emma bought the picture after having watched him gaze, fondly and fixedly, at the canvas during a visit to the Royal Academy. She liked the painting too and imagined that the figures in the landscape – of a husband, wife and child – resonated with Devlin. It was what he wanted, deep-down, she believed.

Devlin felt lost and found, absorbed by the landscape. He imagined himself being the weary traveller coming back home, after a long journey, to Holly. To grace and consolation. To the child, they should have had. To God and Heaven. The leaden clouds would eventually blow away – and the blue sky would remain. Beautiful and serene. Like *her*.

***

Porter barely slept the evening before and woke uneasily, as if the nightmare were continuing into the day. Bleeding into it. Something was wrong or would go wrong, he fervently thought. It was one job too many. Devlin was ill prepared and wasn't in the right frame of mind. What if Five put a watch on Jamal and Ahmadi again? What if one of the bodyguards got a shot off? The sound would toll throughout the hotel like a death knell. If cornered, Devlin probably wouldn't let them take him alive. There were a million ways for things to go wrong. But surely, he was needlessly worrying? Devlin would be professional. Porter told himself to be rational. But his brain prickled with anxiety and superstition.

Porter sat in the conservatory. Pre-occupied. Or plagued. He was fully dressed, as if ready and willing to rush out at a moment's notice. A cigar stub lay in a cut-glass ashtray. He downed the dregs of a whisky, licking any remnants of the single malt from his lips. The weather was sunnier than his mood. He pulled out his phone and was tempted to call his friend – tell him that he'd received new intelligence and Devlin should postpone or cancel the job. But Devlin's course was set, whether there was a storm on the horizon or not.

We are where we are. What will be will be. – The fixer thought to himself, tarred in gloom.

Porter managed a grim smile, as he found himself being tempted to pray that all would be well.

I should rather ask Victoria to pray for Devlin. You will, quite rightly, be more inclined to listen to her over me.

"Everything okay, darling?" his wife asked, coming into the conservatory from the garden - having just filled up the birdbath and hung some food upon the pear tree. She noticed Porter had smoked his first cigar earlier than usual and had waited all of five minutes after midday to have his first drink. He had been distracted the day before too. "You're not worried that I'm going to give you salad for lunch again?"

"No," Porter replied, shaking his head and gently smiling. She always knew when he was troubled – and she knew how to ease his troubles. "I would have poured myself a treble if that was the case. I'm just waiting on some news about an investment," he said, lying.

"I'm sure things will work out," Victoria replied, aware that her husband wasn't necessarily telling the whole truth. "How about we go out for lunch, to help take your mind off things? I'll drive."

By saying she would drive Victoria meant that Oliver was free to drink.

"Thanks. Sounds like a plan. This isn't just the drink talking. I'm not sure what I'd do without you," Porter remarked, with one hand propping up his head. Ageing, but doe-eyed.

"I do. For one, you wouldn't eat any salad," Victoria replied, bending down, stroking his temple and sweetly kissing Porter on his corrugated brow.

***

Devlin picked-up several cigarette butts around Holly's grave and put them in his jacket pocket. He would toss them in the bin at the entrance to cemetery. The widower then carefully – lovingly – placed the bouquet of lilies next to his wife's headstone. The petals shone like fine enamel in the lemony afternoon sun. Devlin now went to the florists close to Garrett Lane Cemetery, having previously bought his flowers through Emma, before they started dating. Ironically Emma became attracted to him for the faithful and touching way he still visited his wife's grave every week. The gesture represented a capacity for love, fidelity and an appreciation of the sacred.

The gold script glinted in the light but Devlin still religiously wiped any flecks of mud away with a handkerchief Holly had gifted him.

"To be beloved is all I need
And whom I love I love indeed."

The quotation was from Coleridge. The words were seared into his breast as much as they had been chiselled into the black marble. Holly had also inscribed the quote into his first edition of Lyrical Ballads.

"I hope I haven't ruined its value. But I want you to keep the book forever," his wife remarked, on the morning of their first anniversary.

"It was valuable. But now it's priceless," Devlin had replied, reverently holding the book of verse and cherishing his wife even more. He loved her with a love which was more than a love.

The grass shimmered in the breeze. Stone angels, perched upon ornate headstones, seemed to have turned their heads towards Devlin. But he noticed them not. He was here for Holly and himself. He closed his eyes and bowed his head, as if in prayer.

So, what's new ? Well I might have a new job. Oliver is right. I've led too much of a life   of leisure. I'm probably telling you things that you know already. But I don't have anyone else I can talk to. I'm not quite sure I've told you this before but I thought you might be interested. Oliver once tabled the idea that I would make a good spy.

Devlin recalled the scene. The two men were drinking late, in a hotel bar in Covent Garden, unofficially celebrating completing a lucrative contract. The burgundy flowed, as did the conversation.

"You would make an effective intelligence officer. All you have to do is sit in a foreign bar and get drunk with someone mildly important. You allow them to talk whilst revealing little or nothing in return. Indeed, once you've mastered the local language you can read the relevant newspapers and glean enough information from them to send back to your controllers and keep the blighters happy... It's far from a glamorous profession however. You're more likely to be propositioned by an ageing Cambridge don than you are a svelte Bond girl. The principle danger too comes from paper cuts, from the brown envelopes of cash you need to pass on to contacts. The cuts can be severe however, given the ferocity with which the cretins will snatch the money out of your hand... Despite your qualities though you may be far too moral to truly flourish. You wouldn't like to leave anyone hung out to dry. Honour is a four-letter word... Arrogant, vulgar Americans ultimately direct resources and policy... Perhaps you're not ready to come in from the cold or go out into it. I always get the two mixed up. Perhaps I've had too much to drink."

Oliver promised he would put in a word for me should I be interested in joining the trade. Or the circus. But I wasn't that keen and Oliver was doubtless eager to keep me on his books, when he sobered up the following day.

Devlin's mouth became dry. He craved a cold beer – and a cigarette. He reached into his pocket and downed half a bottle of tepid mineral water. As he raised his head Devlin noticed a funeral taking place in the distance. They were lowering a coffin into the ground. A white-haired priest stood among the black-clad mourners. Women leaned into men. Children looked solemn, or bored. A teenager was rightly castigated by his father for tapping away on his smart phone. Music played in the background – something by Dean Martin – as the ground swallowed up the polished pine casket. Devlin had witnessed similar scenes during his visits to Holly's grave over the years. A piece of his heart went out to the families every time, to the point where he wondered how much of a heart he could have left. He remembered something Holly once said, however, in reference to a person's heart: "The more of it you give away, the larger it becomes."

I'm not sure how much of my heart I've given to Emma – which is why it's shrunk. You've probably seen me with her. I hope you're not jealous. It's more likely you're disappointed in me by the way I've treated her. I'm going to keep my promise to you and not re-marry. I want to keep my word. A man is only is good as his word. I want to keep you. This. I hate thinking that I'm hurting Emma, being unkind. But I worry that I'll hurt her even more if I break things off suddenly – cruelly. Hyde once told me that I was the bravest man he'd ever known. But, in so much of my life, I have been a coward. And how brave am I being this evening? Does a part of me not want to end my life – suddenly and cruelly? God knows what will happen. He may strike me down – or the greater punishment will be to stretch out my earthly existence, like I'm on a rack. Life is hell. Or the world is hell, filled with hellish people. It's vile and bestial. Dull and deeply shallow. Nothing means anything. And so I've got nothing to lose or gain. There's so much to laugh at in this life, but that's what makes it so tragic.

Devlin realised how much he missed laughing. Laughter was like a song, which he couldn't quite remember the tune to anymore. But he could remember Holly's laugh, sometimes reverberating like a love song but sometimes like a dirge. When she laughed, she did so with her body and soul. The sound was unaffected and infectious. She would bend over, sometimes even holding her aching belly. Tears would glisten in her joyful eyes. She loved sarcasm and silliness equally. Her laugh made him laugh. Her smile made him smile. But now Devlin felt devoid of the strength to raise both corners of his mouth that high again. The closest he came was when Violet jumped up at him after spending the day away from home.

Devlin hacked his way through his melancholy and came to the memory of when he had proposed. Holly had laughed – and cried – simultaneously. Her first reaction was to briefly close and open her eyes – in disbelief. Or at having her faith rewarded.

"You make me so happy. I love you so much."

Emma had never said those words to him. Because she didn't feel that way – or he hadn't given her cause to.

Like a dream mutating into a nightmare however the image of Holly accepting his proposal eventually turned into the sight of her in the hospital, after the hit and run. Her sweet face was swollen, unrecognisable. Tubes enveloped her, like briars. Monitors beeped, dolefully. The smell of bleach – and her perfume – filled his nostrils. Devlin sat by Holly's bedside, as she bled internally. He screwed up his face – and pressed his hands together in prayer – until they hurt. He hurt with a hurt that was more than a hurt.

Devlin opened his eyes and the headstone, with its death date, loomed large. He wanted to kill Jamal. He wanted to kill the driver too, after all these years, even if it was a woman or priest. The afternoon sun disappeared behind a cloud and the temperature dropped. The breeze chilled the sweat on his skin. He wanted God to cut the pain out of him. But no. His grief was real. Grief equated to love. A life without despair somehow seemed fraudulent. An ersatz life.

13.

When Devlin returned to the apartment he went online and booked two first class tickets to Paris on the Eurostar. He also made a reservation at *Astrance*, just off the Rue de Passy. As well as wanting to do something nice for Emma, Devlin had experienced a change of heart, in regards to arranging the romantic break, as it would prove wise to be out of the country. Whilst away Porter would be able gauge if they had identified him as a suspect.

Emma beamed enough for them both when Devlin told her about the Eurostar tickets and restaurant reservation. Her heart skipped a beat as she momentarily fancied that he might be planning to propose over the romantic dinner. Her sweet semblance was a picture of gratitude and anticipation.

"I'm popping over to Samantha's this evening to pick up the keys to the flat. Are you still heading out to dinner?"

"Yeah. I'll be out quite late, so don't wait up."

"Have fun. But not too much fun. You're going to need to save your strength for Paris," Emma said, humorously and suggestively. She wondered if she had time in her schedule to buy new lingerie.

Devlin was determined to play the doting boyfriend for the weekend. He wanted Emma to have a good time. She deserved it. But when they got back he would have to plan-out, as thoughtfully as a hit, how to end things. He couldn't give Emma what she wanted. He no longer window shopped for engagement rings.

If he didn't propose or discuss their future then Emma was determined to broach the subject, either on their last night in Paris or as soon as they got back to London. She intended to tell him that she wanted to have a child. If Devlin wanted a baby too then it would mean they would get married. Neither had lapsed that much as a Catholic. If he said that he didn't want to have a child, or get married, then Emma would at least know how he felt. And that they didn't have a real future together.

A watched pot never boils but still Birch sat in his wheelchair by his kitchen table, glaring at his phone. Waiting for a message from Devlin. He wanted to know that things were still going ahead for tonight. He also wanted to be ready should Devlin send word that he couldn't proceed.

The wooden, uneven table was marked with cigarette burns and coffee stains. A half drunken bottle of beer and crunched-up empty can of Guinness flanked his phone and far from empty ashtray. The ceiling and his fingertips were the same shade of yellow. A bin, overflowing with takeaway and ready meal containers, stood in front of a damp patch, which resembled the shape of Italy. The dying light eked through browning net curtains.

Birch was tempted to travel to Green Park. When the police arrived, he would, like others, congregate around the entrance to the hotel. He wanted to catch a glimpse of the Afghan's corpse being wheeled out the door. But there was a chance that the police might question him. Or he could be caught on camera and, if the investigation team ran him through the system, they would discover a link to their victim. Hopefully a TV crew would reach the scene of the crime early and film things.

Once Rameen was dead he would look to the future. He promised himself he would cut down on his drinking and get a job. There was a nearby veterans group he would sign-up to. He would also use some of the money Devlin had given him to smarten up his flat. He would buy new furniture and brighten things up with a lick of paint. He resolved to get his sense of humour back and not feel like a victim. With Rameen dead, Birch could begin to live again. He hoped that Devlin would feel equally good and free, after doing the deed.

Birch shifted uneasily in his chair. He felt one of his pressure sores begin to bleed again. The sores, which could be easily contracted but difficult to eradicate, had formed due to Birch spending too much time, lying in one position, in bed.

Emma stood on tip-toe and gave Devlin a teasing kiss, before leaving to meet-up with Samantha. Devlin fed Violet, showered and got changed. He placed the Sig Sauer in its holster, the suppressor in his inside blazer pocket and the cap on his head.

Night fell.

He walked halfway down Tower Bridge Road before flagging down a black cab and driving to Oxford St. He popped into Selfridge's, where he bought an expensive platinum necklace, with a sapphire pendant, for Emma, to give to her in Paris. At first, he was tempted to purchase a pair of diamond earrings for her, but thought better of it lest she mistook the box for containing an engagement ring. Once out of the store he slipped the slender box into his pocket, not wishing to be encumbered by any bag.

Devlin strode down Regent St and dined alone at a restaurant in Chinatown. He ordered a pot of green tea after his meal and waited, patiently. He ran through again the different scenarios he would be faced with when he entered Rameen's hotel suite. He also made a mental list of the artworks he wanted to see at the Louvre. And he fretted a little about leaving Violet with their neighbours for the weekend. She had been unsettled for several days afterwards when they returned from their previous holiday. At eleven fifteen Devlin received a coded message on a burner phone, from Mariner, confirming it was safe to proceed.

It was nearly time.

14.

The curtains were closed but occasionally billowed out from the breeze. Plush, elegantly designed rugs lay upon the polished, parquet floor. An ice bucket, filled with an empty bottle of Cristal champagne, rested on a glass-topped table at the centre of the sitting room in the hotel suite. A French carriage clock, bronze statues of a muscular racehorse and a sinuous ballerina, a brass sextant and attractive porcelain vases sat on top of various pieces of finely crafted rosewood furniture positioned throughout the room.

Rameen Jamal paced around and rubbed cocaine into his gums. He wore a chocolate brown silk shirt, half tucked in and out of a pair of black, leather trousers which he had recently bought the previous day at Harrod's. He walked around barefoot. He liked the way his feet felt on the cold floor. It reminded him of being back home. His face was framed with a thin strip of beard running along his jaw and chin. His eyes were just as bloodshot as they had been during the attack in the village in Helmand. His hair was still similarly long and glossy. His teeth had been recently bleached. Rameen was slim and handsome. Narcissistic and vicious. A waspish British diplomat, not altogether inaccurately, had described the Afghan as being like a cross between George Michael and Dodi Fayed.

Faisal Ahmadi blissfully ignored Rameen and sat, rigid, on a soft, floral patterned sofa, finishing off a coded email to a representative of one of his Saudi paymasters. He relayed that his meetings had been fruitful. Funds and instructions had been passed on to imams and other intermediaries, who were responsible for coordinating sleeper cells. Money had also been directed to pay the legal fees of certain terrorists and preachers the British government wanted to deport. Human rights lawyers don't come cheap. But the faithless parasites were worth every penny, Ahmadi chuckled to himself (remaining sour-faced as he did so). The requisite lobbying groups had been paid too. Two Labour Party MPs, a Liberal Democrat peer and a Conservative junior minister were now unwittingly working for his Saudi employer, championing the cause of the primacy of Sharia law in a set of Midlands constituencies.

Ahmadi possessed sharp features and an even sharper brain. He was willing to work with anyone who was useful, or paid well – Sunni or Shia. His agents in Helmand had provided intelligence for the Taliban to deploy against the British and vice-versa. The real enemy was the decadent and heretical West. And Jews. Ahmadi judged that one was either a son of Dost Muhammed or a son of Shah Shuja. One was either a servant of the West, or it's enemy. Wickedness was justified, in the name of righteousness. Ahmadi had amassed a substantial personal fortune over the years but wealth was not his (sole) motivation. What mattered was the will of God, especially when it coincided with his own pecuniary interests. The diplomat wore a grey, Saville Row suit. The colour matched the tufts of hair on his temples. Hooded eyes were perched over a hawkish nose. A thin, cruel mouth was buried within a wiry beard which tapered into a blade-like point.

Ahmadi signed-off on his report by writing that he hoped to send similar good news after his imminent trip to Washington. The Afghan was starting to miss his home and creature comforts in Kabul however. He missed reading and drinking coffee in his garden. He missed the company of his serving boys. Especially Temur, his new favourite. Ahmadi had liked Temur for his innocence at the beginning. But now - thanks to his master - the twelve-year-old knew how to pleasure him.

He was keen to leave London behind. The city was a den of iniquity. Noisy. Smelly. Too many of the women were nothing but brazen whores. Allah would disapprove of their behaviour. Perhaps more importantly, Faisal Ahmadi disapproved of their behaviour. Children disrespected their elders. Nothing was sacred to the infidel. He sneered, internally, recalling how the British had included a Jew in their trade delegation, when they met. He suspected that his kaffir hosts had done so deliberately, to test or goad him. But Ahmadi swallowed his pride – and disgust – by grinning and shaking the hand of the filth. He pictured his grin as being in the shape of a scimitar however. The wily Afghan would have the last laugh.

They underestimate me. Let them.

When Ahmadi was a child he used to pray to Al Alim (God the All Knowing) and Al Qaabid (God the Restrainer). But now the erstwhile agent for Islamic State prayed to Al Hakam (God the Judge) and Al Muntaqim (God the Avenger).

Basel Mourad, Ahmadi's personal bodyguard, dutifully stood behind his employer. The former wrestling champion was square-headed, flat-faced and thick-lipped. A perpetual look of fierceness and disdain shaped his craggy features. The soldier left Karzai's puppet army, after being witness to too many corrupt and dishonourable practises. He considered the British and Americans to be an occupying force. Unwanted guests. Ahmadi provided him with a home and cause. And Ahmadi also paid the ardent son of Dost Muhammed more in a month than he had earned in a year. After proving his loyalty, Mourad was allowed into the agent's confidence. The bodyguard was often granted the privilege and pleasure of interrogating his master's enemies.

The second bodyguard in the room, charged with Rameen's close protection, was Sadiq Tahir. His build was squat and muscular but his face was round and chubby. His dark eyes were glazed over, with tiredness, drink or drugs. Or all three. Tahir had grown-up within Hakim Jamal's household. The two boys had prayed and studied together, from an early age. Sadiq loved Rameen like a brother – and not just because Rameen paid his wages and supplied him with drugs and women. He had acted as his friend's protector, for as long as he could remember - and had served as Rameen's driver and bodyguard since the days of his "rape parties" in Helmand.

The football-loving Afghan was sprawled out on an armchair, watching Sky Sports (with the volume turned down, lest Ahmadi gave him the evil eye and instructed him to turn the television off). A pair of Bulgari sunglasses (Rameen's cast offs) were on the table in front of him, as were several empty boxes of Macdonald's food which he had sent out for. He stared, with glowing contentment, at the new gold watch on his wrist. It was a Rolex. A gift from his employer. Tahir enjoyed being in London, away from his frigid shrew of a wife. He felt he could get used to expensive hotel suites and equally expensive blonde, blue-eyed hookers – who would do things to him that his wife wouldn't even dream of doing. The West wasn't all that bad, Tahir thought to himself, as he poured himself another Jack Daniels and finished off the remaining fries.

Both bodyguards wore black suits, their jackets covering up Glock pistols. Both bodyguards had tortured and killed before. Both bodyguards considered themselves "good Muslims."

"You work too hard, Faisal. Let's celebrate. Have a drink. Allah will forgive you, this one time. The deal is all but signed," Rameen remarked, his voice as smooth as caramel. "I don't want to waste this high."

Ahmadi scowled, baring his sharp front teeth. Not only was he annoyed with the younger man for using the Prophet's name in vain but he had warned Rameen countless times about being indiscrete, in regards to the deal (and other issues). He only suffered the cur out of deference and respect for his father. Hakim Jamal was a lion, wise and merciless. His son dishonoured his name.

"Lower your voice. Or better still, keep quiet. Have you forgotten that we have a guest in the other room?" Ahmadi advised, making reference to the British close protection officer, who was taking a call in one of the bedrooms. Ahmadi was suspicious that the last-minute replacement to their security detail could be an agent of M15. A careless word could compromise their negotiating position. He briefed everyone each morning to keep their phones in their possession at all times. They should also act as if the suite had been bugged by the security services. He would bug the British if the roles were reversed. The keen student of history recalled a book he had recently read - about how Stalin had planted listening devices in the rooms of his allies, during the conference at Yalta. He had gained an advantage of knowing more about his enemies than they knew about him. Although a kaffir, Ahmadi couldn't help but admire Stalin – as well as Lenin, Castro and Martin McGuinness. They were "good" kaffirs. They knew that sheep needed shepherds - and wolves.

"For all your intellect, Faisal, you still need to learn how to enjoy yourself. I'll celebrate for the both of us, if I have to. But live a little."

15.

The Ritz. 111 rooms. 23 suites. Opened in 1906. A grand hotel. The décor was opulent and elegant – an amalgamation of neo-classical, art deco and Louis XVI design. The Ritz was the hotel of choice for statesmen, royalty, socialites and the stars. Noel Coward, Douglas Fairbanks and Charlie Chaplin had regularly dined or stayed at the hotel. Winston Churchill and Eisenhower had held operational meetings over lunch in its restaurant.

Devlin walked through the gilded lobby, neither too hastily or too slowly. The thick carpet felt spongy beneath his feet, in stark contrast to the hard pavement he had been pounding most of the night. The assassin neither looked anyone directly in the eye nor overtly avoided anyone's gaze. His heartbeat and breathing were regular, his palms dry. He was just another guest, returning to his room after an evening out in London. The well-dressed, confident figure blended in and belonged.

Just before they were married Devlin had taken Holly for afternoon tea at The Ritz. It had been criminally expensive – but worth it. Unfortunately, he was unable to spot Noel Coward in the restaurant. But Holly pointed out someone called Cat Deeley. The following week he had taken her to M.Manze, the pie mash shop in Tower Bridge Road. They enjoyed themselves at both venues. Holly, having come from a photoshoot, had been treated like a movie star at the latter. She turned heads. And the staff adored her all the more – thinking her sweet, funny and modest – after chatting to her.

Polished marble, gilded bronze fixtures, mirrors, crystal chandeliers and mega-watt lamps gleamed throughout the lobby. Devlin squinted a little, his eyes aching from the light.

Mobile phones rang constantly and were often succeeded by squealing, inane conversations in half a dozen languages. The air was soup-thick with costly perfumes and colognes. Several guests, often wearing gaudy pieces of jewellery, found it difficult to walk past a mirror without checking out their appearances. Hair was tousled, fringes swept away, skirts were smoothed and ties adjusted. Staff slalomed through the preening guests, wearing fixed, Formica smiles. Devlin fancied that he could be carrying his gun in his hand and people would still be too self-absorbed to notice.

Devlin pretended to read a message on his phone as he stood back and allowed a group of Japanese tourists to enter the lift without him. Once alone he pressed the button to call the elevator with his knuckle, not wishing to leave a fingerprint. The devil is in the detail. The lift was empty as he travelled up to the fourth floor. Perhaps his prayers had been listened to and God was on his side. Before exiting the elevator, Devlin slipped on a pair of latex gloves.

He walked down the corridor towards the entrance to the requisite hotel suite. He could still turn back. But he didn't. The world would be a slightly better place without Rameen Jamal, he judged. The only way he would be free, the only way he could consider honour to be satisfied, was if he fulfilled the promise he made – to God and Birch – all those years ago, in the evac-chopper.

Devlin told himself that his weapon would be reliable and shoot true. As he would. His nerve and skills would not abandon him. If the Sig Sauer somehow failed to fire he would retreat. He was brave, but not stupid. He had his escape route planned-out. His enemies might hesitate, but he wouldn't.

Devlin reached the door. He checked his watch, a CWC chronograph. The same watch he had worn in Helmand. On the day. The professional killer then glanced, in both directions, along the corridor. He listened out for any ping of the elevator or the sound of someone turning a handle to the doors of the adjacent suites. But there was blessed silence. His heartbeat increased. But that was normal. Healthy. Fine. Devlin drew out the Sig Sauer and calmly fixed the suppressor. He then retrieved Mariner's special key card from his trouser pocket.

Remember to count discharged rounds. Two shots each. Centre mass. If they're close, a head shot.

Devlin quickly but quietly opened the door and, as fearless as a bushwhacker, advanced, his gun raised. He had studied the floorplan of the deluxe suite beforehand and knew he would immediately inhabit the lavish sitting room when entering.

His intention was to take out the bodyguards first. It was unlikely (though possible) that Ahmadi and Jamal would be armed. But play the odds.

The brutal-looking Basel Mourad only had time to widen his snarling eyes in surprise before a brace of bullets zipped through the air and struck his large chest. The deep pile carpet cushioned the big man's landing. The marble-adorned walls deadened any other sounds. The Afghan's starched white shirt began to crimson, as if someone had already placed two red roses on the corpse.

Ahmadi turned his head towards his stricken friend and bodyguard. His mouth was agape with horror, as he turned back towards the stone-faced gunman. Or perhaps the silver-tongued diplomat was opening his mouth to speak. To beg for his life. Or offer the assassin a bribe. Or threaten him. But Ahmadi would be unable to talk his way out of things this time. The words stuck in his throat, as did a copper jacketed 9mm round. Blood splattered against the embroidered sofa and antique tallboy, which stood behind the Afghani fixer.

Sadiq Tahir's first instinct was to duck behind the back of the chair his was sitting on. His next instinct was to reach for his Glock and return fire. At no moment did Tahir think to rush and take a bullet for his boyhood friend and employer. Devlin fired the first round into the back of the upholstered armchair, striking the bodyguard's elbow. He then raised his gun aloft to create a better angle – and fire down on his target. The second bullet took off the top of the Afghan's head. Half his brain slapped against – and dripped down – the widescreen TV in front of where the Tahir fell to the floor.

Rameen Jamal stood, petrified, with his hands up in surrender. Mercy. He snivelled or sniffed – either from fear or his cocaine habit. The Afghan was accustomed to being the one holding the gun and having others – especially young women – beg for their life.

Devlin took a few steps forward. The cold killer neither smiled triumphantly nor vengefully. He had no desire to explain who he was or why he was here. All that mattered was to slay the villain who had killed Connelly and crippled Birch. Fulfil the contract.

The bullet travelled through Rameen's left eye socket and chipped a piece of marble off the wall behind him.

Devlin kept his gun raised and scanned the area to check that everyone he shot was out of play. He listened for any noises coming from the adjoining bedrooms and bathrooms. Blessed silence. But just as Devlin was beginning to think the room was clear he saw movement out the corner of his eye. A mirror, hung up in a hallway, picked up the reflection of an arm – and a Hi-Power Browning pistol – moving along a corridor.

Nil desperandum. Instinct, training and experience kicked-in. Muscle memory. Kill or be killed. Devlin darted forwards and - before his opponent could come out from around the corner - created a line of fire. He shot off three rounds. The first spat into the wall but the rest struck their target. The familiar odour of cordite warmed Devlin's nostrils, like the smell of freshly baked bread.

Charles Tyerman lay dead. The Hi-Power Browning pistol was still in his hand, his finger curled around the trigger. A York Security tiepin glinted in the light of the ornate chandelier, hanging from the ceiling. The blood drained from Devlin's face, as if he were a corpse too. He thought the ground might swallow him. Or he wanted it too. His hand and aim had remained rock-steady whilst firing his weapon. But as he reached down to forlornly check Tyerman's neck for a pulse his hand trembled. His stony features cracked.

Devlin gazed around, despairingly. The professional killer in him knew he had to leave immediately. But he was rooted to the spot. Confused. Anguished. Tyerman was supposed to be away in Cyprus. Had MI5 called him in to spy on Ahmadi, using the cover of his personal security company? Was Tyerman looking to get Rameen in his sights and avenge Connelly himself? Or, as he had mentioned at lunch, was Tyerman just covering a security shift himself? The CEO of the company would not want to lose an important government contract. Devlin only had questions. Not answers. If he had known who it was about to shoot he would never have fired his own weapon. But how could he have known? He told himself he was innocent, but unconvincingly.

Devlin remained disorientated. Angry. Guilty. The light seemed to now scorch the back of his retinas. The last time he felt similar to this was when he received the call about Holly's accident. The husband and would-be felt that God was playing a cruel joke on him. He wanted to kill himself. It was the right thing to do. Tears welled in the former paratrooper's eyes but, as well as a debilitating sorrow, the killer experienced a surge of envy as he watched the carpet soak up Tyerman's blood, as it oozed out from the wound in his stomach. He envied him, because he was dead. Whilst Devlin was as far away as ever from finding some peace.

He noticed his watch. It still contained a grain of sand, underneath the glass, that had somehow got trapped there during his time in Helmand. Sometimes it seemed to disappear but sometimes it rattled around in the bold, black and white face of the timepiece. Emma had asked him what he had brought back from Afghanistan. Perhaps it was more than just a grain of sand, he gloomily thought.

Devlin finally took possession of himself, before something took possession of him. He managed to get to his feet and reach the lift. The walls to the elevator felt like they were closing in on him. He couldn't look at himself in the reflective panels. But he knew that a determined expression had turned into a haunted one. Devlin gasped for air when he freed himself from the hotel, like a drowning man breaking through from the skin of the sea. Veering from his plan he headed left into Green Park. He found a quiet corner and leaned against a tree. A passer-by mistook his silhouette for a drunk, about to be sick. Devlin heard the distant sound of police sirens as he exited the rear of the park. He felt light-headed. His stomach churned, like a man in need of a meal or one too full. Devlin flagged down a black taxi. The dour cab driver thought he was just picking up a late-night reveller, a little worse for wear. Still he blended in.

Devlin thought he would feel better once he made it across the river. But he didn't. Sensing that he might be sick he asked the driver to drop him off at Elephant & Castle. He walked the rest of the way home, via the backstreets, avoiding as many people as possible.

Emma was thankfully asleep when he returned. Oblivious. Innocent. The widower loved her, in his own way. But just not enough. He checked his phone, which had been on silent. He had seventeen missed calls from Birch. He sent a text: "It's done". There was nothing else left to say. The alcoholic downed a large whisky and took Violet out for a walk. He still needed some air. Devlin thought that if he somehow encountered Sean Grady and his crew he would kill them. Or allow them kill him.

16.

The Thames was as black as the Styx. The pleasure boats were back at their moorings for the night. The lights were off across the water - candles pinched out by a niggarding churchwarden. Darkness visible. The temperature dropped. But Devlin barely noticed. He had not even complained during the bitterly cold nights in the desert, in Helmand.

Violet lay at his feet. The dog peered up at him with a degree of confusion – as well as devotion – in her expression. She whimpered a little, every now and then, either in sympathy for her master – or she wanted a biscuit.

Devlin took another long drag on his cigarette. He had found a late night off licence and bought two packs of twenty Rothmans. The smoke settled his stomach and helped him breathe normally again. He knew smoking was bad for him. But it felt good. Right.

The killer sat on his bench. Thick, fungal clouds covered the sky. Not a soul stirred. He had just tossed the Sig Sauer in the undulating river. Porter had recommended him to do so, during their lunch, as without a weapon (and CCTV coverage) the police would never be able to bring a case against him - even if they were able to track him down and arrest their suspect. But Devlin disposed of the weapon, as he never intended to fire it again. The gun felt even heavier in his hand, at the end.

He let the smoke flood his lungs again - warm them, feed them – and took another swig of vodka from the hip flask he had brought out with him. He listened to the rhythmic lap of water against the mossy timbers of the riverbank and thought of Matthew Arnold's *Dover Beach*. Devlin remembered how, during his honeymoon, he had recited the last verse of the poem to Holly, as they lay in bed together. He gently closed his eyes and tried to feel again the kiss she had given him, in reply.

The phone, vibrating in his trouser pocket, was ignored. He didn't know, or care, if it was Birch, Porter or Emma.

Emma. Devlin made a promise – to himself and God – that he would end things with her in the morning. It would bring unhappiness to them both. But it was the right thing to do. He dearly hoped she would let him keep Violet. But whether he deserved to or not was another matter, he conceded.

The temperature dropped even more. What stars, which could be glimpsed between the clouds, shone dimly. Police sirens sounded in the distance. But they were coming towards him. Getting louder and louder. Harsher. He wouldn't resist arrest.

God knows I already feel like a condemned man.

We are where we are.

Ready for Anything

Thomas Waugh

"I simply love you more than I love life itself."
Elton John, *I Guess That's Why They Call It The Blues*.

"No human being can really understand another, and no one can arrange another's happiness."
Graham Greene, *The Heart of the Matter*.

1.

London. Bermondsey Square. Pistol shots cut through the balmy, evening air and shattered the party atmosphere. The muzzle flashes and sounds were all but simultaneous, as when thunderclaps follow lightning. The flats, hotel and bars, which formed two sides of the square, trapped and amplified the terrifying noise.

Run. Hide. Tell.

Those were the three words of advice, issued by the authorities, should the public become embroiled in a terrorist attack.

Pint and highball glasses crashed to the ground. Chairs and tables were knocked over. Screams spiralled upwards like tendrils of smoke from chimney stacks. Flip-flops slapped against paving stones. Fearing further gunshots, or a nail bomb, or a savage knife crime, the late-night revellers ran for their lives – scattering like a colony of insects under attack.

It was every man for himself. A stampede. More than one woman was pushed over and trampled upon. One twenty-something, wearing a beany hat and ripped jeans, was more concerned with holding his phone aloft and filming the scene, than helping the girl he floored get back on her feet. He would spend the rest of the evening tweeting about the attack, desperately trying to play the victim (or even hero) in a campaign to glean more likes and followers on his social media accounts. Maybe his ex-girlfriend would get in touch, to see if his was okay, he reasoned. He emailed *The Guardian* to say he was available for comment, enclosing two profile pictures from his Facebook account. In one he was duly solemn, but in the other he was smiling and holding his thumbs up. It had been taken in Australia during his gap year, just before he was about to bungee jump. For half an hour or so his hashtag, #iwillsurvive, even started trending. It was the most exciting moment of the software developer's life.

The stream of people continued to flow out of the square and into Tower Bridge Rd. Traffic screeched to a halt. Hands trembled – and voices broke – as all manner of young professionals called the police. Panic was pandemic. Tears cut through make-up, like scars.

Run. Hide. Tell.

It was a terrorist attack, they fervently believed. A few witnesses reported that they had heard the perpetrators exclaim, "Allahu Akbar."

But one man swam against the stream. The forty-something had been standing, alone, in a corner of the square, keeping himself to himself. Michael Devlin looked anonymous. A no one. He was dressed in unbranded jeans, a polo shirt and sports jacket. Few had given him a second look but some might have thought the man was waiting around for someone. Others might have imagined that someone had just left him. He was drinking. Brooding. Contempt smouldered off him like brimstone, albeit one couldn't quite tell if the contempt was directed towards himself or the surrounding snowflakes. Most likely it was both. The more Devlin thought about humanity, the more he loved his dog.

Devlin still cradled his tumbler of Bushmills as he walked towards *Shortwave* – a cinema and bar – where the shots emanated from. The former paratrooper, having served in Afghanistan, was no stranger to muzzle flashes. As a former contract killer Devlin could also tell the difference between a gangland hit and Islamist terrorist attack. He sucked in the scene as he walked, making a risk assessment and noting the entrances, exits and CCTV cameras.

His red-rimmed eyes narrowed, as he peered over the sea of bobbing heads to take in the gunman and his confederate, standing by their two victims. A cold moon shone down, indifferent to the crime.

The two corpses looked similar. Brothers, perhaps. Eastern European. Probably Albanian. Devlin had heard a rumour they were aggressively moving into the area, peddling drugs and trafficking and young girls. Both victims had shaved heads. Both wore designer tracksuits and diamond-studded earrings. Tattoos decorated their necks – a spider's web and crucifix. The bullets had thudded into their broad chests. They were slumped in their chairs, heads lolling to the sides, as if sleeping. Even when they appeared at peace however in death the two men were unpleasant looking and their thuggish faces betrayed their brutal hearts. Scallop-sized pieces of flesh were strewn on the ground behind them, from the bullets having entered and exited their bodies.

A whiff of cordite stained the air. Devlin breathed in the smell, like the familiar and moreish aroma of cigarette smoke. His hand yearned to grip his Sig Sauer pistol. His trigger finger even made a couple of subtle, reflex pulling motions. But the weapon was now at the bottom of the Thames. Devlin had tossed the pistol after his last hit, when he had accidentally gunned down a friend.

The wiry Jamaican gunman, Isaac "Shanks" Ridley, wore an expression of confoundment more than anger as he noticed Devlin standing a dozen paces or so away from him. His face was thin, greasy, cadaverous. A grin, or grimace, revealed a crooked gold tooth and receding plum-coloured gums. A dusting of grey around his temples coloured his otherwise black hair. The rest of the square was now deserted. The wind whistled eerily through it, like a small town in the old west. His bloodshot eyes were stapled wide-open, with cocaine and sadism. The money was good – his boss would pay him well for the hit, after the Albanians had put one of their crew in the hospital – but money wasn't everything. Ridley enjoyed violence, like some people enjoy wine, computer games or mountaineering. Back in Jamaica he had used a cutthroat razor, whilst making his name as a young enforcer. Violence was visceral, thrilling. He still carried a blade but times had changed. He could have fun with guns too, and there was no need to wash your hands or buy a new shirt after each job. Ridley savoured the sense of power, just before and after pulling the trigger. He relished the look of unadulterated fear in his victim's eyes. His expression would contort in pleasure in direct contrast to the contortions of terror and misery he witnessed – or rather inspired.

Devlin drained the rest of his drink. The whisky warmed his throat and stirred his heart. As well as there being a sense of defiance in his features, he also seemed to be wryly half-smiling at his fellow hitman. Because he knew something his counterpart didn't.

Ridley made a sucking noise through his teeth and the smile turned into a vicious sneer. He shook his head at Devlin, to convey how he thought the drunk was either transgressing or acting dumbly. The white boy should have run. He should have hidden. There are no more heroes left in the world. Innocents had been injured – or killed – in the crossfire during previous jobs. Ridley would still sleep easy at night if he murdered the foolhardy stranger. And he would do it quickly. The police would be on their way and he wanted to get back to his boss' cellar bar in New Cross. Rum, spliffs and girls would be waiting for him there, as well as a plane ticket to a non-extradition island, just in case the hit generated too much heat.

The yardie raised his gun but Devlin didn't flinch, either from fearlessness or fatalism. The stoical contract killer had stared down the barrel of a gun before – one that was loaded too. Instead of hearing the report of a Browning handgun being fired Ridley just registered a click. He even pulled the trigger again, in hope or desperation.

It was now Devlin's turn to shake his head. The gunman was transgressing and acting stupidly at the same time.

Amateur.

Devlin proceeded to walk towards the Jamaican, as if he were a new recruit again, purposefully marching across the parade ground at Aldershot. Ridley let out a curse and reached into his pocket for a spare magazine but as he did so Devlin's empty tumbler glass struck him square in the chest. Ridley was forced backwards and he dropped the gun and magazine. In the meantime, Devlin picked up a glass ashtray from a nearby table, where gobbets of Albanian blood marked various tapas dishes and a jug of sangria. Just as Ridley gazed up and regained his focus he felt the white boy grab him by his shirt and gold chain - and glimpsed the ashtray being thrust towards him. The first blow smashed into his front teeth and knocked him unconscious. Ridley fell to the floor, like a ragdoll. Devlin's expression remained calmly determined, or impassive, as he bent over his opponent and drove the ashtray into his face two more times, as if his arm were a jackhammer. Bone glinted beneath the gashes in the yardie's nose, cheek and chin. The brutal attack lasted just a few moments. Devlin neither knew – nor cared – if the figure at his feet was dead. Adrenaline began to course through Devlin's body but he still had the presence of mind to place the ashtray in his pocket. He'd retrieve the tumbler too. He didn't want to leave any trace evidence.

Ridley's young confederate, Justin Gardner, took in the sudden change of events, his mouth agape. It was the first time the teenager had taken part in a hit. Tonight was supposed to be another test. He still needed to prove himself. Earn the respect of his fellow gang members. Ridley instructed that there was no need for the youth to carry a gun.

"Just watch and learn, young cub," the older man said, with a mischievous and menacing gleam infusing his doped-up expression.

Drugs had yet to ravage Justin's features, or dull the teenager's aspect. But he believed his path was set. He could make more money in a month than his father had made in a year, before he left. After tonight he could put a down payment on the car he wanted – and get his girlfriend the lingerie she (or rather he) picked out on the *Victoria's Secret* website. He would order the latest iphone and only wear designer labels. But the money wasn't just for himself, he vowed. He wanted to buy his mum a new flat, in a better neighbourhood, and send his younger brother to a better school. But first he would get the keys to the Mitsubishi Evo. Justin had dreamed about the car, ever since he first played Grand Theft Auto when he was eight.

Devlin quickly, professionally, loaded the gun and levelled the weapon at the petrified teenager. The hit wasn't supposed to turn out this way, for Justin. It felt like a dream. Or nightmare. His bottom lip trembled and his soul eked out an inelegant prayer. Whilst Ridley was being savagely, or clinically, assaulted by the stranger the young gangster had

216

pulled out a blade from his inside coat pocket. He had threatened to cut someone before, but had never actually bloodied the weapon. Gardner stood at the crossroads, caught between fight or flight. Beads of sweat wended their way along his down-filled cheeks.

"You've brought a knife to a gunfight," Devlin drily remarked. "Go. Or if you're going to come at me, come at me now."

Police sirens sounded in the background. At any one time forty vehicles, containing armed officers, patrolled the streets of London – ready to respond to violent crimes and terrorist attacks. The aim was for the authorities to reach any possible scene within eight minutes.

Part of Devlin wanted the youth to attack him, stab him. He was ready to die. *Nothing is good or bad but thinking makes it so.* He deserved to die. Life weighed upon his chest like a tombstone. He wanted to die, as much as a bridegroom desired his bride on their wedding night. Devlin had sinned, more than he had been sinned against. Guilt scythed through him like a bolt of lightning, every day... And the widower would only be able to see his wife, Holly, in the next life. Not in this one.

The teenager's heart skipped a beat but then galloped. His breathing became irregular – and there was a moment when he nearly lost control of his bowels - but somehow Justin began to shuffle backwards. Self-preservation was sovereign over any loyalty he felt towards his confederate. His eyes flitted between the coal-black pistol and the stranger's flinty aspect. Justin resisted the temptation to turn around, out of fear of being shot in the back, but retreated into the bar. Spilled kettle chips and cashew nuts crunched beneath his feet. The speakers still piped out acid jazz. Once he made it to

217

the kitchen door Justin ran – and didn't look back. Cutlery and crockery crashed to the floor. He dreaded breathlessly explaining events to the getaway driver, parked close-by on Long Lane. He further dreaded having to explain events to Onslow, his unforgiving boss, waiting for him back at the bar – *The Rum Punch* - in New Cross.

Devlin slipped the Browning into his jacket pocket. He would dispose of the weapon in the Thames.

The police sirens grew louder. Wailing. Out of the corner of his eye he could see a few curtains, in apartment and hotel windows, peel back a little. But no one secured a good look at the man who hadn't run or hid.

Devlin calmly, unassumingly, left the square. Head bowed down. His hands buried in his pockets. Most people were too glued to their smart phones to notice him. Devlin already had his route home planned-out, one which avoided any CCTV cameras.

The moon disappeared behind some thick grey clouds, congealing across the sky like a scab. Police cars began to light up the scene, like a disco, in the background. But Devlin didn't look back as he tabbed down a poorly lit side street and the night swallowed him up.

2.

Devlin threw the gun in the river. The Thames gratefully gulped it down. He now lay curled up, in a foetal position, on his sofa. A large brandy sat on the coffee table in front of him, as did a full ashtray and well-thumbed copy of Bernard Malamud's *The Assistant*. He closed his eyes and exhaled. His conscience smarted not from having injured, or killed, the recidivist in the square. He was pleased however for having spared the trembling adolescent. He was young, but not innocent. *There are no innocents left in the world.* If nothing else, the lapsed Catholic believed in original sin. Devlin believed in God too. He just couldn't serve Him.

The curtain rhythmically billowed out, as if someone were standing on the balcony with a set of bellows. Warm air – and the abrasive sound of police cars gunning down Tower Bridge Rd – entered the room. Devlin reached over for the remote control and turned down the volume on the stereo. *The Bob Dylan Playlist* was on, again:

"*Most of the time*
I'm clear focused all around
Most of the time
I can keep both feet on the ground
I can follow the path
I can read the sign
Stay right with it when the road unwinds
I can handle whatever
I stumble upon
I don't even notice she's gone

Most of the time."

Devlin thought how it was almost a year to the day since his last hit. The target had been Rameen Jamal. The Afghan, who had murdered and maimed his friends during a routine patrol of a village in Helmand, had been staying at *The Ritz*. Devlin had arranged, through the fixer Oliver Porter, to have the cameras hacked and temporarily disabled at the hotel. As well as Jamal, Devlin also assassinated Faisal Ahmadi that night. Ahmadi was travelling in Jamal's diplomatic party. He was a person of interest for MI6, for his involvement with various Islamist terrorist organisations.

But not all had gone to plan. Devlin was unaware that his former commanding officer, Charles Tyerman, was serving on the Afghani's security detail. He unwittingly shot the man who, a few days before, offered him a job. A future. Afterwards Devlin told himself that Tyerman should not have elected to work for Jamal (even though it could have been the case that his ex-CO was there that night under the auspices of the intelligence services, to keep watch over the Afghanis). Devlin had to shoot his final target in the hotel suite quickly, else he would have been shot himself. He didn't know it was Tyerman, before he fired. He told himself it wasn't his fault. *But there are no innocents left in the world.*

After the hit a year ago, in the dead of night, Devlin had gone for a walk and sat upon a bench, by the shimmering Thames. Police sirens echoed out in the night then too. Devlin promised himself that, should somehow the authorities come for him, he wouldn't run and he wouldn't hide. He also wouldn't tell, in regards to giving up Oliver Porter in return for a shorter sentence.

It was also nearly a year to the day when Emma walked out on him. If he would have asked her to stay she may have changed her mind. But he didn't. The end came after Devlin cancelled their trip to Paris. Emma had nurtured a hope that the man she loved would propose there. But she asked the question: does he love me? The inconvenient truth was that Devlin was still in love with his late wife, Holly. He still visited her grave every week, played her favourite songs, stared at her picture and re-read old letters. Devlin still had one foot in the past. Or rather one foot in her grave. Tears streaked down Emma's face, of despair and anger, as she confessed how she felt. She wanted to hurt him – and said a number of things she later regretted. Her throat became sore. Whilst Devlin remained calm. Or cold. He understood how she felt and it was indeed best that they end things, he remarked. His tone was laced with more relief than regret, which only made Emma despair – and grow angrier – all the more.

There were times when Devlin missed Emma – and was tempted to get in touch to apologise to her. Try to make amends somehow. Atone. But what good would it have done? She had found someone else and he would still ultimately keep his promise to Holly, never to re-marry or fall in love again.

It was almost six months to the day, when his foster-mum, Mary, passed away. Cancer ploughed through her body like a plague of locusts and death came three months after diagnosis. Devlin made the funeral arrangements and gave the eulogy. Before she died Mary made her son promise that he would regularly visit his foster-dad in the care home. The couple had been married for over fifty years. Devlin tried to visit every few days, but Bob Woodward's condition grew worse after his wife's death – and lately he barely recognised his foster child. Tragically Bob often forgot that his wife had passed away and he would ask Devlin where she was - and break down on hearing the news, as though he were being told for the first time.

Devlin would take his wheel-chair bound father out into the care home garden for a cigarette and navy rum. His mind and body were diminishing by the week, curling up on themselves like an old, mouldy slipper. Moments of lucidity were rare, precious and increasingly infrequent, like a sunny day in March or October. Everything is born to die. The inevitable truth provides little consolation however. Bob Woodward's skin was stretched over his face like parchment. His grey hair was now snow white. Liver spots flared up on the back of his hands and temples, like daffodils blooming in spring. His foster-dad's once wide, toothy grin had grown narrower, or had disappeared altogether. Devlin's father was sinking further into the black hole of vascular dementia and there was nothing he could do about it. He felt guilty on the days when he didn't visit the widower – and depressed on the days he did.

Violet, who had been laying on the floor by Devlin, suddenly got up. She padded into the kitchen and then came back again, gazing at her master expectantly. The black and white mongrel had a sweet temper, expressive face and lively manner. Somehow, she had the power to pull Devlin out of his own black hole, when it began to suck him in. He got up from the sofa, walked past the bin in the kitchen, overflowing with bottles of vodka and takeaway cartons, and filled-up her water bowl. Perhaps Emma knew how much Devlin needed Violet, which was why, in one last act of love, she let him keep her after they separated. It broke her heart, but it would have broken his more. Devlin stared down at the mongrel, a former stray. Small beads of water dripped from her chin. Her tail wagged, cutting through the fog of his listlessness. For the first time that day the former soldier managed the semblance of a smile. It was a weak smile, but a smile nevertheless.

"*I can survive and I can endure*
And I don't even think about her
Most of the time."

3.

Oliver Porter stood in his parlour and sampled a glass of the Claret he decanted earlier in the evening. Moonlight washed over a manicured lawn as he peered out through his conservatory window – and caught his own reflection as he did so. He had lost weight and kept it off, he thought to himself, gently pleased. Not even his bitterest enemies, of which the former fixer might have owned a few, could call him "paunchy" now. His doctor said that his blood pressure was "sterling" – and he no longer needed to be proscribed statins.

Porter was wearing a camel-coloured summer suit from Chester Barrie and a crisp, white Huntsman shirt. Not a hair, black or steel grey, was out of place on his head. The former Guards officer had regained a little more of his military bearing and gait since regaining his figure. A tan, gleaned from a recent family holiday in the Seychelles, gifted him a further air of vitality and happiness. Partly he had ventured to the island paradise to go sea fishing. The middle-aged conservative suddenly had an appetite to try out new things. He had started writing a novel, about a wily diplomat serving the Byzantine Emperor Alexios Komnenus during the First Crusade. Porter was also learning to tie his own flies and every Friday night he took pleasure in cooking a three-course meal for his family. Retirement was not the hell he once thought it might be. Few things perturbed Porter. Fly-fishing taught him the virtues of patience and stillness. If he had lost his head, as an officer or fixer, then others would have lost theirs. Being "passionate" was vulgar. The Englishman believed in retaining his sangfroid, even when he didn't feel like doing so. It was good for business and his soul.

The furniture was somewhat eclectic in the room, but things still worked and played off each other. His wife had been responsible for furnishing most of the house. Her excellent taste was the least of her admirable qualities however. Victoria was waiting for him upstairs. The children were away for a few days, staying with friends. She had asked him not to be too late in coming up to bed. The fixer didn't need a cryptologist from MI5 to decode what she meant.

Porter emitted a contented sigh and smiled. A number of investments he'd made a decade ago had just matured. Money makes money. His children were performing well at school and thankfully reading outside their narrow curriculums. He recalled his son's laughter last night, when Porter had told him a joke whilst they put away his air rifle:

"Margaret Thatcher, Tony Blair and Jeremy Corbyn are all standing in a line. You have a gun but only two bullets – and your mission is to save the country. What do you do?... You shoot Jeremy Corbyn, twice."

The precocious boy laughed and then cheekily replied:

"I'd need to watch that the bullets don't go straight through, as there's nothing between his ears."

Porter's smile widened as he glanced at the newspaper on the arm of his wingback leather armchair. Derek Hewson, the Tory MP for Cheltenham, had resigned from office – and Porter hadn't even needed to fix the welcome outcome. Porter had been hired by Hewson and a group of lobbyist a couple of years ago. A freelance journalist was about to sell a story - concerning the politician having sent lewd photographs, via text messages, to underage girls. Porter bribed the journalist –

and arranged to put him on staff at a major newspaper – in return for burying the story. When he returned home that evening, having fixed things, Porter found it difficult to look his wife and daughter in the eye. He's leapt, before he's been pushed, Porter thought to himself. He imagined the sleazy MP, standing before the party chairman, wringing his hands and trying to worm his way out of things. In the article, the dutiful politician claimed that he wanted to spend more time with his family. Knowing how much his wife rightly despised him though, Hewson was at least starting to receive his just desserts, Porter idly thought.

He wrinkled his nose briefly, deliberating on whether to smoke a cigar or not. He had cut down on his smoking and drinking over the past year or so, but Porter was still far from puritanical in his habits. Ultimately though he resisted the temptation. There was mettle more attractive upstairs and he didn't want his breath smelling of smoke when he made love to his wife.

It had been their wedding anniversary a week ago. Porter took Victoria to the same restaurant, near Warminster, where he proposed.

"As much as I admire you Oliver for having given up certain things in your diet, which you used to harp on about not being able to live without of course, the thing I most appreciate is that you have given up your work for me and the children. We're all enjoying your retirement."

Victoria had never asked too many questions concerning her husband's work. Perhaps she knew the truth would frighten or appal her. He called himself a consultant, which wasn't altogether a lie. But Oliver had spent over a decade consulting on ways to launder money, ruin reputations, cover-up scandals and even assassinate people. When his life – and that of his family – had been put in danger by some particularly unsavoury clients – the Parker brothers – Porter decided that it was time to untie the Gordian Knot and extricate himself from his profession. He had saved himself. But Devlin had saved him too, having gunned the gangsters down before they could get to Porter and his family.

Devlin. His former associate was an old photograph he would take out of the draw every now and then. Sepia-tinged. Devlin was the most honourable man Porter knew – and the most tragic. The two things were linked. His vow to his late wife, never to marry again, had condemned him to a life of loneliness (albeit one could preside over a harem and still be lonely, Porter conceded). Through keeping his promise to one friend in Afghanistan – and assassinating Rameen Jamal – Devin had ended up killing another.

The two men had attempted to keep in touch after their last job together. Porter invited Devlin to lunch at *White's* but his guest turned up drunk and they largely sat in silence. A fortnight later Porter invited Devlin to stay over at his house for the weekend. But something was missing. Perhaps the two men reminded each other of their previous lives, which they would have preferred to forget. Victoria noticed the change in her husband's friend immediately:

"He's there but he's not there... Is he on some form of medication? He's like some burned out candle or empty shell case... Michael looks older as well. You can tell he's been drinking... The children seem wary of him too, where they used to find him fun and fascinating."

After that weekend Porter determined not to contact Devlin again, unless he contacted him first. The fixer had come out of retirement for the assassin once, to help with the Afghani hit. But the first time would be the last. His debt had been paid. Honour had been served. He was not his brother's keeper, Porter declared to himself.

Devlin was just waiting around to die now, although one could have argued that we are all guilty of that. But Devlin was ready to die – and not just in a spiritual sense. He had already purchased the suit he wanted to be buried in. His plot was picked out too, one close to his wife's grave. He just needed someone's permission to end things, it seemed. Was he waiting for a sign? Perhaps from his God, Porter mused.

Just before Porter was about to head upstairs his phone rang. *Unknown number.* He was tempted to ignore the call, but it might have been one of the parents his children were staying with for the weekend.

"Hello," he remarked. If the word was expressed as a question as much as a greeting then Porter didn't like the answer.

"Hello, old boy. It's the ghost of Christmas past, Mason Talbot, here. I apologise for calling you at such a late hour. I hope I've not disturbed you and your good lady wife, Victoria."

His skin prickled and a chill slithered down Porter's spine as he heard the CIA operative's voice. Especially when he casually – but deliberately – mentioned his wife's name. She had never met the American, not did Porter ever want her to.

"No, it's fine," Porter replied. Polite, but far from warm.

"I was wondering if you would be free for lunch tomorrow? And I won't take no for an answer."

Talbot's tone was collegiate, charming. Faux English. But beneath the civilised veneer of the agent from New Hampshire there resided a black, serpentine soul. Talbot came from what passed as aristocratic stock, for America. Old family money, originally earned from molasses and later oil, had paid for the finest education at Yale and Oxford. Talbot's father, a priapic Democrat congressman, had then used his influence to grant his son an entrée into the world of military intelligence. Mason Talbot did possess an official job title, although no one quite knew what it was, but more so he worked in the shadows – a law unto himself. The senior CIA operative, who had recently celebrated his forty-ninth birthday, had been stationed in London for over a decade. He oversaw, or instigated, black-ops in Britain and the rest of Europe. Talbot also ran assets and gathered intelligence, with or without the cooperation of MI5 and MI6. Although the American was not beyond sharing information with his allies, he always made sure he received more than he traded away. "As with when I convert my currency, I like a favourable exchange rate," he would smoothly remark.

In some regards Porter regarded his American cousin as a fellow fixer. Just a more powerful and menacing one. The two men had several meetings and meals together, around five years ago. Talbot had offered the Englishman a stipend, with the promise of further payments to follow, should Porter be able to provide him with poignant intelligence on his clients.

"Think of yourself as becoming a professional gossip. We are both aware that you work in the service of various people of influence, whether it be in the worlds of commerce or politics. I would just like you to be paid twice for your labours. I would like to know what you know, or who you know... I like you Oliver. We are cut from the same cloth. Indeed, we even share the same tailor do we not? As Thatcher once said of Gorbachev, we can do business together."

Porter had no intention of being drawn into the American's web and politely declined the offer to become one of his assets. It had been over three years since he had even spoken or seen the CIA agent. Wariness – or fear – eclipsed a sense of curiosity as to why he was getting in contact again. Talbot was one of the most dishonourable – and dangerous – men Porter had ever met. He pictured the man behind the convivial voice on the end of the phone. His slim, almost feminine, jawline and cleft chin. His blond hair, which he probably now dyed. His turquoise eyes, bright and yet cold at the same time. Bleached teeth. Handmade shoes. His gold signet ring, bearing his family crest, which he often stared at – as he assessed whether he needed another manicure or not. Talbot could smile, re-fill your class and fraternally clasp your hand – right up to the point, or after, of sheathing a knife in your back. Even his compatriots spoke ill of him, albeit they only did so when whispering. Mason Talbot was akin to an unctuous villain from an unfinished Eric Ambler novel.

Porter noted down Talbot's precise instructions, after agreeing to meet the American for lunch. His skin prickled again when he mentioned Devlin's name in passing. Porter firmly pressed "call end" on his phone, hoping that if he pressed it hard enough he might never hear from Talbot again. The smile on his lips had fallen, shattered, like a piece of fine porcelain dropping to the floor. He sighed, wearily. To help settle his stomach Porter poured himself something stronger than wine. He gave some thought as to why the American would contact him, accessing a rolodex in his mind of reasons as to why their paths should now cross. The scene outside darkened, as the moon seemed rinsed of light. Brittle. Porter eventually trudged upstairs. The stairs - or his bones - creaked. His shoulders seemed more rounded. His head was bowed down in prayer or logical thought. The husband would apologise to his wife. He would explain that he was tired, or had a headache. But the last thing Porter felt like doing right now was making love.

4.

There was no CCTV footage of any suspects, regarding the incident in Bermondsey Square, the authorities lamented. Eyewitness reports were contradictory. The photofit of the man the police were looking for resembled a Slavic Jason Statham. Ridley had been put into an induced coma in order stabilise his condition. It was unlikely the gangster could, or would, aid enquiries once he recovered. If he recovered. As disturbing as the crime was however there was a general mood of relief that it was not another terrorist attack. The gangland killings would soon be yesterday's news.

God is smiling on me, Devlin ironically mused as he turned off the television. As he readied himself to go out he glanced at a framed print on the wall, of Anton Mauve's *A Dutch Road*. The picture was a replacement for one that Emma had taken with her when she moved out. After surveying the artwork, he glanced in the mirror (if the picture wasn't already a mirror to his soul). His eyes narrowed, or face winced, as took in his unconditioned figure. His t-shirts used to stretch a little across his body due to his broad chest. But now they did so due to a burgeoning pot belly. Devlin often used to run in the mornings when he was with Emma. He would push himself. Lactic acid would be replaced by endorphins. He would gulp down tap water as if it were liquid ambrosia. On his return, should Emma still be home as opposed to working in the florist, they would make love in the shower. The couple might then go to the park and just sit and read, with Violet curled up in between them. Contented.

Devlin left the house. He walked with his head down, as though he were a clergyman, deep in prayer. He had no desire to meet anyone's gaze. Connect. Should Devlin have looked up – and around – he might have spotted two CIA watchers following him. They hovered about at a distance, like a brace of vultures riding the thermals.

To further shutout the bleating world he inserted his headphones and turned the music up. At first, he switched on *Holly's Playlist*, a collection of songs his late wife used to listen to:

"Love has truly been good to me
Not even one sad day
Or minute have I had since you've come my way
I hope you know I'd gladly go
Anywhere you'd take me
It's so amazing to be loved
I'd follow you to the moon in the sky above."

The music conjured up all manner of memories for the widower. Lazy summer afternoons spent in Hyde park, resting her head on his chest like a pillow as they drank ice-cold lemonade and read pot-boiler novels. Illicit sex in women's changing rooms as she invited him in to see how an outfit looked on her. Sighing quietly yet intimately. She often told him how much she loved him, during or just after climaxing. Tears sometimes in her eyes. Sometimes giggly. Sometimes tingling or shaking. Sometimes desperately wanting to be hugged. On flights home from trips away she would lift the arm rest between them, lean into him and share the music she was listening to by dividing up her headphones. Holly was the only one he could ever talk to about how lonely his childhood was – and what it felt like to be abandoned by his natural parents. She would always remind him of how much he was loved now though, by his foster parents and herself.

Devlin's bittersweet reveries grew more painful however, as the wrack continued to turn. He changed the playlist. He pictured Holly again, lying in the hospital bed. Her comely features were swollen - bloody and ashen in different places, like the patina on a slab of marble. He closed his eyes and felt again the slight squeeze of her fingertips as he spoke to her, whist her life ebbed away – swirling down the drain. The doctor said it was a reflex action, but he believed otherwise. She was responding to his voice. There was still hope then. Faith. But that was then. The garrotte of grief continued to choke. But Devlin embraced the pain. It was all he had, or all that seemed real. True. It proved how much he loved her. That love exists in the world. This wicked, vain and plague-ridden world.

"If I could only turn back the clock to when God and her were born

Come in she said I'll give you shelter from the storm."

Devlin stood in Garratt Lane cemetery, staring at Holly's gravestone. An asphalt sky augured rain.

Vincent Cutter sat on a bench, in the distance, watching Devlin. The CIA operative, who had worked under Talbot for over five years, opened-up his laptop and updated his report on the Englishman. His orders were to just observe, unless it looked like Devlin was going to leave the country.

"Just get to know him. Make sure he isn't on drugs, or physically and mentally burned out. If he has any other weaknesses though, we can use them to strengthen our hand," Talbot instructed his agent.

Cutter was squarely built, but agile. Like a Humvee. His crew cut was severe, as often was his expression. The forty-year-old former marine was professional and precise in his conduct. The ardent patriot was loyal to his country and employer. His wife had come second to his job, which is why she divorced him. Talbot had taken Cutter under his wing, after the agent had failed the psych tests during his application to join the Secret Service. Talbot was his mentor – and even after five years Cutter would avidly listen to the older man's words of wisdom (he was also grateful for the regular bonus payments his handler gave him, outside his government salary):

"The rules of engagement should be shoot first, so that you only have to shoot once... Who needs to win hearts and minds when you have them by the balls?... Know your enemy, before he even knows you're his enemy... It's when you don't lie to Congress that they think something is wrong... Plausible deniability. They should always be your ultimate watchwords."

Cutter updated Talbot by leaving his report in a draft folder of an email account he shared with his employer - that way no correspondence was actually sent (and potentially intercepted). The CIA operative, or one of his colleagues, had been following their person of interest for a few days now. Cutter reported that the Englishman drank heavily. He spent several afternoons or evenings at his local pub. In terms of his routine he regularly walked his dog, visited his life wife's grave and attended to his ailing foster parent at a nursing home. He didn't work but rather lived off a generous income from monies earned as a contract killer. Having read about his service record in Afghanistan and some of the hits attributed to Devlin the agent granted the Englishman some grudging respect. He was a fellow professional. Talbot also read with interest about the events of the previous night. Any reservations the agent might have had about the target losing his edge had been quelled. The English hitman had ice in his veins, to face down the Jamaican gunman as he did. Or Devlin possessed a death wish. He certainly possessed good taste in women, the American thought, as he clicked open the photographs of Emma and Holly. Cutter briefly thought of an ex-girlfriend who had been crippled in a car accident recently, as he read about the death of Devlin's wife. *God only knows what the bastard went through.* Any admiration Cutter harboured for Devlin would not colour his judgement however should Talbot order him to take the Englishman out. He had killed better men, during sanctioned and unsanctioned operations. Talbot told him where to point – and Cutter fired. No questions asked.

Semper fidelis.

Devlin picked up a few pieces of litter, lying next to Holly's grave, and replaced the old bouquet of flowers with a new one. He read the inscription on the gravestone once more, a quote from Coleridge:

"To be beloved is all I need

And whom I love I love indeed."

The words had carved themselves into his soul, as surely as they were carved into the expensive marble. He spoke to her. As much as Devlin knew what his wife would say to him back, he still would have loved to hear her voice again. Just once even.

If he had drawn another gun last night, I still would have walked towards him. I felt like I was walking towards you. I'm not sure I even confronted them out of a desire to save other people. In the end, we're all dead.

Devlin's phone vibrated in his pocket. Usually he turned it off, whilst talking to his wife, but as he was expecting a call from the care home about his father's latest blood test he checked the screen. He duly ignored it and placed the device back into his pocket on viewing the missed call – and then text message – from Birch.

"It's been a year. Let's celebrate."

John Birch had served with Devlin in Helmand – and had been injured during Rameen's attack on the village. Birch had also been the one to alert Devlin of the Afghan's presence in the London last year. He reminded the contract killer of his promise that he would kill Rameen, if ever the opportunity arose. Devlin wasn't in the mood to celebrate the anniversary however. He winced, as if he were in physical torment, as he remembered Tyerman. It was the anniversary of his death too. The sins of the past can cling to you, like leeches. Bleed you dry.

After visiting Holly's grave Devlin smoked a couple of cigarettes outside the gates of the cemetery and then flagged down a black cab to take him to the *Huntsman & Hound* pub. He needed a drink.

Cutter and his watch team followed in a charcoal grey BMW.

The *Huntsman & Hound* pub was located just off the Old Kent Rd. Black, iron horseshoes and yellowing photographs of how the pub looked in the past adorned the walls. The polished brass fittings and rows of glasses, hanging from the bar, gleamed in the improving sunshine. A smell of beer, chicken goujons and furniture polish infused the air.

A couple of locals sat at the far end of the bar, whilst a few medical students worked their way through a second bottle of wine in the corner. Devlin gave the locals a friendly nod and then caught the eye of Terry Gilby, the pub's genial landlord. Devlin made a subtle swirling motion of his finger, signalling that he was happy to buy a round of drinks for everyone.

Shortly afterwards the door to the pub opened and an American ordered a drink. He sat himself at a table, read the newspaper and glanced at his phone and watch – as if he was waiting for someone.

Devlin downed half his pint in a few desperate and thirst-quenching gulps. Frequenting the pub had become one of his few pleasures in life. He often took Violet along with him. It felt more like home than home.

"How 'ave you been?" Terry asked, confident that, unlike some of his other customers, Devlin wouldn't launch into a Jerimiah. The landlord had almost become the postcode's sin eater, listening to his patrons' various problems: marital issues, the ineptitude of the local council, work troubles, Millwall's loss of form and the rising price of cigarettes.

"I'm fine," Devlin casually replied, as if he didn't have a care in the world, as he also waved his hand in acknowledgement of the locals at the end of the bar thanking him for the drink. "How have you been? Busy?"

"Busy enough. When it gets quiet I often wish that it'll liven up. But when it gets busy I long for it to be quiet again," Terry replied in good humour, clinking his pewter tankard against his friend's. "L'chaim."

"L'chaim," Devlin enjoined – and finished off the remainder of his pint.

"So, did you hear about the shooting last night in Bermondsey Square? A yardie gunned down a couple of Albanians. And then the yardie was beaten to within an inch of his life by a mysterious bystander – with an ashtray of all things, according to some reports. There are worse tragedies. At least it wasn't another poxy terrorist attack. There's a chance you might have even heard the shots from your flat."

"I saw something on the news this morning but I wasn't really concentrating. I also slept through the whatever happened. I heard enough gunfire in Helmand to last me a lifetime. Hopefully the government might now be encouraged to bring back smoking in pubs, given the security benefits of ashtrays."

"Amen to that. You must have seen a lot during your time over there. Did you ever have to shoot at anyone? I won't be offended if you tell me to mind my own business," Terry said, as he poured his friend another pint. He subtly shook his head when Devlin motioned to pay, indicating that the drink was on the house.

"I fear I might bore you to sleep should I start recounting some old war stories. Suffice to say I fired off a few shots in anger, whilst over in Afghanistan. One of the councillors over in Helmand once asked a sniper what he felt, when he fired off a shot and killed an enemy. "Well, depending on if I haven't had breakfast that morning, I feel hungry," he replied... After the Iranian Embassy siege in the early eighties the SAS were all asked to submit a report of their actions during the assault. A soldier was quizzed as to why he shot a single terrorist more than thirty times. His answer: "I ran out of bullets." I knew soldiers in Helmand who discharged their weapons by accident, or out of nervousness. Others did so out of anger or a sense of vengeance for fallen comrades... If you don't shoot the enemy, the enemy will shoot you... Soldiering is a job. And controlled aggression is part of the job description... Sometimes war can bring out the best in people, sometimes it can bring out the worst..."

Devlin thought how, more than perhaps any other regiment, the Paras brought out the best and worst in people. The motto of the regiment was *Ready for Anything*. The Paras went forward when others would take a step back, or retreat. They fought for one another like brothers. Fearless. Often decent. Often noble. Montgomery had called the Paras, "Men apart." But Devlin had witnessed the darker side of "men apart" – behaving like animals. Few squaddies gained their red beret without a bout or two of milling. Devlin had stepped into the ring himself. He had been both a lion – and punchbag – at the same time. His arms hung off him like two sacks of potatoes afterwards. His expression creased in disgust every time he recalled the "gunge" contests of his fellow squaddies. Shit was eaten, piss was drunk. 1 Para prided itself on being the best, or worst, "gungers". The other great contest between squaddies, to separate the men from the boys or Paras from the craphats, during his time in the regiment had been the Dance of the Flaming Arseholes. Soldiers would strip naked, roll-up a magazine and shove it into their arse. It was then set on fire. As the rest of the room chanted a song called "The Zulu Warrior" the Para would dance on the table and try to let the magazine burn down as far as possible, until he couldn't endure the pain anymore. Devlin tried to remain a man apart on such nights. He would retire early and catch up on some reading, or maintain his weapon and kit.

"Truth as Circe: Error has transformed animals into men: is truth perhaps capable of turning man back into an animal?"

Devlin recalled the quote from Nietzsche as he remembered the incidents of beastings and punishments beatings throughout his training. Man's inhumanity to man is the dye that's impossible to whitewash from history. We're human, all too human after all. Devlin himself had executed Taliban fighters and turned a blind eye to acts of sadism. He still couldn't be sure if he lost or found himself during his tours. Most of the horror stories about what the Paras did to captured IRA members in the seventies also contained kernels of truth. But the IRA were also men apart, Devlin judged. Vile, brutal, conceited thugs – adopting a romantic cause to mask a criminal organisation which pedalled drugs and ran one of the largest protection rackets in Europe. When Devlin was offered the contract to take out a former IRA brigade commander he willingly accepted.

"Where's Kylie? Is she not working today?" Devlin asked, curious. He also wanted to steer the conversation away from his time in the army. It was another part of his past he wanted to bury. Kylie was a barmaid. Devlin had known her from when she used to work in *The Admiral Nelson*, a pub close to his flat. He had slept with her then. He had slept with her again, about a month ago. She had recently broken things off with her boyfriend. It had been late. They were both drunk. Both lonely. Devlin visited Holly's grave the following morning and said that it had meant nothing. A few days later Kylie was back with her fiancé. When Devlin and the barmaid saw each other again they duly acted as if nothing had happened.

"She asked for the day off. Her idiot and selfish shit of brother has taken what spare cash she has and disappeared again. She came in earlier, crying her eyes out, saying that Paul Simms and Chris Chard were demanding that she pay her brother's debts. If you didn't already know Simms and Chard work for Tony Jackson, the local loan shark and drug dealer. The two businesses complement each other. I'm not even sure if Tony knows that they're hassling Kylie for the money. It's not his style to go after women. Simms and Chard may be doing it to earn some extra cash, or they're just getting their kicks from terrorising her. I'd offer to help her out but her brother owes over five grand. She doesn't want to ask her fiancé either, in case it causes an argument and he break things off again."

Devlin compressed his jaw and pursed his lips. His stomach tightened into a fist. He pictured Kylie's heart-shaped face and bright, coquettish eyes. There wasn't a mean bone in her body. She couldn't afford five grand. But it didn't matter. Devlin would make somebody else pay.

"I think I've seen Simms and Chard about before. Do they still drink in *The Plough*, off Deptford High St?"

"Aye. Simms is shagging the landlady there. Hopefully she'll give him a dose of the clap and he'll be too ill hassle Kylie. Fancy another drink?"

"No, I best be off. I need to feed Violet and take her for a walk."

"Will you be back later?"

"I'm not sure. I need to take care of some business first."

5.

Devlin paced – or stalked - around his living room and smoked another cigarette. Music played in the background. After returning home Devlin had fed and walked his dog. He also cooked himself a meal of some grilled trout and steamed broccoli. He resisted the temptation of drinking a bottle of wine with dinner and just had water. He wanted to rehydrate and sober up. Be sharp.

Devlin remembered the brief look of rejection on Kylie's face when, as they lay in bed, she asked if things would ever get serious between them - and he replied that they couldn't. He then thought of Holly and turned his back to the barmaid. But the girl's hurt expression now scorched what was left of his soul. He hoped he would now be able atone for the hurt he caused. Absolve himself. Kylie would never know how he helped her. But that didn't matter. Devlin would know. God would too.

The ex-soldier told himself he wasn't suffering from bloodlust, having gained a taste of violence again from the previous night. It was just an unfortunate coincidence. *I'm still retired.* He didn't want to scratch the itch but he was left with no choice. Simms and Chard needed to pay.

And Devlin would be able to forgive himself for what he was about to do. Holly would forgive him too. If God was unable to forgive him, so be it. Devlin had still not been able to forgive Him for taking his wife away.

Devlin finished off his cigarette, retrieved the claw hammer from his tool box and headed out.

Years of soldiering had taught Devlin how to be patient. After having walked past the pub and confirmed that Simms and Chard were present he crossed the road and sat by the window in a late night Turkish kebab house. He ordered a coffee, mixed grill and read the newspaper, whilst keeping one eye on the doorway to *The Plough*.

A few cheers and jeers filled the restaurant as a group of young men sat and watched a Galatasaray match in the corner. But Devlin tuned them out. His eyes were as keen as a croupier's, keeping track of all the bets, as he focused on the job at hand and played out various scenarios. What if there was a lock-in at the pub and the two men stayed there for the night? What if they didn't leave together and went their separate ways immediately after leaving? What if they turned left together? What if they turned right? What was their likely route and destination?

The waitress, Helena, approached him again to re-fill his coffee. They had spoken earlier. She was a mature student, studying European Literature, and worked in the restaurant at night to help pay her tuition fees. "I'm giving myself a second chance in life, trying to better myself," Helena remarked. They briefly chatted about Balzac and Flaubert. She was impressed. He was courteous, attractive and, from the looks of his watch, wealthy. Helena was a blend of Asiatic and Arabic good looks. Long, glossy black hair hung down her back like silk drapes. She was alluring, even in dark jeans and a cheap t-shirt (with the name of the kebab house, *Kebabylon*, emblazoned across it).

"Anything interesting in the newspaper?"

"It's all bad news I'm afraid, aside from the fact that one of the stars from a programme called Made in Chelsea has died of a drug overdose," Devlin drily joked. He figured that anyone who liked Balzac would have a healthily dark sense of humour. "It's the only bit of news they're not blaming on Brexit. Although I'm sure someone will write into the letters page and correct that mistake."

Helena laughed and her lips curled-up into a cat-like smile.

"You have nice, kind eyes," she suddenly and flirtatiously expressed, surprising herself a little by how forward she was. Usually the customers hit on her. But here she was chatting a customer up.

"I'm sure it's just a trick of the light," Devlin replied.

"You're modest too."

"I have a lot to be modest about, unfortunately"

Helena laughed again - and tucked her hair behind her ear.

"I'll be taking my break soon. Would it be okay to sit with you for a while?"

Devlin was tempted. Perhaps it was time he started dating again. Enjoying himself. He was attracted to her. It had been a year since he had shared a nourishing conversation over a nice meal. He would enjoy making love to her, going on holiday together. Visiting art museums and seeing plays. Spending the night on the sofa, watching a film. Laughing.

But Devlin had a job to do tonight. As well as Helena, standing in front of him, an image of Kylie came into his mind. Duty called.

"I'm afraid that I might have to suddenly leave soon, I'm due to meet someone," Devlin politely replied, placing his hand on the table so that his wedding ring came into view.

The waitress said she understood – and forced a smile – before retreating to the counter.

Devlin left Helena a tip which was equal to the price of his meal and drinks – and headed out into the street, having spotted Simms and Chard leaving *The Plough*. He decided to keep his distance to begin with. As he crossed the street he noticed a brace of rats scuttling along the curb and was reminded of something one of the regulars, a pest control officer, said in the *Huntsman & Hound* a week ago:

"You can't kill every rat. You need to accept them, like the air you breathe. To even get close to wiping them all out you'd have to use so much poison that you'd probably kill off half the good burghers of London too."

The street lighting was poor as they walked towards the *Pankhurst* housing estate but Devlin was still able to take in his prey. Simms possessed a pasty complexion, even in summer. He was gaunt, rake thin and swaggered rather than walked, imitating the gait of some of his favourite rap artists. Although approaching forty Simms was still dressed in a tracksuit, baseball cap and a pair of garish Puma trainers. Simms had been dealing – and consuming – drugs since his mid-teens. He was far from the best advert for taking weed and coke – given his unpleasant character and appearance – but Simms knew his business and customer base. Most of the sentences that came out of Simms' mouth contained two – or three – swear words. The small man liked to play the big man. He was relentless and ruthless when it came to collecting debts for his boss, Tony Jackson. The first warning was merely verbal. But should a customer not pay the required sum on the second time of asking Simms would pull out his knife and slice the webbing on his victim's fingers. On the third time of asking Simms unleashed Chard. Thumbs or arms were broken. Goods were also removed from the debtor's home. Simms was also proficient at carrying out his boss' orders of occasionally giving his product away for free.

"Concentrate on getting them hooked first. Sooner or later we'll make them pay double. And if they can't quite afford to do so, we can happily lend them the money of course," the rapacious Jackson instructed, providing a business plan for his small army of dealers and enforcers.

The brawny Chard dwarfed his friend, almost comically so. He wore a Paul Shark jacket over a chequered Ben Sherman shirt, elasticated jeans to cater for his large waist and a Dunn & Co flat cap, which had once belonged to his costermonger father. Ten years of boxing gave the enforcer a flat, crooked nose and cauliflower ears. His neck was thick, his hands were as large as bear paws and his knuckles scarred. When the big man hit someone, he stayed hit. Either sinus trouble, or an addiction to cocaine, caused the enforcer to constantly sniff.

Devlin made an educated guess that the pair were ultimately cutting through the housing estate to reach a late-night bar on Deptford High St. He made the decision to break off following the two men – and took a different path through the estate – having settled on a narrow alleyway where he could ambush his prey. There would be no room for the two men to manoeuvre or escape. The passage was situated between the estate's generator and one of the walls of the children's playground. No one could look out their window and witness the attack, should they hear any screams.

He reached his destination, hiding just behind the generator at the mouth of the passageway, and waited. He knew he wouldn't have to wait long. Devlin, like a number of other soldiers or criminals he had encountered over the years, possessed an internal switch - a kill switch – which he could turn on at will to get the job down. Violence and immorality became a necessity. Doubt, decency, cowardice and conscience were all switched off. They would be fine to be switched on again, after the job was finished.

Devlin heard their voices and footsteps approaching. He took a breath and gripped the pimpled handle of the claw hammer. Holly had bought him the hammer, as part of a toolbox, many years ago. He had used it to hammer in the nails to hang-up various works of art.

He was wearing black jeans, a black shirt and dark blue summer blazer, with a spacious inside pocket. Devlin had retrieved the balaclava from his pocket and placed it over his head. The soles of his shoes were rubber, having had them changed from the original leather, lest he slipped and lost his footing. The devil is in the detail.

It was dark. The attacker owned the element of surprise. And the victims' reflexes were dulled from drink and drugs. Devlin paused not to let his opponents take him in as he appeared before them.

Chard was first hit with a powerful kick to the groin. He was winded, disorientated – in too much pain to retaliate. Before Simms had a chance to react Devlin grabbed the spindly drug dealer and smashed his head against a brick wall – just forcefully enough to knock him down rather than out.

As Chard began to straighten-up and absorb things he received another agonising blow to the groin. This time the big man fell. Devlin quickly snatched the flat cap from his head and placed it over his mouth as he pounded the hammer on his kneecaps. Once. Twice. His large body jolted, from head to toe, with each savage blow.

Devlin muffled the screams but then removed the cap and loomed over the stricken enforcer. Tears moistened his eyes. He seethed and puffed out his cheeks. His knees – legs – felt like they were on fire.

"Keep quiet. If you make a sound or move I'll crush your windpipe. Nod if you understand."

Chard grimaced and nodded.

Devlin swiftly transferred his attention back to Simms. Blood seeped out of the back of his throbbing head and stained his baseball cap. He was just coming out of his daze when he felt his attacker remove his trainers. Devlin removed a sock too and forced Simms to insert it into his mouth, threatening to smash his teeth in if he failed to comply. The eyes looking out from the balaclava were far from kind.

There are over twenty-five bones in a human foot. Devlin broke most of them as he ferociously struck both of Simms' feet, like a blacksmith pounding on his anvil. Bone and cartilage snapped like bracken. The drug dealer's remaining cream sock quickly turned red. Simms moaned, twisted and turned – but to no avail.

"You tell Jackson that Deptford now belongs to Spinks," Devlin remarked, speaking loudly and forcefully through the balaclava. Spinks was a rival operator to Jackson, whose territory encompassed Woolwich and Thamesmead. Devlin calculated that Jackson might retaliate and start a war. Hopefully the two men would go to war. It was a dog eat dog world. But either way he was confident Kylie would be free from suspicion, as to the being the origin of the attack.

Devlin relieved the two men of their mobile phones and a large roll of cash. He walked away, wiping away any spots of blood from the hammer and his hands. The assault had taken no more than two minutes – but it's legacy would endure. Simms would now hobble, rather than swagger. Chard would also be out of action for some time. Jackson might even write his two employees off – and demand payment for the money Devlin took from them.

As he reached the high street and flagged down a cab his phone vibrated with a message, from Porter.

"We need to talk."

Devlin messaged back that he would call his friend in the morning. He renewed the promise he made to himself however:

I'm still retired.

It had been like old times. Before his retirement. Porter had returned from London and lied to his wife about his day. He had met with Talbot but said to Victoria that he had visited *Farlows* in Piccadilly and ordered new fishing rods and tackle (he had bought various pieces of equipment online to give credence to his story). Porter wasn't a proud liar, he was just a proficient one, he thought. He came through the door early evening and forced a smile, pretending that all was well. For her part Victoria pretended not to notice that there was something that her husband wasn't telling her. Just like old times.

Victoria rested on her bed. A book lay open in front of her but she couldn't concentrate. The words seemed dead on the page. She bit her nails and felt like clasping the cross around her neck. And praying. She imagined how her pragmatic husband would have argued that praying wouldn't do any good. But she would have countered that it couldn't do any harm either.

Porter sat at the dining room table downstairs. He wanted some time alone, to brood, think, frown and hold his head in his hands. The fixer only forced a smile when his dog, Marlborough, nuzzled his leg and whimpered – either in sympathy with his master or the hound heard the fox padding across the lawn outside.

His phone buzzed. Porter read the text message from Devlin, to say that he would call in the morning. He wished he could have kept his friend out of Talbot's plans – but he was central to them. Both men would meet with the American tomorrow. He was too tired, or despondent, to think of another deception tonight to tell Victoria, to explain away another trip to London.

Porter downed another mouthful of brandy and took another drag on his cigar. But he took little pleasure in his familiar vices. They delivered little consolation. He felt like his head was in a noose – and Talbot's hand was on the lever which worked the trapdoor. His could lose everything. For once the fixer was at another man's mercy. Porter was used to manipulating events, not being manipulated himself. Suffice to say he preferred the former. Only Devlin could save him. He needed to say yes to Talbot's proposal. Do the job. Porter knew that he had to help save Devlin in return however. He was his brother's keeper.

6.

Devlin called Porter first thing in the morning. On the surface of things the conversation was a normal one. Porter mentioned a time and location to meet – to discuss a possible business opportunity. At the beginning of the exchange however Porter asked about the health of his foster parent, which was a pre-arranged code between the two associates to signal that one of their phones or emails might be being monitored.

Devlin hung up, briefly closed his eyes and sighed.

We are where we are.

He walked and fed Violet, whilst idly speculating on his forthcoming meeting with Porter. No amount of money could tempt him to come out of retirement, he determined. He no longer owned a weapon. He could no longer be a gun for hire. Out of a courtesy to his friend he would meet with Porter though. He owed him that. The tone of his voice suggested that it might be something different to the fixer offering him a contract as well, especially since he still thought Porter was enjoying his retirement. It was not completely out of the ordinary for his former employer to enact the simple security protocol. But it was rare. Better to be safe than sorry, Porter would argue.

Midday. The address Porter gave Devlin was for a house on Boston Place, close to Baker St tube station. The property was large but anonymous looking. He rang the bell. His heart beat a little faster than normal but Devlin's expression remained impassive. He was briefly tempted, earlier in the morning, to bring a weapon to the meeting but he trusted his friend. There were other protocols Porter could have enacted in a coded way. He could have warned Devlin that he was in danger, or to get out the country immediately, through various pre-arranged phrases.

Cutter opened the heavy black door and invited Devlin in with a nod of his head.

"Raise your arms please," the American instructed, neither politely nor rudely, before padding the visitor down for any concealed firearms. "If you could also remove your phone and any other electronic devices from your pockets."

Devlin left his phone in the allotted plastic container on a table by the door. Cutter pulled out a paddle-shaped scanner and ran it over the Englishman's person, checking for cameras or bugs. As the agent did so Devlin caught a glimpse of the man's Glock 43 beneath his suit jacket. Or perhaps Cutter allowed him to catch a glimpse of the weapon, as a threat or warning. Devlin remained unfazed by the rigmarole and security procedures. He'd experienced them plenty of times before.

Cutter scrutinised Devlin, looking for signs of shock, surprise or fear. But the hitman remained unreadable - unhackable.

The agent led Devlin upstairs to a clean, spacious living room, where Porter and Talbot were waiting.

"Good afternoon Mr. Devlin. I hope I can call you Michael. My name is Mason Talbot. I work for the CIA, for my sins. Oliver will be able to vouch for my credentials and character. Thank you for meeting with me on such short notice. Firstly, would you like something to eat or drink? Vincent here can get you something," Talbot amiably remarked, smiling on more than once occasion. Hopefully everything could be civil. Or as civil as humanly possible - in light of the blackmail and other crimes which were about to take place.

"I'm fine, thanks."

Devlin glanced around the smartly furnished room. A big, flat screen tv next to a cabinet full of DVDs dominated one corner. A blood-red Dyson air purifier hummed in another corner. A row of bestselling paperbacks sat over an ornamental fireplace. Porter was sitting on one of two expensive, comfortable leather sofas which faced one another. The blinds had been pulled down over the windows and the room was illuminated by a pair of tall, brass floor lamps. Inoffensive works of art hung on the walls. Family photographs and personal effects were absent. Devlin figured that the property was usually used as a safehouse.

As well as quickly surveying the room Devlin took in his host. White. Anglo-Saxon. Protestant. The American was well-groomed and well-conditioned. He was dressed in a navy-blue Brooks Brothers suit, pristine white shirt and red silk tie (held in place with a gold, but not garish, tie pin). His shoes were as polished as the wooden floor he was standing on. Devlin caught a whiff of both cologne and moisturiser on the senior CIA agent. He looked good, even great, for his age. His voice was clear and authoritative. He could have been an American news anchor for Fox News (as opposed to CNN). Devlin suspected that his forehead had been botoxed on more than one occasion – and that the agent bleached his teeth. Talbot was not so much a car salesman, as someone who owned an entire dealership, Devlin later considered.

Porter stood-up and greeted his friend. He appeared a little sheepish. Outfoxed. His expression was creased in worry – or contrition – as he shook Devlin's hand. Porter somehow seemed diminished, deferent, in the American's presence.

"It's good to see you again, Michael," Porter said. It remained obvious, but unsaid, that he wished it was under different circumstances.

Devlin nodded, in a non-committal way, in reply.

"Please, gentlemen, take a seat. My apologies, Oliver, if I repeat some of what we discussed during our previous meeting. You seem like a straight talking – as well as straight shooting – kind of man, Mr. Devlin. As such I will come straight to the point. I want you to carry out a job for me."

"I'm retired," Devlin remarked, not quite rudely but matter-of-factly.

Talbot smiled in reply, almost unctuously, as though he had won a private bet with himself as to predicting the Englishman's reaction to his opening salvo.

"I think you might find that you've just been on a long sabbatical. It was Oliver's first thought too. But then, wisely, he had second thoughts when I made him an offer he couldn't refuse, to quote a phrase."

Devlin turned to look at Porter, who was sitting beside him on the sofa, but the fixer averted his gaze and bowed his head, in shame or otherwise.

"You only have yourself to blame, one might argue," Talbot continued, after taking a sip of coffee and fastidiously smoothing his tie down. "You came to my attention as a result of your last job. Your principle target was Rameen Jamal, I believe. But you also took out Faisal Ahmadi, a person of interest to me. Incidentally, I was surprised, impressed or appalled by you shooting your former commanding officer that night. In another lifetime I would have gazumped Oliver and recruited you myself, when you left the army. But as to Ahmadi it was my intention to turn him, or at least extract sufficient intelligence from the agent. I wanted to know who his paymasters were – and who he was giving money to. You rendered my operation obsolete however. Ahmadi's death didn't upset me, God and Allah knows the cretin deserved to die. But I found it irksome, to say the least, when some cowboy moseyed on into *The Ritz* and gunned down my target. I do not like to have my time and energies wasted. Now you and Oliver here were clever enough to shut down the surveillance systems of the hotel during the hit. But our equipment was still working fine when you entered and exited the building. Man plans, God laughs. It took some time but we managed to track you down. We duly discovered your connection to Oliver and I built up a file on you both. I've condensed the highlights of your files into these two folders, which you can peruse before you leave. Or you may want to glance at them now, so you are fully aware of the unfortunate position you're in."

With a nod of his head Talbot instructed Cutter to hand over the two manila folders, containing photographs, intelligence reports and facsimiles of bank records and other documents. The CIA operative had been thorough. He often compared his agency to "the great Eye of Sauron," which saw and knew everything, eventually.

"I have considered you both prospective assets for some time. You just didn't know it. I felt fine to put you on ice, until now. I want you to help me make a problem disappear. Once done, those files you are holding will similarly disappear. Now before you think of chirping up and saying that you are still retired, Michael, I want you to think carefully not just about yourself, but think of others in your life too. The authorities can use what's in that binder to freeze and appropriate all your assets. A long prison sentence is inevitable. Who will then pay for your father's care home? Who will visit him in your place – and give him his cigarettes and navy rum? Your former girlfriend, Emma, will be devastated too. Not just because of a sense of betrayal and humiliation. But did you know she is currently applying to work for an NGO, dealing with foreign aid? How much would you rate her chances of success once the word gets out that she was intimately involved with a contract killer? And who will be left to tend to Holly's grave, after you're gone? Should you insist that you are still retired there will be consequences for Oliver, your partner in crime so to speak, as well. I'm not sure how much he – or his family - will enjoy his sunshine years from a drear jail cell. I take no pleasure in mentioning such unpleasantness but I believe it's best that you are apprised of all the facts before you make your final decision," Talbot remarked with sympathy. Unrepentantly.

Devlin remained outwardly calm – but inside he experienced an urge to make the CIA agent his next target. But that would only make his situation worse. He flicked through the pages of the file to discover photos of him leaving both Bermondsey Square and the *Pankhurst* estate. Perhaps if he still insisted that he was retired the American would threaten to send the relevant photos to the local yardie boss – and Jackson. His family – and the likes of Emma, Terry and Kylie – could suffer a worse fate than just seeing him go to prison. *And what would happen to Violet?*

Devlin always knew the past would somehow catch up with him one day. Perhaps the past caught up with him every day. It wasn't even the past. It was his present. We are where we are. The past can, like malaria, lay dormant for years. But every decade or so the disease will rear its ugly head. Make you suffer.

7.

Devlin agreed to take on the job.

Talbot rubbed his hands in satisfaction and beamed, as if he had just closed a business deal of mutual benefit to all parties.

"I'm pleased, gentlemen, that we are all on the same page. You'll also be pleased that your target is neither a good nor innocent man, although we have all worked in this trade too long to grow a conscience. You are familiar with Ewan Slater…"

Porter pictured the fifty-year-old former MP for Bradford West. He was scruffy-chic and could often be seen wearing a corduroy cap, which he claimed had once belonged to John Lennon (although he had been quoted years ago as saying the cap belonged to Donovan). A former trade unionist and member of the Labour Party, Slater had run as an independent candidate a decade ago and, against all odds, had won a seat. He called his party "Vision." He had only served one term as an MP but Slater was currently experiencing a renaissance in support, mainly due to his appearance on the television show Strictly Come Dancing. He was willing to make a fool of himself – and a large section of the audience loved him for it. Vision was gaining some traction in the polls again and Slater had just announced that he would put himself forward as a candidate in the next election (albeit he remained coy about which constituency he would be running in). The BBC seemed to grant him as much favourable coverage as he desired and his team were adept at using social media (both to spread positive stories and shout down any critics). Most critics of the party were trolled and labelled "fascists" or "racists". *The Observer* half-jokingly described Ewan Slater as "slightly to the left of Jeremy Corbyn". The article also stated how the "socialist Nigel Farage" had won a poll relating to which political figure the public would most wish to have a drink with down the pub (despite the fact that Slater was a teetotaller). Porter had once met the rabble-rouser at a dinner in Mansion House. He was the guest of the Venezuelan ambassador. Porter had noticed over the years that even the most ardent communists were happy to break bread with capitalists, providing the spread was lavish enough and they didn't have to pay. Slater turned to championing his friend's country and its political system, arguing that "Venezuela is the fairest nation on Earth. Nigh on everyone is the same." Porter was tempted to reply, "Aye, nigh on everyone is poor and is an enemy of the state," - but desisted.

Talbot continued with his character assassination:

"Slater is vegetarian, against foxhunting and has spoken of a worldwide Jewish conspiracy on more than one occasion. He also fanatically believes the state should control the means of production. And he has the audacity to compare Donald Trump to Hitler. I am not at liberty to divulge the reason why we have commissioned this job but suffice to say you will be doing your country a great service. Slater may well be the single most dangerous man in Britain right now."

Porter painted a scenario of the target's resurgent party winning a few seats at the next election (in northern towns and constituencies encompassing large student populations). He would be able to prop-up a Labour government, if the polls were correct, in exchange for enacting certain policies and being given a prominent post in the cabinet. Slater's avowed enemy was "western imperialism". Capitalism was to blame for all the worlds' sins, according to the activist's political philosophy (although what Slater really desired to propagate was a political religion). He called *Das Kapital* his Bible and Marx was a prophet. The proletariat were the chosen people and socialism, national or otherwise, was the promised land. In terms of who should play the role of God, the evangelical atheist had no doubt pencilled himself in for the role. But only he had the vision to make things work. He could be a new Mao or Stalin, but he would learn from their mistakes. The CIA couldn't countenance such a figure having influence over foreign or trade policy relating to the United States, Porter mused. For years the establishment had rightly treated the radical socialist as a joke. Ewan Slater couldn't be afforded to have the last laugh however.

The CIA couldn't be caught carrying out an assassination of such a figure on British soil, Porter reasoned. Devlin provided them with plausible deniability. He was their scapegoat. A patsy.

"You have both been in the game long enough to know that, if apprehended, you will be on your own. And should you feel tempted to divulge any inappropriate information your families will suffer a far worse fate than just some financial insecurity."

Talbot hardened his features briefly – and Devlin fancied that he looked a little like a gargoyle - but then donned his mask of civility again. For the most part, the Englishmen sat in silence, like two chastised but truculent schoolboys outside the Headmaster's office. They would be unhappy about it – but they would take their punishment. Cutter brought a bottle and glass of wine over.

"This is your favourite Burgundy is it not, Oliver?" Talbot remarked, as an aside. His intention however was to stress to Porter just how much he knew about his new associate – and therefore control him.

Despite ashtrays being conspicuous by their absence – and Talbot pulling a face when the Englishman retrieved his cigarettes – Devlin lit-up and filled the pine and cranberry scented room with smoke. For his own sense of worth, he needed to assert his will and defy the arrogant CIA agent. Even it if was a meaningless victory.

"Now I appreciate how you have planned your jobs in the past but this operation has a strict time frame. Our window of opportunity will be open in two days. But rest assured the plan is sound. Should you have any reservations – or you discern any holes in the operation – we will duly listen. But Cutter will serve Slater up on a plate for you. We will provide you with a clean weapon. You will just need to arrange for your own extraction. But that shouldn't be a problem for you to fix, Oliver. Who knows, this could be the first of many jobs together. We could form our own special relationship... Cutter will brief you further on the details. We have a file on Slater, which we can show you. I want you to have full disclosure. In terms of intelligence, what's mine is yours. But I am afraid I need to leave, to attend another important meeting. No rest for the wicked. If a shark stops swimming, it dies," Mason Talbot confidentially exclaimed, like a man in control of his own fate - and the fate of others.

Cutter was thorough and professional in his briefing. The former Guards officer and ex-Para rolled back the years – and were under orders again like common soldiers. Cutter provided them with maps and laid out when and where

Devlin would execute the kill shot. He had done most of Devlin's work for him, including recommending an escape route.

"I have studied your service record and other hits that we've attributed to you. You are more than capable of making the required shot."

The American ran through a list of rifles, suppressors and sights he could furnish the Englishman with, depending on his preference. All would be untraceable, should Devlin need to abandon the equipment during his exfiltration. Devlin also requested he be provided with a handgun – a Sig Sauer P226 – for the operation. Cutter paused to consider the request but then assented to it.

"We will meet again here for a final run through, the day after tomorrow. If you have any questions, now is the time to ask. Mr. Talbot and I do not tolerate failure or disloyalty. But you are both smart and professional enough to already know that, I imagine," the operative asserted, martinet-like, with more than a hint of warning in his voice. His expression was as taut as a bowstring.

"Rest assured, Mr. Cutter, I have no intention of ruining what Mr Talbot called our special relationship."

Yet.

8.

"Drink?" Porter suggested, mustering what little cheer he could in his being, as the two men stood outside the house on Boston Place.

"I wouldn't say no," Devlin replied, with understatement.

They headed down into the tube in order to employ some counter surveillance measures and shake off any watchers. It didn't really much matter whether they had a tail or not now but it was another small act of defiance. Travelling by tube again reminded Porter why he couldn't abide travelling by tube. He turned his nose up at the odours, as well as the ill-mannered and ill-dressed passengers. *The great unwashed*, he snobbishly thought, quoting Cicero to himself.

The pair alighted at Oxford St where Porter bought a couple of mobile phones. They decided that the best way to communicate over the next few days would be via *Whatsapp*. The system was nigh on impossible to crack, even for the intelligence services. After leaving the phone shop Porter hailed a black cab and instructed the driver to take them to the Special Forces Club in Knightsbridge.

Porter was a member of several clubs in London – including The Garrick, The Athenaeum, White's and The Savile Club. Although he seldom now used the Special Forces Club he was warmly greeted by one of the managers as he entered the establishment. The spic and span figure resembled Capt. Peacock from *Are You Being Served?* Devlin fancied.

"Afternoon Mr. Porter. It is good to see you again. I hope you're keeping well. Thank you so much for the signed and personalised copy of the Frank Kitson book. It's much appreciated."

There were some things which Oliver Porter still didn't mind fixing.

The two men went upstairs, ordered a couple of drinks and sat in the corner.

"I'm sorry, Oliver," Devlin exclaimed, his expression contrite and pained. If not for Devlin's insistence on carrying out the hit on Rameen Jamal then they wouldn't be in their current parlous state.

Porter waved his hand in front of his face, as if brushing away a fly. Part of him was indeed upset with his friend but the blame game wouldn't do anyone any good at present. Pragmatism was the order of the day.

"What's done is done. We need to concentrate on the job at hand and make sure we can extricate ourselves from acting as assets for our American cousins in the future. I have no desire to sell my soul to Mason Talbot. As little as my soul may be worth, I warrant it's worth more than that. His leverage will remain, once we've completed the hit. A small mercy may be that he's intending to return to the US next year, to run for Congress. But that doesn't mean he won't turn over our files to his replacement."

Devlin nodded his head in acknowledgment, agreement. But his face betrayed a sense of resignation to his drear fate. All is for the worst in the worst in the worst of all possible worlds, he morbidly thought.

"We're going to have to complete this job," Porter continued, as he fastidiously straightened the cutlery on the table in front of him. "Are you confident of making the shot?"

"That won't be a problem. It seems strange that they would want to kill Slater in such dramatic fashion though. They could easily engineer things, given an extended time frame, to make it look like an accident."

"There does seem to be something else going on. Surely Talbot cannot consider Slater to be such a dangerous figure, who could have such an adverse effect on America's interest? The election is some time away. It's more fantasy than reality at the moment that Slater would be in a position to do a deal with Labour and get into power," Porter posited, thinking how he would look into any personal connection Talbot had with their target. Something was amiss.

"And will you be fine to arrange our extraction?"

"Mariner should be able to immobilise any local CCTV, if needed. I'll also contact Danny Tanner to organise a vehicle. He should be able to dispose of the car and weapons at a designated drop-off point too. I'm actually relieved that we'll be responsible for arranging our exit. I don't wholly trust our new friends. But tell me, how have you been keeping?" Porter asked, emitting a different type of concern in his voice.

"I've been better and I've been worse," Devlin answered, shrugging his shoulders slightly. He'd certainly been better, though he was at pains to remember a time when things had been worse. "And how's the family?"

For the first time that day a fond smile shaped Porter's features as the image of his wife and children came to mind.

"They're well, thank you. They're doing far better than I am at present it seems. Have you heard from Emma?" he asked, in hope more than expectation.

"Emma's due to visit the flat tomorrow, strangely enough, to pick up some papers which she left there. I'm planning to be out when she comes around though. She's engaged to be married. And you just heard today how she's applying for a new job. I'm happy for her. She's moved on," Devlin remarked, but a twinge of anguish sliced through his expression as he pictured his ex-girlfriend's face.

"And have you moved on? Do you have anyone special in your life?"

Devlin was tempted to reply that he had Holly, but he merely shook his head.

Porter took in his friend once more. He was like a worn piece of carpet, where the pattern could no longer be discerned.

"Are you keeping busy? Are you working on anything at the moment?"

Devlin nearly replied that he was working his way through half a bottle of Talisker a day.

"Fitzgerald said that there are no second acts in American lives," Porter continued. "But he didn't say anything about British lives. You'll find someone else, Michael."

"I know," Devlin solemnly replied, lying.

9.

The two men had a quick lunch and took their leave. Porter needed to get home and fix various things. For the first time in a long time he would work in his office in the garden.

Devlin took a cab home but then decided to get out prematurely at the Elephant & Castle. He needed some air. He resisted the temptation of stopping off at the *Charlie Chaplin* pub for a few drinks. As many sorrows as he had to drown he needed a clear head. He walked the rest of the way home, collecting his thoughts. He felt like he was in a maze – and he hadn't even reached the centre yet, let alone found a way out. Before, when plying his trade as a soldier or contract killer, he had the semblance of a choice to pull the trigger. But this was worse than his time in the army, when he had killed for a cause (however misguided that cause may have been). He had also killed to prevent the enemy from shooting himself and his friends. And as a hitman he had selected his targets. But now he was being forced to take another man's life. He was trapped, like a performing monkey in a cage. He wasn't scared of prison, or even solitary confinement, but he couldn't countenance making Bob or Emma pay for his sins.

Devlin told himself that he had killed better men than Slater, as well as worse, and that the self-serving politician deserved to die.

When he got back to his apartment Devlin checked beneath his carpet, to see if the crisps he had left there had broken beneath a trespasser's foot. Similarly, he checked if the ash he had left on part of his laptop had been disturbed. He swept for bugs and cameras on a device Porter had given him a couple of years ago. The flat was clean. But Talbot had little need to surveil Devlin now anyway. He had him where he wanted him.

After walking Violet along the river Devlin grabbed a bottle of water from the fridge and researched Ewan Slater on his computer.

The politician had been born in Mells, an affluent village in Somerset. His father had been a senior civil servant, his mother a ceramics teacher. Despite his self-proclaimed solidarity with "the ordinary, working man" Slater was schooled at Harrow and Keble College, Oxford. After university, he joined various activist and militant organisations, including the League Against Cruel Sports and the Surrey Socialist Chapter. His general political stance throughout the years, which remained either nobly or stubbornly consistent, was that the state should aim to curb, or abolish, capitalism. The establishment directed world affairs – started wars, caused economic crashes, rigged elections through the media – to keep themselves in power (Slater also hinted on occasion that the world was directed by a cabal of Jews, as opposed to American capitalists). Government should control the means of production. The state should also punitively – or "fairly" – tax anyone in a higher income bracket to himself. The people with the broadest shoulders should bear the heaviest burden. "It should be a crippling burden," Slater had even once venomously remarked off air, whilst his microphone was still on. The former editor of the *Morning Star* implemented a U-turn recently however on his proposed policy to target highly paid footballers – blaming them for all that was wrong with society. He dropped his proposals of a special wealth tax after his Director of Communications ran several focus groups on the issue, which concluded that the policy wasn't gaining traction. He duly reverted to blaming bankers and "fat cats" for the country's woes. "The most important challenge facing this country is battling against the few, who oppress the many. Trade Unionists – and the activists involved in organisations like Vision – must man the barricades and fight the good fight."

Slater's first wife was Katerina Schiller, who, it was rumoured, had strong ties to the Baader Meinhof gang in the nineteen seventies. Together they had one son, Rupert, who attended one of the country's top grammar schools (despite it being party policy that grammar schools should be abolished). Also, despite the charges of cronyism and nepotism that Slater levelled at the establishment, Rupert worked as an assistant to the leader's number two in Vision, Pat Snyde – the fair-weather Marxist and apologist for Sinn Fein.

Katerina divorced Slater in the mid-eighties. She claimed that the prominent member of CND and Amnesty International physically abused her during their marriage. Slater even, allegedly, punched his wife and broke her jaw on the night of Thatcher's landslide victory in 1987. Although the final settlement was undisclosed, it was said that Slater had to withdraw money from his family's trust fund to finance the alimony – and he was kept from selling the family pile, Cypress Manor, by the skin of his teeth.

Slater's second wife, who he was still married to, was the journalist Stella Brighton. When Owen Jones wasn't available, Sky News would call her up for her passionate and progressive viewpoints. For years Brighton had worked as an ardent campaigner for LGBT rights, gender equal pay and the criminalisation of all forms of hunting (including fishing). All the great and important issues of our time. She had an enviable amount of twitter followers and would often boast, whilst at the same time play the victim, about how she had received death threats online from trolls. But she would not be silenced, unfortunately. Brighton's focus of campaigning in the last year had revolved around visiting Syrian migrant camps (but only if she could be filmed at them and the BBC paid her expenses and a modest fee). On more than one occasion Brighton had stated how she would be willing to take in a migrant refugee family. "It's the humane thing to do." When a journalist recently asked her why she had still failed to take in anyone, or even apply to do so, the self-titled "neo-feminist" tetchily countered that, "this tragedy isn't just about me – you should focus on the big picture... There are children dying... You should be ashamed of yourself... As my husband recently said, the refugee crisis is the most important single issue facing the country today."

The refugee crisis was last years' news though. Her next crusade would be against (white) people guilty of cultural appropriation. She was already in talks with Channel 4 about a documentary. She had been tempted to address the subject of female genital mutilation, but her husband would need the Muslim vote in the forthcoming general election.

The couple made a formidable team, in terms of gaining air time. Brighton's Irish brogue and time spent being bi-sexual ticked plenty of diversity boxes. It helped that several of their friends from university now worked at *The Guardian* and the BBC as well. Ewan Slater's star was shining bright, since Strictly Come Dancing. The politician made the front page of the Sunday papers for the first time in his career, dressed up in a fat suit as the Prince, from Beauty and the Beast. After being voted off the programme he had brought in an image consultant to sharpen up his act - and softened some of his more radical views. During a recent interview with *The Independent* a reporter had done his homework and challenged Slater about some of his previous opinions and affiliations. During the eighties the activist had taken part in fund raising rallies for the IRA – and stated that any soldier who had participated in the Falkland's conflict should be prosecuted for war crimes. Israel was also "a stain upon the world's conscience" – and that "Stalin is the most misunderstood figure of the 20th century." Slater's reply was to argue that the reporter should, "Look to the future rather than dwell upon what was allegedly said the past. Most of this is fake news… A vote for Vision is a vote for hope. I want to see a new kind of politics. That's the most important thing you should convey to your readers. I want to be judged by the electorate - the kind of people who watch Strictly Come Dancing - not the right-wing media."

When the subject of Slater's party came up the journalist raised a couple of issues. Firstly, had he been aware that the BBC were sitting on a documentary exposing how Vision had targeted certain anti-Israel student bodies to recruit and campaign for the party? Also, was he aware of the fact that members of Vision were briefing students on how to vote twice in the general election, both in the constituency of their university and that of where their family home was located? Slater denied any knowledge of the documentary and remarked, for the record, that voter fraud was a crime: "Young people are our future. We should invest in them, not criticise them." In reply to allegations of anti-Semitism among party members Slater was forthright in his condemnation of any form of prejudice: "Vision has a zero-tolerance policy on such misdemeanours and will expel any party member guilty of hate speech or anti-Semitism." When asked how many members had been expelled in the past Slater replied that he didn't have the figures to hand. The answer was later found out to be none.

Devlin's search of images for Ewan Slater brought up an array of photographs of him shaking hands with "edgy" (but politically correct) stand-up comedians and past performers from the Cambridge Footlights. When he stubbed out another cigarette Devlin wished he could stub out half the world. Or himself. He thought about pouring himself a large whisky but he continued drinking water as he found a series of speeches and quotes by the self-proclaimed "man of the people". It was often the case that the more the assassin knew about his target the more he judged that they deserved to die. *But that might be the case with everyone*, Devlin grimly half-joked.

"Inequality is unnatural. All property is theft. The state is a tool to compel people to live in harmony... I care about the NHS more deeply than anything in the world. It is our oldest, greatest institution. Despite these recent stories about abuse, corruption, waste and unlawful killings, it is still the best health service in the world. Every staff member, especially the migrant workers, should be given a badge with "angel" written upon it... We must live within our means, even if we need to borrow money to do so... Because of the courage and goodness of the IRA we now have a peace process... I believe in trade unionism, social justice and nationalising the railways. That's my religion. And I want my congregation to be the entire country... This is not a time for self-aggrandisement, but Vision is my vision... Have you been to Cuba? Well, I have. And everyone in Havana walks around

with a smile on their face. If Fidel Castro was a dictator, he was a benign one - who cared about his country as much as I care about mine... There are times when I can sympathise with the caliphate. America is Satan... Providing all-female carriages on our trains is the most important issue dominating my time at the moment. It's not segregation, it's emancipation. Why? Because I say so... Price and wage fixing, high taxation and five-year plans can work. If you just have the vision, pardon the pun. If you just have hope."

Devlin reacted with amusement, boredom and worry at different junctures during his browsing. Eventually tiredness started to get the better of him – and Violet deserved his attention, far more than Ewan Slater. But he didn't want to succumb to sleep quite yet. He had a proper drink – and then another – before having a cold shower. Devlin closed his eyes and imagined the water washing his sins and troubles away. The plughole burped, with satisfaction, as it swallowed them down. But as Devlin opened his eyes he knew that there were some sins that could never be washed away. Or forgiven.

10.

Porter removed his reading glasses and pinched the bridge of his nose. It was late. His head ached. His stomach rumbled. But there was still work to be done. He put his glasses back on, drained what coffee was left in his cup and continued to read the intelligence reports on Mason Talbot that Mariner had sent over in a secure file. He just needed one nugget of evidence or information to use as leverage against the American. He needed some "treasure", as George Smiley might have called it, Porter wistfully thought. He searched in vain however for a compromising link between Talbot and Ewan Slater. He was even tempted at one point to contact Slater and confront him on the issue. But it was too risky. He didn't want to just hazard a guess that there was a connection between the two men.

Porter had spent most of the night reviewing the agent's career and profile. Searching for a chink in his enemy's armour. He was unsurprised to discover that, before his posting in London, Talbot had worked in Iraq, overseeing the set-up of "Camp Redemption" at Abu Ghraib. He had also been involved in several of cases of rendition. Porter noted how late amendments to the reports stated categorically that Jack Straw and David Miliband had no knowledge of any of the operations Talbot and his agents participated in.

Porter recalled the paddle-shaped scanner again Cutter used to check for electronic devices. It reminded him of the wooden paddle his Housemaster had used on him at school, years ago. The fixer wasn't prone to violent thoughts, but he felt an urge to throttle Talbot with the scanner (or his old Housemaster's bat) when he was at the house in Boston Place.

As Porter reviewed Mason's character and career he felt a nagging sense of shame, as well as revilement, as he noticed parallels between himself and the American agent. Had he not blackmailed people in the past and exploited assets to secure his objectives? Had he not acted as a middle-man in carrying out numerous contract killings? Porter had as much blood on his hands as anyone. The words "charming", "cultured" and "ruthless" were employed to describe the American. The same words had been used to describe Porter.

He glanced at the family photo next to his computer and felt an invisible blow to his solar plexus, winding him, as he imagined what would happen if he defied Talbot. The story might make the tabloids, as well as the broadsheets. The summer party invites would dry up, although he would be attending in spirit as a central topic of conversation, no doubt. His clubs would revoke his membership, although not all of them. Some would still be happy to take his money. It would be difficult, after all, for him to show his face at an establishment whilst also serving a long prison sentence. Those who already knew about his profession – and had hired him – would act with the most pronounced shock and opprobrium, he fancied.

But Porter had experienced enough "society" to last him ten lifetimes. His wine cellar was equal to the Garrick's too. His dog Marlborough was sufficient company – and far more loyal and trustworthy than any politician or magistrate.

Porter's heart sank, however, as he thought of his family. His children would be shunned or bullied – and asked to leave their schools. Victoria's friends would turn their back and look down their noses at her (women are the fairer – and crueller – sex). She would be cast out of her church, as if she were a witch from Salem. The charities she was involved in would ask her to resign – for the good of the organisation. He would be responsible for ruining her life. Why wouldn't she leave him? Why shouldn't she leave him – and take the children? They would have to sell the house – their home. The authorities would utilise new terrorist legislation and aim to appropriate his assets.

Some of it may be considered blood money, but it's still my money.

More importantly Porter knew that, should Talbot leak information about the contract killings he oversaw, his life could be forfeit. Although he had neither ordered the hits, or pulled the trigger, the associates and the families of the victims could hold him responsible. Half his business had been generated over the years from a sense of grievance and vengeance, on the part of his clients. Nothing was sacred to them, except the need for the debt to be settled. For justice to be done. Porter believed that revenge should have some usefulness, utility, rather than just be a crime of passion. But he long ago conceded that he wasn't made like other people. His enemies would consider his family a justified target as well, to repay the debt they owed Porter. And Talbot knew that too.

The fixer found himself grinding his teeth and cursing Devlin's name. The widower had nothing to lose. Whilst the husband and father had everything to lose. But he breathed out and quickly forgave his friend. Devlin wasn't the enemy. Talbot was.

All was not lost, Porter told himself in a feeble fit of logic or optimism. Mariner had messaged to say that he was still digging up information on the CIA operative. The fixer had called in a favour from a contact at MI6 to pass on any intelligence too. From the sigh Porter emitted – and his hollowed-out expression – all seemed lost however.

"Darling, it's getting late. Would you like me to leave you some supper out on the kitchen table?" Victoria exclaimed, from the other side of the door to his office in the garden. There was a chequered strain of fondness and falsity to her tone. She wanted to convey that everything was as normal, but she really knew that something was wrong. Her anxieties would remain bubble-wrapped and boxed-up though. A marriage can't survive without its secrets and small – or large – deceptions.

Porter dabbed at the film of sweat across his corrugated brow with a handkerchief his wife had given to him on his last birthday. He then sculptured his features into a crescent smile before opening the door.

"I'll be finished up soon, I promise," Porter remarked.

"It's a beautiful night. I may stay up and have a glass of wine on the terrace," she replied, hoping to further coax her husband outside.

It was indeed a fine evening. The stars seemed as polished as the buttons on his dress uniform. The sky was a glossy sable. Birdsong threaded its way through the hedgerows and trees. Lilting, lulling – as opposed to just loud.

"It is beautiful." Porter agreed, without really noticing or caring.

Yet he thought to himself how his wife was beautiful and a welcome sight. Her skin was bronzed, but as soft as velvet. She wore a simple floral-print dress which fluttered in the breeze and yet quite rightly also wanted to cling to her elegant figure. He caught the scent of her shampoo in the air and breathed it in. He tried to identify the constituent parts of the whole: cinnamon, jasmine, coconut, lemon. Porter increasingly thought how much older than his wife he must now look, but took consolation from the fact that no matter how old he got she would make him feel younger. The former officer knew that some people thought him as dry as piece of flat-bread. But with Victoria he could be romantic – and even sentimental. Porter didn't much care if others considered him cold or stuffy – because he knew that she knew the truth.

Porter would ultimately beat Talbot, he vowed. Because he had something worth fighting for.

11.

Morning. The city was shrouded in a dirty grey mist, as if everyone had been chain smoking since dawn. A watery, jaundiced light eventually seeped through, like puss secreting from a wound.

Devlin pretended to be a friend of Kylie's brother. He composed a short note, enclosed with ten thousand pounds (which he retrieved from his bug-out bag at the bottom of his wardrobe), explaining how Kylie could use the money to pay back her brother's debt. She should then use any money left over to help pay for the wedding.

He checked for a tail - and ran a few counter-surveillance moves for good measure – before heading over to the barmaid's flat and posting the letter and money through her door.

As Devlin walked home he sketched out a schedule for the day ahead. After taking Violet for a walk he would vacate the flat, before Emma was due to turn up, and visit Bob at the care home. After a couple of drinks in the pub he would then visit Holly's grave. Once back home he would check-in with Oliver and run-through the plan for tomorrow.

Devlin's schedule – and innards – span out of kilter however as he opened the door to find Emma already in his apartment, wrestling Violet for possession of a plastic bone.

He briefly stood dumbstruck, or enamoured. His mouth fell open, forming a perfect O – as if he were a goldfish. He was a little shocked – as opposed to angry – that Emma had turned up so early and let herself in. Indeed, he quickly realised how pleased he was to see her. There was a surprising lack of awkwardness. Maybe it was her calm and heartfelt smile, putting him at ease.

"I'm sorry, I know I'm early. I hope you don't mind that I let myself in. I was lucky with the traffic," she warmly remarked, crimsoning a little. Emma hoped Devlin would believe that she had arrived early by accident, rather than design.

"No, it's fine. I'm not the only one who's pleased to see you it seems," Devlin suggested, nodding towards to an ebullient Violet. The stupidly happy mongrel wagged her tail and excitedly paced up and down. Her claws made tap dancing sounds upon the wooden floor. The animal constantly alternated her gaze between Devlin and Emma – perhaps hoping that Emma had come back to live with them again. Devlin was reminded of the enormity of Emma's selfless act, to let Violet stay with him after they separated. It was probably the nicest thing anyone had ever done for him.

The first thing he noticed about Emma was how she had grown her hair long. Her fire-red tresses seemed to burn brighter, and cascaded down to her breasts. Her freckles were in bloom too, as they had been last summer. What little make-up she wore complimented her prettiness. Her lips were the colour of strawberry ice-cream, as opposed to strawberries. Her eyes were neither alluring nor demure. But her eyes were attractive and striking because they were kind.

Emma had given herself an extra spray of her favourite perfume that morning. She was wearing a cream, A-line thigh-high summer dress, belted at the waist to accentuate her figure. She had only bought the outfit, in *House of Fraser*, two days ago, along with the dark blue strappy heels she had on. Devlin thought how she was probably due to have a meeting, or attend an event later. He was too tired, modest or innocent to think how Emma had dressed-up to impress him. Whether consciously or unconsciously she still wanted him to find her attractive still - or show Devlin how she was flourishing without him. But not from a motivation of spite.

"I was about to take Violet for a walk. Would you like to join us?"

"I'd love to."

The heavy cloud cover lifted like a curtain in a theatre, to a musical – and the sun came out. Small waves slapped against the bank of the Thames, as the pleasure boats began to cruise along the moss-green river.

Anyone might have mistaken Devlin and Emma for a newly married couple as they walked their dog, chatted and laughed together.

At first, upon seeing Devlin, Emma thought he had changed. And not for the better. He appeared tired, defeated, like a man twice his age. He was, for him, out of shape and a little overweight. His t-shirt needed tucking in and his hair was slightly unkempt. His eyes were dark, almost bruised, from sleeplessness or drink. His voice seemed rougher. Yet essentially Devlin was still the same, she realised. Melancholy. Dry-witted. His face – being – was still a swirling, cracked mosaic of strength and vulnerability. He still needed saving.

"And how's your mum?" Devlin asked, as they caught-up with various things.

"Oh, she's still her usual, unbearable self. She might even have a nervous breakdown one day, instead of just always being on the cusp of one. My dad should be given a medal for putting up with her. Although I'm sure he'd prefer just to lower his golf handicap."

Emma failed to mention how her mum disapproved of her fiancé, Jason. During their first lunch together she had asked her daughter's new suitor if he was Catholic. He wasn't. God was a "cultural construct" for the tax lawyer.

"I can accept that someone called Jesus Christ existed. I just think he was a carpenter rather than the son of God," Jason asserted.

"He's an atheist," she had said, with some alarm, after the boyfriend left. "It could be worse though, I suppose. He could be C of E," she added, without a hint of humour – which was what made it funnier for Emma and her long-suffering father.

"Daddy misses you, of course," Emma remarked to Devlin, just after throwing another biscuit up in the air and having Violet catch it in her mouth. "He talks about you as if you were a fish. The one that got away. He's got no one in his life now to chat about military history with... How's Bob?"

"Unfortunately, he's gone downhill since Mary passed away. He can't really hold a conversation anymore. He gets confused. He barely eats... And he cries when he remembers Mary. He just lays in bed most of the time with the TV on, although he can't really take things in. The easiest way to describe it is that he seldom laughs or smiles anymore."

Devlin mumbled rather than spoke – and for the first time since Emma had known him the ex-soldier looked like he was going to break down and cry. He felt buffeted and burdened, plagued by the harpies of grief, guilt and Mason Talbot. Everything invisibly attacked him at once and the combatant couldn't fight back. His features crumbled in on themselves like a crushed polystyrene cup. Her heart went out to him, as did her fingertips as she gently placed her hand upon his arm.

Devlin realised just how much he needed the touch, once he felt it.

"You must be glad you've found someone else, given the state I'm in?" Devlin joked, doing his best to raise a smile.

Emma nearly answered "no".

"I'm sorry," he then said, simply and sincerely.

"That's okay, don't be silly. You have been through a lot recently, what with Bob's dementia and Mary passing away."

"No, I mean I'm sorry – for everything. For hurting you. I wanted to be the man you wanted me to be. But couldn't. I regret how I treated you – and how things ended – but I don't regret getting to know you. Being with you, Emma."

Tears glistened in her eyes. She had rehearsed what she wanted to say to Devlin, if she encountered such a scene, so many times. But silence seemed apt. If he would have asked her to keep him company all day – and all night – she probably would have said yes. They both leaned towards each other, as they sat on the bench. Propping each other up. Emma squeezed his hand. Devlin was responsive and squeezed hers in return. Their heartbeats and breathing synchronised.

"I hope you're happy now," Devlin said, his voice still a little broken.

"I am," Emma replied, lying. She increasingly preferred to spend time by herself, rather than be in Jason's company. She told herself that this didn't matter. But it did. He was a junior partner at a law firm in Holborn. He still had a lot to prove, to himself, his successful father and the partnership. Every discussion – or argument – between them was akin to a small court case. And he needed to win it, either through semantics or plea bargaining. He felt lucky to have her – and Jason loved the woman he asked to marry – but Emma sometimes felt she was little more than an adornment, a piece of eye candy who could hold an intelligent conversation around a dinner table with clients and associates. But he was decent and stable. And Emma wanted to marry him, she told herself – although her decision was slightly coloured by a desire to have children. At least he had never been married before. All the time, when Emma had lived with Devlin, she felt like she had been competing with the ghost of his first wife – and she could never live up to Holly. She was sacred. Perfect. Yet Emma missed how Devlin would put her first when they were making love. Jason couldn't compete with her first love in that respect, either from a lack of technique or selflessness.

"I know that other people say how they'd like to remain friends, but I would. I've enjoyed this morning, despite me just making a fool of myself and doubtless depressing you. But not many people I know can hold their drink like you, or have read Graham Greene. It'd be a shame to lose you altogether."

Emma smiled and the tears began to glisten in her eyes for a different reason.

"I'd like to see you again too. Not many people can put up with me complaining about by mum. And I've got no one to discuss Graham Greene – and, of course, Jane Austen - with as well. And I've missed Violet," she remarked. At the sound of her name the dog jumped up and Emma let her lick her face.

She was tempted to mention, either casually or more seriously, how much she missed Devlin. But she didn't. Yet.

"What's the form on an old boyfriend buying a present for his ex for her wedding day?"

"How about you just take care of yourself? That can be your gift to me.""I'd much prefer to buy you a microwave or fridge freezer. It'll be a lot easier for me, than taking care of myself," Devlin said, with a piratical grin.

Emma laughed, albeit underneath she still worried about the lapsed Catholic – and wanted to save him.

12.

Devlin and Emma decided to have lunch together in one of their favourite restaurants, overlooking the river. As they parted, after their meal, Emma kissed him on the cheek and embraced Devlin, in more than just a casual fashion, before finally saying goodbye. Both Devlin and Violet gazed longingly at Emma, as her heels sounded across the wooden decking and the breeze played with lose strands of her silken red hair. Devlin sighed and then breathed in her perfume, as if he was doing so one last time.

The next notable smell to prickle Devlin's nostrils was that of the mix of bleach, lavender and cauliflower cheese – when he entered the foyer of the care home. Despite the bright décor of the home a sense of joy could only be a fleeting visitor, rather than permanent resident, in the building. Even the plastic flowers, located on the desk at the main reception, seemed to be withering, Devlin fancied.

He headed upstairs to Bob's room, passing other residents along the way. Most sat calmly and quietly in God's waiting room, gently rocking or talking to themselves. Yet a few still had a glint in their eye – a divine spark - and smiled and said hello to the familiar face.

Devlin forced a smile onto his careworn countenance and greeted his foster parent. Bob Woodward appeared both decrepit and child-like at the same time. His rheumy eyes peered out at the world with a blend of innocence, vacancy, disorientation and sorrow. The aged, dementia sufferer reminded Devlin of photographs of WW2 prisoners of war, which he had seen as a teenager. Bob was wearing chocolate brown trousers, a flannel shirt and corduroy slippers. Most of his clothes were now too big for him, due to his recent weight loss. What little hair he had left was cobweb-grey. His liver-spotted hands loosely held a remote control and banana skin. White, wiry hairs hung down from his chin, similar to a Billy goat. Certainly, he could be as gruff as a Billy goat on occasion, Devlin thought to himself. Bob was sitting in a wheelchair, as the nurse advised that the frail patient was too weak to walk unaided and unaccompanied now.

"Would you like to come out to the garden and have a cigarette?" Devlin asked, akin to a father encouraging his son to do something.

"Okay," Bob replied, croakily, whilst nodding his head. Devlin took consolation from the flicker of recognition and desire in the old man's expression.

The air was awash with buttery sunshine. Ferns, yuccas and rosebushes bordered the tennis court-sized garden. Devlin politely – even cheerfully – greeted the staff and other residents enjoying the clement weather. He wheeled Bob next to a beechwood table on the lawn, with a parasol over it providing some shade. His pale face it up in conjunction with Devlin lighting his cigarette for him. As well as retrieving his cigarettes from the top of the wardrobe in Bob's room he had also picked up a steel hipflask, containing a measure or two of navy rum. Devlin poured out the elixir into a glass for the former merchant seaman.

"You're a good boy," his father said, lovingly.

Devlin's face creased-up and for a moment he was caught, betwixt and between, smiling and sobbing. He couldn't quite decide if life was a comedy or a tragedy. If it was a comedy, that was sad. If a tragedy, you had to laugh. Devlin was grateful for the kind words – and happy at witnessing Bob's contented expression. But tears welled in Devlin's eye because he knew just how much he hadn't been "a good boy".

After a few drags on his cigarette – and a couple of sips of rum – something seemed to click into place inside of Bob's brain and he spoke with purpose and feeling:

"I know I'm turning into a silly sod. I keep falling asleep and talk all sorts of bollocks. I keep forgetting things too. But I don't want you to forget how proud your mother and I are of you."

The lump in Devlin's throat prevented him from replying.

"And how's that nice girlfriend of yours, Gemma?" Bob added.

"She's fine. We had lunch together today."

"Good, good," the old man said, whilst nodding and gazing off into the distance, the cigarette burning itself down to the butt.

Devlin thought how his foster-dad still, just about, resembled Michael Caine. He had looked and sounded like the cockney actor most of his life – and even wore similar glasses. It had been just after watching *Zulu* when Devlin had mentioned his intention of joining the army. Bob neither encouraged nor discouraged his son in his decision.

"You're a man now. It's your choice. Just don't go getting shot, otherwise you mother will kill you. And me too."

Devlin looked back fondly on the afternoons they had spent together, fishing, drinking down the pub or watching football (because the "poxy commentators" often got on his nerves Bob would watch the matches with the sound off – and listen to Neil Diamond, The Drifters or Frank Sinatra instead). Devlin also remembered how Bob had introduced him to

John Buchan, having given the teenager a copy of *The Thirty-Nine Steps* one summer. Perhaps the book led him down his path. In which case, Devlin didn't know whether to blame or thank Bob. He missed Mary. And he missed Bob, even though he was still alive and saw him every week. But dementia had eaten away at his humour and dignity. The postman had been honest and hard-working, two traits which Devlin found scarce, outside of the army. He also loved his wife with an old-fashioned affection and devotion which this age was probably incapable of understanding, let alone duplicating.

Devlin was pleased that, for part of an afternoon, he had his father back with him. But ultimately a mournfulness gripped his heart as he stared at the pitiful figure. Death in life. Dementia had borrowed itself deep into his bones, like a cancer. There would be no Lazarus-like, miracle recovery. It was just about managing decline, fighting a losing battle. But it was one that had to be fought. The reward for a long life is not altogether so much of a reward, Devlin gloomily thought.

The two men largely sat in silence for the next hour. Bob issued the occasional confused utterance, or gave monosyllabic answers to Devlin when he tried to start a conversation. The weather continued to be fine though and the old man enjoyed a cold glass of milk, as well as his navy rum.

When Bob started to nod off Devlin wheeled him back upstairs and positioned him in front of the television. The son then bent down and kissed his father on his waxy forehead, before taking his leave – with tears brimming in his eyes once more.

It was getting too late now to visit the cemetery, Devlin told himself. Or perhaps he didn't want to discuss his day with Holly, given the amount of time he had spent with Emma.

During the can ride to the *Huntsman* Devlin dozed off a couple of times. He first dreamed about Bob. Devlin had come into his room at the nursing home and found him on the floor, having fallen out of his chair. Despite his emaciated figure Devlin found it a burden to pick him up. He shoulders burned, like he was back in the regiment again, carrying a backpack of bricks during basic training. Also, when he tried to place Bob back in his wheelchair the contraption kept toppling over. It was like trying to balance a bullet on its head.

The second dream was about Emma. The couple were having dinner by the hexagonal shaped swimming pool in the resort in Gambia they had holidayed at for a week. Not another soul was around, as though Devlin had booked out the entire restaurant for the night. She was wearing the two-toned Karen Millen dress which Devlin had bought for Emma before the trip. The outfit clung limpet-like to her lithe figure, yet could fall from her body like silk. He wanted to tell her how much he wanted her but his mouth was sown shut. His feet were nailed to the floor, preventing him from going to her. Or kneeling before her, either in the act of proposing or pleasuring her. Or supplicating her, to ask for forgiveness. Her lips were moist with champagne. Emma was equally desirous and desirable.

"I want to tell you something," she part teased, part prepared to confess.

Devlin wondered if she was going to ask if he would marry her, or tell him how much she wanted him - or reveal she was pregnant.

But before Emma could say anything else the taxi braked sharply, as it pulled up outside the pub.

Terry poured Devlin a pint before he even entered, having spotted his friend through the window, paying the cab driver. As he got to the bar Alan and James, the couple who lived next door to the pub, were having a discussion cum argument about whether to attend a Star Trek or Star Wars convention later in the year.

"Terry, we're never going to agree about this so why don't you decide for us?" Alan proposed, keen to settle things either way, if only because he wanted to go outside and smoke another cigarette.

"That's a good idea. Which is a first for Alan," James replied, only half-jokingly. "What do you think, Terry?"

"Well, having listened to you both for the past half an hour I can honestly say that I genuinely – and passionately – couldn't care less about which conference you go to," the landlord jovially exclaimed.

Alan and James grinned and nodded in sympathy, whilst "Welsh Mick", another regular, let out a cackle and tapped his silver-handled walking stick on the floor a few times as a form of applause. Mick, a former Royal Engineer, had the uncanny ability to vent bile and get upset about any and everything in the world – but then, aided and abetted by a couple of ciders, he would then duly laugh at any and everything happening in the world.

Devlin got a round in for the group of friends at the bar and, for a blessed hour or so, he was able to drink a measure from Lethe's cup and forget about Bob, Emma, Holly and the job he would have to do the next day. The tension in his shoulders dissipated, like an aspirin dissolving in water. He laughed out loud several times and took an interest in the lives of his drinking companions. But he knew he would have to drink again from the river Acheron, sooner rather than later. Despite the protestations of Terry and the regulars Devlin excused himself after only a few drinks. He needed to return home with a clear head and contact Porter. The two men, employing coded phrases, confirmed arrangements for the next day.

For better or worse, Ewan Slater was as good as dead.

13.

A fleet of battleship-grey clouds anchored itself in the sky. The rain pelted and hissed. Relentlessly. *Perfect weather for killing*, Devlin drily posed. People kept their heads down in such weather, oblivious to what was going on around them. The only thing they were concerned about was getting out of the rain. Even more usually he would travel about in the capital, unnoticed. Devlin rifled through a cupboard and retrieved his large, black, Fulton umbrella. Porter would no doubt carry his own umbrella – and both men would be able to shield themselves from London's prying CCTV cameras.

Devlin woke-up early that morning. After showering and dressing in some black jeans and a plain blue shirt he smoked a couple of cigarettes and drank a cup of strong coffee. He was wired, but not too much. A small element of edginess was fine, natural. He walked Violet and chatted to a couple of other dog owners he knew. They spoke about the weather and he feigned interest in their plans for the weekend ahead. All the while Devlin imagined himself taking the shot. The rain would not change anything. The room he would shoot from would provide sufficient cover. The trajectory was fine. The distance was relatively short, compared to other shots he had taken over the years, and he had no need to factor in bullet drift or the Coriolis effect.

Cutter sent a message from a burner phone, reminding him of their rendezvous. Should Devlin somehow be running late, he should let the CIA agent know immediately.

He took the tube to Baker St. Rain fell down the cheeks of the sullen, harassed passengers like teardrops. Devlin gently tapped his wedding ring against the wooden handle of his umbrella, either nervously or impatiently. A couple of hipsters blamed the summer rain on climate change (if they could they would have blamed Brexit). Devlin wryly smiled to himself as he recalled the afternoon before, in the *Huntsman*. Someone, a newcomer to the pub, asked if he was a climate change denier.

"It's not that I don't think climate change exists, it's just that I don't care about it," Devlin responded, with a nonchalant shrug of his shoulders.

The regulars laughed, much to the chagrin of the po-faced stranger.

The contract killer shook the incident out of his mind, like a forester macheting his way through the jungle, and thought about the vehicle Porter would arrange for them. Like the fixer himself, the car would be practical, reliable and modest. Danny Tanner could be trusted to dispose of the vehicle too. Porter met the former Royal Engineer during his time in the army. If Tanner liked you – and your money was good – he was a useful and loyal associate. The rest of the world however was fair game to fleece. Tanner owned a string of garages across London which, by day, also served as chop shops. Occasionally, at night, the upstairs offices of the garages doubled-up as pop-up poker bars, replete with serving girls and mixologists. And cocaine, of course, which only the house was permitted to sell.

The heavens continued to open as Devlin came out the station, not that he believed that God was ever on his side. He met with Porter on the corner of Glentworth St. He nearly didn't recognise the former Guards officer, such was his casual dress. He looked like a plumber. Devlin had never seen Porter wear jeans before, or indeed anything with a Nike swoosh emblazoned across it. Casual, for Porter, usually meant leaving the house without wearing a tie or pocket square. The two men nodded at one another, beneath their umbrellas.

"Nice weather for it," Porter drolly remarked, although like his associate he was all too aware of the benefits from the persistent showers.

"We know more than most how it never rains but it pours," Devlin replied, smiling lightly as he noticed how his friend had swapped his Patek Philippe, for a digital Casio watch, for the day.

As the pair walked towards Boston Place Porter made small talk by asking if Emma had come over to his flat the previous day. Devlin answered that she had, but failed to mention they had spoken and had lunch. Perhaps he would say something at the end of the week, after he processed how he – and she – felt.

They were met at the door to the house in Boston Place by the American who had followed Devlin into the *Huntsman*, a few of days ago. They were then led upstairs, where Cutter was waiting for them. He had taken his jacket off, revealing his gun and solid torso. His build and square head made him look like a turret.

"Is Mason not going to grace us with his presence today?" Porter queried, noting his absence.

"Mr. Talbot is attending an important meeting elsewhere," Cutter flintily replied, conveying his dislike for English irony and sarcasm.

Plausible deniability, Porter thought to himself.

Cutter got down to business straightaway, keen for everyone to be ahead of schedule. He unceremoniously pulled out a British Army issue L115A3 sniper's rifle, complete with adjustable bipod, an all-weather telescopic sight and suppressor. Cutter also handed over a 5-round box of 8.59mm bullets.

Cutter issued the asset with an equally untraceable Sig Sauer P226 – with shoulder holster, magazine and suppressor. Devlin squeezed the guard of the pistol more than he needed to, as if giving a firm handshake to an old friend.

The American invited Devlin to check the weapons and ammunition. He disassembled and reassembled the rifle on the kitchen table. Once Cutter saw that the Englishman was satisfied he ran through the plan, again. His voice was hard, galvanised. His thoughts and speech worked in straight lines. At any moment Porter fancied Cutter might revert to being a marine and start bellowing orders, or shout "Oorah" as a stirring refrain.

"We will drive you to Shelley St, a couple of streets away from where your vehicle is located, on Derwent Row. You will then drive to the house on Cooper Rd. We currently have a car parked outside, which we will remove just before you arrive. The property is empty – but I have posted a man in line of sight of the address, just in case someone attempts to knock at the door or loiters outside when you enter or exit the address. The second-floor back bedroom to the house looks out onto Lewis St and the front of Hayden Mole's home. You have been given photographs, maps and diagrams of the address – and the surrounding area. Mole is our target's campaign manager. Ewan Slater has set aside the afternoon to conduct meetings in the office on the ground floor of the house. At precisely 14.00 a call will come through to the office. Slater will be asked to come to the phone, which is situated by the window. You will be able to clearly see his silhouette. The phone is an old-fashioned one, connected by a wire, so the target will remain in view for a required period of time. Once I give the order you will take the shot. Failure if not an option. Even if you claim that the rifle has misfired, or the shot goes amiss, I will expect you to draw your pistol and fire a cluster of rounds at the target. Your marksmanship is at a standard to do so. We will leave it to you to ensure that you do not leave any evidence in the room. You are responsible for your own extraction. Do not attempt to contact us after the operation. We will contact you in our own time... Any questions?"

The personal bled into the professional after Cutter's debriefing, as the CIA operative smirked-cum-sneered at Devlin. Cutter wanted him to know that he was the master – and the trigger man was the dog. He wanted to posit that the marine was superior to the squaddie, the lawman was superior to the criminal – and the American was superior to the Englishman. There had been moments when Cutter had sized up his counterpart – and wondered about the extent of his training and number of kills to his name. Unlike many of the other assets Talbot was responsible for running Cutter was curious, or frustrated, in regards to knowing what made the ex-soldier tick. Devlin had the air of a wild horse, who still wouldn't let anyone ride him. He needed to be broken.

"Don't worry, this will all soon be over and you will be able to go back to your old life – or what little life you appear to have. You can spend your days drinking again," Cutter remarked, unable or unwilling to disguise his animosity towards Devlin.

"As Sinatra once said, "I feel sorry for people that don't drink, because when they wake up in the morning, that is the best they are going to feel all day.""

Devlin internally doffed his cap to Bob Woodward, for sharing the quote with him many years ago.

Cutter sneered again, like he was looking at a failed recruit, and shook his head disapprovingly. Reprovingly.

"You have no code, no honour. You fight for nothing. Or for a few measly bucks. You're half the man you once were, since leaving the army, I imagine."

"Be all you can be. Isn't that the mantra of the marine corps? If you're not being all that you can be now, you might want to go back for some basic training. But should you be being all you can be at the moment then your life may be considered just as tragic as mine," Devlin said, the corner of his mouth raised in a smile. Rather than treating the American with contempt, Devlin wanted to convey how much Cutter amused him – which only riled and antagonised the agent even more.

"You don't want to make an enemy of me," Cutter threatened, approaching the Englishman and puffing out his chest. Eyeballing him. His breath smelled of gum and cranberry juice.

"It might prove preferable to having you as a friend," Devlin wryly, unflinchingly replied.

Cutter initially screwed up his features in disdain but then forced a smile. He didn't want to give his opponent the satisfaction of seeing him losing control or reveal or any weak spots.

And they still had a job to do.

14.

Porter glanced at Devlin, out the corner of his eye, and noticed the look of concentration or concern on the assassin's face. He quickly shifted his focus back to the road however as Porter drove the car through the streets of Islington and switched the windscreen wipers to on to intermittent. The fixer wasn't quite sure if the silence between the two men was comfortable or eerie. He offered up a brief prayer to God, or the cosmos, or Good Luck, that they would come through the day unscathed. Porter justly understood however that his prayers to God might fall on deaf ears, for assorted reasons.

Devlin lowered his window and allowed a blast of fresh air to revitalise his skin. A thick, soupy humidity accompanied the rain. He had overheard two people on the tube earlier describe the heat as "oppressive" and "unbearable". Devlin recalled the heat in Afghanistan, which could sap a man's strength and will to live. The sun would hang upon the shoulders like a set of stocks and cook you in your body armour. Sticky, salty sweat poured down faces like rain. One needed to constantly gulp down water, like a camel stopping off at a wadi.

The heat and humidity would not bother him. He could kill in all weathers. But something did begin to bother him – a gadfly buzzing around in his head - although he couldn't quite put his finger on what it was. Devlin compressed his jaw and re-focused on the task at hand. He castigated himself a little for forgetting to bring a small towel, which he liked to place between his shoulder and the rifle stock. He wondered if the recoil of the weapon would feel familiar or alien to him. It had been eighteen months or so since he had fired a L115A3. Cutter had offered to arrange a practise session for Devlin, to re-introduce him to the weapon, but he declined. Had he done so out of pride or arrogance? Normally he would have been meticulous in his preparation. The harder you practise the luckier you get. Train hard, fight easy. Due to the time frame and parameters of the job however Devlin hadn't reconnoitred the target or location properly. He was just being asked – or rather ordered – to point and shoot.

"We're here," Porter announced, as he turned into Cooper Rd. The road was lined with terrace houses. Most had been split up into flats, some were still council properties - and some were homes to middle-class families, with two cars, a Filipino nanny and a Somalian cleaner. As Cutter had promised, the parking space, directly outside the property, was free. The agent had provided Porter with a tracker and radio after the debrief.

Both men put up their umbrellas after getting out the non-descript vehicle. Should any neighbours have noted the two figures they were unable to catch a proper view of their faces. Porter retrieved the rod bag from the backseat whilst Devlin carried a fishing tackle holdall containing latex gloves, hairnets and his Sig Sauer pistol. Without appearing to be overly rushing they quickly entered the empty property.

The two men put on their latex gloves and hairnets. They had no desire to leave any trace evidence. Porter had considered putting plastic coverings over their shoes but he had instructed Tanner to destroy all their garments, when disposing of the car and weapons, and provide new clothes at their drop-off point.

The musty-smelling house was half-furnished with bits of old furniture and worn carpets. A film of coarse dust and dirt covered the stairs and surfaces. Mouse droppings and cobwebs decorated skirting boards and crevices. The property was due to be sold in September.

Without a word said Porter and Devlin ascended the stairs. Onwards and upwards. Porter briefly comforted himself with the thought that he would be carrying his own rod bag tomorrow, fly-fishing on the banks of the Kennett. He looked forward to emptying his mind, or filling it with plans of getting out from under Talbot's influence. The American had of course promised that their association would end after today, but he would rather trust a Turk, or Tory, than the CIA agent.

The back bedroom contained a metal-framed single-bed, a table by the window and a pine tallboy, housing a chipped figurine of a racehorse and jockey. The floral wallpaper was yellowing and peeling off in places, due to damp, and several of the wooden floorboards were warped. Motes of dust hung in the air like a congregation of flies over a mound of garbage.

A dull light crawled through the window, which was half covered by a new bark-brown roller blind (which Cutter's people had recently fitted). Both men surveyed the scene. Either through luck or judgement Cutter had picked a favourable spot. Hayden Mole's house was directly opposite. Beneath them resided a row of backyards but the rain ensured that no one was sitting out in them. In between the yards – and Mole's terrace house – was Lewis St, containing a few parked cars. Recently painted iron railings stood at the front of Mole's home. To the right of its red door was the large window to his office. Devlin and Porter could already

302

observe a couple of figures moving about, behind the net curtains.

Mole, an avowed Marxist and "fan" of the Stasi, had arranged a slew of meetings for his leader. Some related to press interviews, some to campaign funding and others to introduce Slater to people of potential influence (who they could buy, or be bought by). Porter was already familiar with Mole. A mockney accent disguised Mole's heritage of being educated at Stowe and Balliol College. He was the son of Tarquin Mole, former head of programming for Radio Four. Mole worked as a Fleet Street journalist for a decade or so, before becoming a senior press officer for the National Union of Miners in the mid-eighties (during which time he accused the SAS of assassinating half a dozen of its members). After resigning from his position at the NUM (his justification being that they were neither militant nor radical enough for him) Mole went back to being a political commentator, although his reputation was tarnished when he was caught falsifying evidence for a story. His long-term mentor and ally – Ewan Slater – quickly hired him as Vision's Director of Strategy and Communications. Mole described himself in his recent autobiography, "Left Standing", as a cross between Alastair Campbell and Gerry Adams – as though such a creature should be lauded and admired. Should Devlin's bullet somehow travel through his target today – and fell Mole too – then Porter promised himself he would drink two large brandies that evening, instead of just one.

Whilst Devlin pulled down the blind fully and commenced to assemble his weapon Porter paced up and down the room, craving a cigar. This was the first time he had accompanied an associate on a job. Usually he was miles away. Plausible deniability. Although Porter was slightly anxious, he was in no mood to panic. Because of his time as a Guards officer (or other regiments might joke that despite his time in the Guards) Porter was no stranger to gunfire or death. Although he hadn't pulled the trigger himself, he was aware of how much blood he had on his hands in relation to previous contract killings too. But it would soon all be over, the fixer told himself. Porter also took heart from seeing Devlin in action. The ex-soldier was a picture of determination and professionalism as he methodically attached the bipod, suppressor, telescopic sight and magazine to the tried and tested L115A3. He was akin to an artist, readying his easel. More than anyone else he knew, Devlin could be relied upon to get the job done.

Cutter's stentorian voice came over the radio. It was 13.50.

Devlin pulled the blind and window up to the required height. The rifle's bipod rested on an oblong table. Devlin was standing, directing the weapon downwards. His features were neither relaxed nor tense. The barrel of the weapon remained inside the room. The butt was nestled comfortably in his shoulder. With his free hand, Devlin adjusted the telescopic sights. The ground-floor window loomed even larger in front of him. He closed the blind and informed Cutter that he would be in position at 13.58.

Devlin waited, as patient as a priest – waiting for his flock to arrive. Or for someone to enter his confessional. But beneath his calm, focused exterior the gadfly still unsettled him. He remembered the last time he fired the sniper rifle. He had assassinated Dermot Cahill, the IRA brigade commander. It had been a righteous kill. George and Byron Parker, Rameen Jamal and Faisal Ahmadi. The world was better off without them and Devlin hadn't lost any sleep over their deaths. But would the world be better off without Ewan

Slater? Probably. But it was too late now to worry about breaking the sixth commandment. His own voice, or that of a devil, chimed in his ears:

Thou shalt kill.

The philosophical assassin could have argued that, had he not taken out some of his targets, then his homicidal and tyrannical victims would have caused more death and suffering than he ever could.

Devlin briefly wondered that, if he looked in a mirror right now, would he see a vile and atrophied figure? Or, in his latex gloves and hair net, would he resemble a clown more? One to be laughed at, or pitied.

If only Talbot was the target. The bullet would have been worth its weight in gold.

It was time. Cutter's voice crackled on the radio again.

Porter pulled the blind up and Devlin readied himself. The butt was buried in his shoulder once more. His index finger rested on the trigger guard. Devlin briefly closed his eyes and regulated his breathing and heartrate. He bent his knees slightly – but owned the strength and technique to hold the slightly unnatural pose. The ground floor window loomed large in the telescopic sight again. If the gadfly was still buzzing in his ear then Devlin was besting it, ignoring it. Swotting it.

The world would continue to spin on its axis should Ewan Slater perish (he should have died hereafter, Devlin thought, misquoting a line from Macbeth). Nature would be indifferent to his death and – as some believed that God was Nature – then God would not condemn the act either. Ewan Slater would trend on social media for twenty-four hours or so but then that would be it. He would be history. Or not even that. Although his wife would doubtless want to sign a book deal and carry on the mantle of his campaigning work. The world would still have its Vision.

14.00.

Devlin watched as someone came to the window and picked up the phone.

Breathe normally. Squeeze, don't pull. Keep your face close to the stock and do not jolt with the rifle.

The phone was handed to another figure – silhouette.

Cutter's incisive voice came through the radio:

"Take the shot."

The figure loomed large in the telescopic sight. Slater seemed to be facing him, presenting as big a target as possible.

The sound of the 8.59mm round leaving the weapon was a mix of a thud, a puff and a hiss. It was and it wasn't like the movies, Porter thought to himself. He watched the bullet ping through the window (which didn't smash) and the silhouette disappear from view, in the blink of an eye. It was all far less dramatic than one might have imagined, the fixer posited. Life doesn't end with a bang. But rather with a whisper. Whimper.

Whilst Porter pulled down the window and blind Devlin commenced to place the rifle back into the rod bag, after having pocketed the shell casing from the floor. They briskly – but not too hastily – descended the stairs. After taking a breath, they removed their hairnets and gloves – and then opened the front door, wiping any prints away as they did so. The police would work out that somebody had used the empty property to take the shot but the trail would end there.

Umbrellas went up. Car doors were opened. Bags were put inside. They drove away. Job done.

15.

A sombre silence hung in the air, as did a pall of cigarette smoke, as Porter drove to their rendezvous point with Danny Tanner. His stomach churned. He didn't know if he was famished, or if he wanted to be sick. He swallowed a couple of times, his Adam's apple moving up and down like a boat bobbing upon a choppy ocean. The fixer thought about saying "good job" to Devlin but it somehow felt inappropriate, or even patronising. Instead he gratefully breathed in Devlin's secondary smoke and imagined the scene back at the house. People would be confused and terrorised, fearing for their own lives. Perhaps they all rushed to the back of the property, or lay on the floor. Even – or especially – the atheists would be praying. The police and ambulance service would be called. The operator would try to urge calm from the hysterical voice on the other end of the phone. Ewan Slater would be pronounced dead. The police would scratch their heads a little, until the specialists arrived. Could they label the assassination as a right-wing terrorist attack? The BBC and press would soon descend upon the scene like vultures. They would need to cordon-off the house – and surrounding streets. Find evidence. Interview neighbours. They would be unable to set-up a security cordon around the city however, to catch the shooter. It was London. The culprits would easily be able to vanish, like Robin Hood and his Merry Men disappearing into the evergreen.

The car sloshed through another puddle. Porter glanced at Devlin. As ever his expression was inscrutable. He would have made a good poker player, albeit he probably wouldn't have much cared whether he won or lost. Or maybe Porter could read his friend. Devlin was just sad most of the time. Angry. Grieving. He was a man unwilling and unable to climb out of the hole he had dug for himself. Or he was unwilling and unable to nourish himself, like Kafka's Hunger Artist:

""I have to fast, I can't help it... I couldn't find the food I liked. If I had found it, believe me, I should have made no fuss and stuffed myself like you or anyone else.""

They arrived at the drop-off point, an empty industrial estate on the outskirts of Walthamstow. Danny Tanner was there himself to oversee things. His team were professional. Most of them were ex-army. Tanner offered the two men the use of his own car and driver.

"Just tell him where you want to go. It's all part of the service," he remarked with a wink.

The impulse to be rid of the murder weapon was, for Devlin, matched by a desire to keep the Sig Sauer pistol. As well as disposing of the rifle, vehicle and their clothes Porter also handed over the tracker and radio to be destroyed, as per Cutter's instructions. He was now free. It was job done, except for the lingering stain on his conscience. Porter wondered how many stains Talbot had on his conscience. In his mind, he might have worn them like medals – badges of honour.

Once safely ensconced in the car – and driving towards Paddington St station – Porter checked for news of the shooting on his phone. The blood drained from his tanned face as he scrolled through the various online reports. He passed the phone to Devlin. For a moment, it felt like the world had fallen off its axis. Talbot had not only blackmailed the two men, but lied to them as well – tricked them into murdering a potentially innocent man.

"Broadcaster and activist Stephen Pinner has been shot dead in Islington... Police are not ruling out a professional hit, or the crime being terror related... Pinner was shot at the home of Hayden Mole, the Director of Communications for Vision... Strictly Come Dancing's Ewan Slater was attending a meeting with Pinner at the time of the shooting."

Porter sifted through the rolodex of his mind and recalled what little he knew about the left-wing academic. He pictured his pinched features, tortoiseshell glasses, tweed suits and long, silver hair. He looked like a cross between A.C. Grayling and Charles Hawtrey. *The Observer* had called him a "British Bernie Saunders". Every week Pinner hosted a podcast which unpicked the policies and propaganda of Donald Trump's administration. He had also recently made the news by proposing a day of protest outside the new American Embassy, due to open in Battersea:

"This day will not be about me saying "no" to America, nor even about London or Britain saying "no". But the world must say "no" to Trump and his racist, bigoted and populist agenda."

Porter kept reading the ongoing reports. Pictures were emerging of journalists door-stepping the home of Pinner's wife and children. Tributes were coming in from the likes of Tariq Ali, Russell Brand and J.K. Rowling. Even Gary Lineker had sent out a tweet, condemning the heinous crime. Hayden Mole had been quick to give a comment too:

"It would come as no surprise to me if British or American intelligence agencies were found to be complicit in this murder."

For once the former hack was telling the truth, Porter mused. Although previous paranoid and unsubstantiated outbursts from Mole, during his long and un-illustrious career, meant that he had cried wolf too many times before to be listened to now. The Director of Communications was but the warm-up act for the main event, as Porter watched Ewan Slater, dressed in a tie for once, give a press conference.

"I am shocked and appalled... We must show solidarity... His day of protest should still go on, in his honour... The Labour Party treated my socialist brother as a pariah or extremist. But I was always proud to campaign and share a platform with Stephen... Hope must not give in to hate... Our meeting today was about working together more closely... Stephen was part of our family and vision..."

Porter judged how the term "political opportunist" could be considered a tautology. He put the phone back in his pocket and pensively stared out the window, engrossed in thought. As tragic as the situation might be – the turn of events provided Porter with a glimmer of hope. He hadn't been able to find any intelligence connecting Talbot to Slater because there wasn't any to find. There was every chance of finding some compromising intelligence linking Talbot to Pinner though.

All was not lost.

16.

A week after the shooting Bob Woodward passed away in his sleep. Devlin made the funeral arrangements. He had already organised a joint plot so he could be with his wife, Mary. Oliver and his family came to the service. Along with a few other people the Woodwards had taken on, as foster children over the years, Devlin gave the eulogy. His voice sometimes cracked but he stopped, drank from his glass of water, and carried on:

"…I'm not sure exactly when I started considering Bob to be my father, instead of a foster parent, but it happened. And it was a long time ago… He embodied a sense of quiet dignity, which encompassed the ability to laugh at himself… As evidenced from today I was not the only beneficiary of the Woodward's generosity, love and plain-speaking wisdom… Before he passed away Bob said to me that I was "a good boy". If I am in some way good, then credit must go to Bob and Mary. They may not have been overly concerned with the likes of climate change or the gig economy, but they did believe in courtesy and decency. The young these days are often inclined to blame society's ills on the old. I remember Bob laughing at a cartoon I showed him in *The Spectator,* shortly after the Brexit vote. It showed a row of decorated veterans on a Normandy beach, with the caption beneath, "What have old people ever done for Europe?" Young people nowadays are prone to taking pictures of themselves and looking in the mirror, but they seldom see their faults. What they believe are instances of virtue, or victimhood, are usually instances of vanity. Perhaps it's just not young people who are prone to such folly though. But nobody ever accused Bob of being vain or playing the victim. He was proud to be British and proud to be working-class. But that didn't mean he wasn't smart or well-read. One of the first memories I have of Bob is him taking me to the library and showing me the History section… And Mary was of a similar character. Except she swore less and could cook… Together they were greater than the sum of their parts. Together they could teach young people a few things about love and sacrifice – and that marriage isn't just about booking the right photographer for your wedding day… I like to think Mary was waiting for him, with a bottle of stout and shepherd's pie on the table. They are having a laugh and chinwag now, no doubt. And they would want us to do the same. Maybe she called to him in a dream, which is why he didn't want to wake up… We should celebrate his life, as opposed to just mourning and missing him."

After the funeral service and laying of the casket Devlin arranged for everyone to come back to the care home – for a party. Staff and residents were invited. A *Chas & Dave* tribute band played in the garden. Terry furnished the party with a couple of kegs of beer. Manse's Pie & Mash provided the food. Half-way through the afternoon Devlin unveiled a bench and brass plaque, in memory of Bob and Mary Woodward.

Whether due to the death of Stephen Pinner, or his father, Devlin began to drink more heavily. He ignored most of Porter's messages and turned down an invite to spend time at his house.

Terry and the regulars saw plenty of Devlin however, to the point where the landlord advised his friend that he might be drinking too much, as he helped prop him up most evenings to get him into his cab home. Mick saw Devlin's decline as no laughing matter. The old soldier knew a case of burn out when he saw it. Even Alan and James were in agreement – for once - that something was troubling their drinking companion.

Devlin desperately wanted to see Emma. Be with her. But he realised it would have been wrong and inappropriate to contact her on her honeymoon. He wanted her to be happy, more than he wanted to free himself from his own unhappiness. He thought about tracking down Helena. But what was the point?

Sleep seemed to be the only balm for his despair and depression, provided that the same ghosts who haunted his waking hours didn't occupy his dreams. Devlin began to consider sleep as the moreish bouquet, before tasting the wine of death.

He read the end chapters of Graham Greene's *The Heart of the Matter*, twice.

He stopped reading the news. The world was an awful place. He also wished to avoid seeing pictures of Pinner's wife and children on the television. Whether Pinner was wholly innocent of sin it was difficult to tell, but his family were.

The soldier often lay curled up on his sofa – or unable to get out of bed, save for walking Violet or picking up a few groceries. He'd lost his appetite for many of his favourite foods however. Devlin felt hollowed out. When he walked he felt like his body was pulling his heavy, ragged soul behind it, like a knight with his foot in the stirrups being dragged behind his horse. When he forced a smiled occasionally, out of politeness, his grin resembled a rictus. He realised that, years ago, he had given his everything to Holly. And you can't give your everything more than once. Since her death he had been playing a part in a dumb show.

For a time, just after Pinner's death, he had thought about taking out Talbot and Cutter. They deserved to die, more than most. But the switch inside of Devlin could no longer be turned on or off. He was too tired, too morose, to plan and execute another hit. The bullets could stay in the gun, for now. Although he pictured meeting Cutter in an empty, secluded car park at night. He would challenge the American to a fight. He had read-up on how the CIA agent had boxed at college and studied Krav Maga. As the two men stood in position however Devlin would remark how his opponent had brought his fists to a gunfight – and slot two into his chest in the blink of an eye.

Out of a sense of desperation, or to fuel a sense of finality, Devlin finally scratched an itch and visited the small, local Catholic church which Emma used to attend. *St Jude's*. The spire still vaunted upwards, like a spindly forearm reaching for a star, but the cross and masonry had lost its majesty. The church was a great, but doddering, thespian - who could no longer bring in the audiences. The voice may have still been soulful and sweet, but the lungs were no longer strong enough to reach even the middle aisles. Yet Devlin went in, with an age-old sense of fear and shame. The smell of damp was more prevalent than incense. He couldn't help but note how the marble font was chipped - when he dipped his fingers into the tepid holy water. Devlin felt like a child again as he devoutly closed his eyes, crossed himself and genuflected. He slowly took a turn around the church – reverently surveying his surroundings as if he were attending a museum or art exhibition. He brushed his hands along the wooden pews and marvelled at the spectacle of the stained-glass window and artistry of the stations of the cross. Although the lapsed Christian had never been to the church before the air was potent with nostalgia. The memories were so thick he needed to brush them away from his face, like flies. No matter how quietly he tried to walk his footsteps still sounded on the smooth flagstones, reminding him that God hears everything. Could the Almighty see the sinner more clearly too, now he was present in his house? Churches always brought out such conceits in him, Devlin judged.

He patiently waited in the background for someone to finish their prayer, but then approached the row of votive candles. Gleaming. Golden. Welcoming. His hand trembled and Devlin accidentally – comically - lit two candles. He found he couldn't commit to one prayer, let alone two. He placed a £50 note in the box, to compensate for his error - and walked away feeling embarrassed. And anguished, that he had forgotten how to pray and talk with God. Faith was a self-lighting candle, that Devlin had lost or thrown away some years ago. When Holly died. Or when he fulfilled his first contract for Porter.

The priest was hearing confession. He briefly remembered his old parish priest, Father Matthew. Irish. Decent. He could still smell the whisky on his breath. Devlin now realised that his rosy cheeks were caused by the burst blood vessels beneath his skin. A handful of elderly parishioners, mainly women, were sat on the front pew, waiting their turn. A couple fingered their rosary beads, in advance payment of any penance. Devlin flirted with the idea of joining them but there wouldn't be enough hours in the day for the priest to hear his sins. There were others who needed to see him - everyone was a far more deserving soul. And Devlin had no desire to be forgiven, indeed he thought how, should he go back, light a candle and pray to God – the soldier would implore the Almighty to punish him. Kill him.

The invisible weight grew too burdensome and Devlin sat on a pew, near the back of the church. The bench was more comfortable than he remembered, but the years had put some padding on his posterior he fancied. He picked up a faux-leather, dog-eared copy of the Bible from the seat in front. The pages were wafer-thin and it seemed like the book might fall apart in his hands at any moment, blow away like ashes. But it didn't.

Devlin stared at the altar after carefully putting the Bible back in its place. The musty fragrance of books and distinctive aroma of burning candles flickered in his nostrils, as welcoming as the smell of freshly baked bread. The credence table, tabernacle, ambo, chalice and baptismal font owned an air of strangeness and familiarity, piety and majesty. He was reminded of being a teenager again, sitting next to Mary Woodward. Wearing his Sunday best. Sometimes bored and sometimes struck with wonder. Shivering in Winter (and often in Spring and Autumn). Love and God sometimes in his heart.

The large crucifix naturally attracted Devlin's attention. Christ was a picture of agony and compassion. Devlin experienced an overwhelming sense of admiration and guilt in its – or His – presence - and had to turn away. Tears welled in his eyes. He missed Holly. He missed God. But they were still with him too. Just not enough. The statue was ageing but had been lovingly maintained. The blood from his wounds glistened in the candlelight from where someone had freshly painted the figure. His suffering was but a drop in the ocean compared to Christ's. Yet he seemed to be perpetually drowning from that drop in the ocean.

Devlin idly wondered if he was too Catholic or not Catholic enough to kill himself. But it didn't matter now. His mind was set. He would leave the church with an age-old sense of hope and holiness.

"Oh, that the Everlasting had not fixed His canon 'gainst self-slaughter" – he used to think.

17.

Talbot was as effusive, as he was insincere, in his apology, when he contacted Porter a fortnight after the botched – or seemingly botched – operation. Porter knew he was lying – and Talbot knew Porter knew he was lying – but form had to be preserved and the game played out. The American assured the Englishman that all debts had been paid. Ewan Slater was now his problem to deal with, alone.

"We should have lunch soon," Talbot added, hoping that just the offer of lunch would serve as sufficient goodwill.

"We should indeed. How about tomorrow? Come to the Savile. I'll reserve us a quiet table," Porter replied, a paragon of charm and generosity, having accepted Talbot's forthright apology.

"I'm not sure. I will need to check my diary," the American said, hoping the stock response would convey his lack of enthusiasm to meet.

"I insist. It'll be in your interest, as well as mine, to say yes."

There was a conscious hint of a warning, or threat, in the Englishman's voice. Porter wasn't quite altogether being the soul of politeness. Talbot knew he was hiding something – but to see his cards they would have to meet in person rather than just talk on the phone.

"I have a meeting but I can cancel it for you," the American remarked, pretending to consult his diary, when really, he flipped the pages of a sailing magazine which was to hand on his walnut desk.

Porter arrived at the Savile early, the following day. Offering to make a generous donation to the club's chosen charity – he booked out the entire first-floor terrace for the duration of lunch. Porter explained that he was hosting an important guest and needed some privacy. The manager was duly obliging but cited that, no matter how important the guest, he must abide by club rules and be dressed correctly in a jacket and tie.

Talbot, accompanied by Cutter, arrived fifteen minutes late, at 1.15. The two men squinted in the glare of cloudless summer's day as the manager led them out to their table where Porter was patiently waiting, with a glass of gin and tonic in his hand. Talbot and Porter warmly greeted one another. Both were dressed in navy blue blazers and mustard coloured corduroy trousers. Oil held their hair in place.

Talbot eyed the manila folder, beneath the salt and pepper pot, with curiosity and suspicion.

"Please, Mason, have a seat. I am afraid I am going to have to ask that we lunch alone. I have arranged for your associate to sit by the door, away from the grown-up's table," Porter said, garnishing his honeyed tone with a dash of vinegar.

Cutter's eyes bulged at the insult and the corner of his mouth subtly twitched with rage. Just as he was about to reply, or snarl, Talbot stepped in.

"I'll be fine, Vincent. Order a glass of wine. Lunch shouldn't take too long. Mr. Porter and I do not have a great deal to discuss. Our business has already been concluded."

Talbot had already decided that he would not call on his new assets to work for him again, until the dust had settled. They could have time off for good behaviour, he had joked to Cutter in the aftermath. Unless of course certain circumstances prevailed and he would need to utilise their skills again.

The former marine nodded his head. He would follow orders and not make a scene. Porter fancied that if he pursed his lips any more however they might bruise, or bleed. It was just a slight shame that Devlin couldn't be present to watch Cutter be denuded in such a fashion, Porter fancied. He had considered inviting his friend to lunch. But then reconsidered. He was too unstable. Devlin might have been tempted to throw Cutter over the railings of the first-floor terrace. Management would have frowned on such behaviour.

Talbot and Porter sat in silence and perused the menu as one of the waitresses, Maria, poured the wine. Talbot covertly glanced over his menu however to take in his host. The fixer no longer seemed sheepish. Perhaps his over-confidence stemmed from being on home turf. No matter how confident the Englishman seemed though he could but bluff with the cards he'd been dealt. The American held all the aces.

"Ah, they have veal. There is no other choice. Perhaps its due to my belief that the herd are better off being kept in the dark," Talbot remarked, his cold eyes momentarily twinkling from being pleased with his own joke.

Maria took their orders and then took her leave. Once she was safely out of sight and earshot Talbot leaned forward and spoke, baring his bleached teeth a little to show his animus.

"I do not appreciate being summoned. I sincerely hope you've not invited me here to dish out some mock indignation at what happened. Sometimes mistakes are made in the field. You and your associate know this all too well, given what happened a year ago. Any feelings of remorse which you might attempt to instil inside of me Oliver I will duly mistake for indigestion. If, however, you are here to warn me that your boy has gone off the reservation then I will be grateful and act accordingly. I imagine that Cutter will take great pleasure in tracking him down."

It came as second nature for the senior operative not to admit specifics during conversations which he couldn't be certain were wholly private. Plausible deniability. Yet he felt he got his message across to the fixer – and he had re-established his authority. He ran assets. Assets didn't run him.

"I've not invited you here to give your dog a bone. Rather I'm here to bring his master to heel."

Talbot momentarily sneered, viciously, before relaxing his features and offering up a fake chuckle.

"Ha. How many of those gin and tonics have you had, Oliver? Be careful with your jokes though, as I make it a rule in life to have the last laugh," the CIA agent warned, both darkly and playfully.

"I've not nearly had enough to begin to celebrate with. And I suspect that I'm going to be far more amused by what I have to say that you will be, if you'll permit me the floor for a few minutes," Porter countered, steely and playfully.

"I'll indulge you for a few minutes, Oliver. But I'd take care not to cross any red lines. People who get out of their depth often drown. Watch what you say, old chap."

"I'm always careful to watch what I say, as I know you are, Mason. But in your line of work you have doubtless been asked before, who watches the watchers? I may have cause to apologise to my old Latin master and Juvenal, but "Quis custodiet ipsos custodes?" In answer to the question I watch the watchers, especially when I suspect that they are watching my friends and I. After our initial phone call the other evening I went to bed. Understandably, I had trouble sleeping. I decided to get up again - and contacted several associates of mine. Having mentioned Devlin over the phone I suspected that you had put a team on him. So, I had my team follow yours, the following day."

A flicker of irritation came across Talbot's face but he nodded and forced a smile, indicating that Porter should continue.

"Thankfully, at one point during the observation of their target, your friend sitting over there logged-on to one of your accounts on his computer and gifted the password to us. Using slight variations of the password my associate was subsequently able to hack into several other files and accounts you use. I'm now a veritable font on knowledge, concerning CIA operations conducted on British and European soil during the past ten years. But that information pales in comparison to what the company doesn't know. That you've been a busy but naughty boy - using company money and resources to fund off the books black-ops for personal gain. I've condensed the highlights of your files into the folder on the table, which you can peruse before you leave. Or you may want to glance at it now, so you are fully aware of the unfortunate position you're in. In terms of intelligence, what's mine is yours. Congress would frown on such behaviour. I have friends in the press, on both sides of the pond, who wouldn't be afraid to run the story. Ewan Slater will have more chance of getting elected as Prime Minister than you will have of becoming a congressman, should I air your dirty laundry in public. Suffice to say I also gained access to one or two of your bank accounts but, as much as I may be a rogue, I'm no common thief. Although I was tempted on more than one occasion to make a donation, in your name, to the charity Alice Pinner has set-up, in honour

322

of her late husband. But, please, before you say something in mock indignation Mason, allow me to continue. I'm about to come to the best bit."

Porter took another sip of his wine and wiped the corner of his mouth with his napkin, to help prolong his guest's ordeal. By now Talbot's face was fixed in a permanent scowl. Beetle-browed. His hands were equally rigid, as they gripped the table like talons.

"Now I must give you some credit, from one devious bastard to another, for your plan. Like Napoleon before Waterloo, you humbugged my Wellington by having Michael take out Pinner instead of Slater. I didn't see it coming. One silhouette looks the same as another. I can understand how you were more confident of us killing Slater than his saintly associate. I would ask that you enlighten me however as to why you wanted to take Pinner off the board. I have a theory, which any silence on your part may speak volumes to. I suspect that you were once Pinner's handler. Either you blackmailed or paid him to provide intelligence, concerning some of his more left-leaning associates. But at some point recently Pinner grew a pair of balls and wanted to be free of you. Or he had heard about your ambitions to run for congress and believed he could blackmail you. If it came out that you were responsible for having funded the man leading the day of protest for when the US embassy opens in Battersea then your political career would fall at the first hurdle. God knows you have made enough enemies, who wouldn't think twice about putting a knife in your back. So, you thought it best to silence Pinner, before he had a chance to talk. It wouldn't be the first asset you've burned. And you decide to sub-contract the job out, so you and the company could evoke plausible deniability should anyone investigate the killing and Pinner's connection to you."

"I'm impressed Oliver. Well played. I'd clap, but I fear that your club has put a ban on any applause or show of emotion," Talbot remarked. Simmering.

"And quite rightly so too."

"Given your resources and smarts I should perhaps try even harder to recruit you now. But I trust you about as much as a Sunni or Shia religious cleric. I forget who is the most untrustworthy and vicious out of the two. It almost changes each day. So how do you propose we move forward? Are you expecting to blackmail me, treat *me* as an asset? You must surely know that, should you attempt to leak anything, you will be signing your own death warrant? Before you embark on a journey of revenge, dig two graves."

"I'm not sure I could consider you to be an asset, in any definition of the term. And revenge is a grubby business. As is blackmail. We're in a position of mutually assured destruction, should we press our respective buttons on each other, so to speak. Should you be tempted to sign my death warrant then you must know I've taken certain steps to make you think twice. You know the drill. I have set up measures whereby if I, or an unknown associate, do not log in a code each day then my files on you will be released to various major news outlets. Should any accident befall me it will trigger instructions – and a payment – made to another associate of mine, who will make sure that you suffer a similar accident. We might be both as trustworthy as Donald Trump or Hilary Clinton – I forget which one is the more untrustworthy out the two, it almost changes each day - but we are also both firm believers in self-preservation. So, do we have an accord?"

Talbot shifted uncomfortably in his chair for a moment and paused, thinking about the ramifications of Porter's words and proposal. But he then nodded his head in agreement, seething as he did so. He gulped down some wine but it couldn't wash away the bitter taste in his mouth. Although in a position of stalemate, the American felt like he had lost. Been outplayed.

"We have an accord, as you pompously say. You must know that I'm not one to forgive and forget though, Oliver."

"You're in good company. Neither am I. Let's be honest, we have no desire to stomach being in one another's presence right now. But I'm happy to for you and your associate to have lunch, on me. Just make sure you leave Maria a handsome tip," Porter said, as he got up from the table.

"As little as you may think of me – and as much as you may have cursed my name over these past weeks - just remember that we have more in common than you would like to admit. Neither of us would make our grandparents' proud. We're both no strangers to grubby business practises. And we have the same blood on our hands."

Talbot removed a piece of fluff from his lapel and adjusted his tie and cufflinks as he spoke, as though if he appeared immaculately groomed his soul would be less tainted.

"I know. But whereas you and your ilk cause problems, Mason, I try to fix them."

Porter made his way off the terrace, although before he left the club he sought out Maria to give her a £50 tip, just in case his guest failed to do so.

18.

Porter was looking forward to getting back home. The Sword of Damocles was no longer hanging over his head. He wanted to see his wife and children again. He would take them out for a meal this evening – and propose a family holiday. No more secrets. No more lies. He could enjoy his retirement again. Breathe freely. Thankfully he had the first-class carriage to himself on the train back to Windsor. He treated himself to reading a few more chapters of Runciman's History of the First Crusade and made some notes for his planned historical novel.

He was also looking forward to giving Devlin the good news. Talbot would just be a bad memory for him now too. He could move forward.

Porter kissed his wife when he got in the door – and hugged her for a few seconds more than normal. He even felt like lifting her up, as if they were characters from a West End musical.

"You're in a good mood. I take it your lunch meeting went well?" Victoria asked, bathing in the rays of her husband's sunny disposition.

"That it did," Porter cheerily replied, resisting the temptation to add that the meeting went well because he would never have to do business with or see his lunch guest ever again.

"Michael Devlin called by the way. I said you were out and would call him back later."

"Did he say anything else?" Porter said, a little surprised and curious, as he had never known Devlin to call the landline before.

"We chatted for a bit. He asked how the children were – and mentioned he would be going away soon and would it be too much trouble if we looked after Violet. I said it'd be fine. I hope that was okay?"

Porter's sunny disposition suddenly became overcast with storm clouds of concern. Devlin hadn't mentioned going away at all to him. Indeed, when he had suggested that his friend go travelling, six months ago, Devlin had assuredly replied, "I've seen enough of the world not to want to see any more of it."

He immediately tried to call his friend. He also left emails and text messages for him to urgently get in touch.

"What's wrong?" Victoria asked, seeing her husband visibly distressed. Porter paced up and down the hallway and his hand trembled as he poured himself a small brandy. Deep furrows lined his brow. His skin seemed to hang off his jaw, like it had turned into melted wax.

"Nothing, I hope. I'm sorry, but I need to head back to London."

"What for?"

"I'm worried about Michael," Porter replied, realising that, for the first time in a long time, he wasn't lying to his wife about the reason he was travelling into town.

"I'll drive you to the station," she immediately resolved, lovingly placing her hands over his in comfort and support. Victoria didn't need to enquire why her husband was worried about not being able to contact his friend. She already knew.

Porter endeavoured to call Devlin multiple times from the train. He even dialled the numbers of his burner phones. But there was no answer. As he got into Paddington and saw the traffic he decided to suffer the underground, as it would take him over an hour to get to Devlin's apartment by car during the rush hour. As he stood up, being buffeted on the District & Circle Line, listening to the inane conversations of his fellow passengers, he started to appreciate why his friend often wore headphones while he was out, to cut him off from the world.

It had been a long day. His lunch with Talbot that afternoon seemed like a lifetime ago. He was bone-tired. Yet Porter still mustered the energy to walk briskly as he alighted from Tower Hill tube station and crossed the bridge, weaving his way through groups of tourists and city workers alike.

As he breathlessly strode over Tower Bridge, in what some might have deemed a mercy dash, Porter took in the Tower of London and remembered how he had taken Victoria there on a date, when they had first started courting. He had read a book on the Tower beforehand, hoping to impress her with his knowledge of the historic building.

Porter cut a desperate figure when he reached Devlin's apartment complex. His tie was askew, he had lost a cufflink on the tube, hair oil and sweat glazed his forehead and his shoes were scuffed. But he didn't much care. He just needed to see Devlin. Put his mind at rest.

He pictured the scene of knocking on his friend's door and waking him up, from a drunken stupor or otherwise. He would recount his meeting with Talbot and take Devlin out to celebrate with a meal and a bottle or two of Sancerre. He thought he might run some ideas by him, regarding his novel.

He valued his opinion. He regretted not telling him how much.

Porter's stomach churned – and his legs nearly gave way – as he pictured an alternative scene - of finding his friend dead. His body sprawled across the floor, next to the Sig Sauer pistol. Violet licked his fingers and face trying to wake him up.

Neither scene prevailed when Porter reached Devlin's apartment. But Devlin had committed suicide.

19.

Derek, the grey-haired Pakistani concierge to the building, found the body. Or rather Devlin had arranged for Derek to find the body, after giving instructions, earlier in the morning, for the concierge to pop-up to his apartment at a given time. Devlin had also arranged for a neighbour to dog-sit Violet for the day.

Porter arrived ten minutes or so after Derek had called the emergency services. The concierge sobbed as he spoke and reported what had happened. He was clearly still in shock - and distressed. "He was a good man."

He peered into the room from the doorway. Derek explained that the police had instructed him not to let anyone into the property, until they arrived. And Derek, in his freshly dry-cleaned uniform, was a stickler for the rules.

Life doesn't end with a bang. It ends with a whimper. The air smelled of furniture polish. Devlin had recently cleaned the flat. Death wouldn't be given a chance to fester in the place he and Holly called home. Porter briefly wondered how much Emma had called it home. Devlin lay curled-up, or contorted, on the sofa. He was dressed in a sky-blue shirt and beige trousers. Sunlight flooded the room, almost screechingly so. His pale face resembled polished ivory, or the death mask of a Roman nobleman. Porter couldn't quite decide if he was smiling, or if his mouth was twisted from having suffered a stroke. But Porter told himself his friend was at peace. In some ways, he was happy for him. Devlin's wedding ring glinted in the light, as if winking at Porter.

Showing him a sign. A couple of bottles of pills sat on the floor, by the sofa. No doubt Devlin had researched which ones would be most effective. Fail to prepare, prepare to fail. There would have been method in his madness. But how mad had he been? He could still tell a hawk from a handsaw. A framed photo, of Devlin and Holly on their wedding day, lay clutched to his chest. He also noticed a few candles, which looked like votive candles from a church, alight on the window sill.

Porter recalled the last time he and Devlin had spoken. It had been at night, over the phone. Devlin had been drinking and, rarely for him, he opened-up a little to his friend. Porter had mentioned how he didn't want the hitman to go to war with Talbot and Cutter. Devlin replied, "Don't worry. I trust you to fix things, Oliver. The only war that's left is the one with my soul."

Porter couldn't be sure whether, by dying, his friend had won or lost his war. If he had been courageous or cowardly. It was all such a waste.

Music played in the background. As ordered, Derek hadn't touched anything. Not even the volume button on the stereo.

"Now, I've heard of a guy who lived a long time ago
A man full of sorrow and strife
Whenever someone around him died and was dead
He knew how to bring him on back to life
Well, I don't know what kind of language he used
Or if they do that kind of thing anymore
Sometimes I think nobody ever saw me here at all
Except the girl from the Red River shore."

Over the music Porter heard the lamentable sound of Violet moaning from the neighbouring apartment, as if the mongrel already knew something was wrong. He would take the dog home with him.

It's the least I can do.

Later that evening Porter broke down in tears in front of his wife. And quite rightly so too.

The day before he passed away Devlin disposed of the pistol, wiped his computers and removed all other evidence of his profession from his home. He also pre-arranged for his lawyer, Milton Fiennes, to oversee his finances and will. Milton also served as Porter's lawyer. The two men had nicknamed him "Jaggers".

Devlin left his apartment and the bulk of his estate to Emma. She was welcome to keep the capital or sell off his assets and give the money to charities of her choosing. It was up to her. His one stipulation about the house and its contents was that Emma should pass on the framed print of Holbein's *The Ambassadors* – and any books that he wanted from his library – to Oliver.

Certain sums of money were also set aside for John Birch, Terry Gilby and Derek, the concierge, by way of an apology for putting him through the trauma of discovering Devlin's body.

Porter fixed it with Father Matthew so that his friend could have a Catholic funeral. During the service, it was mentioned that Devlin died in his sleep, from heart failure.

More people turned up to the funeral than Porter expected. Neighbours from his apartment block. Regulars from the pub (and a bottle-blonde barmaid who sobbed hysterically; at one-point Porter feared she might even try and drape herself over his coffin). Brothers-in-arms from the regiment, some of whom owed their life to Devlin's bravery and skill in Afghanistan. Porter was pleased that Emma attended the

332

funeral too. He couldn't help but note how she was without her husband.

Porter delivered the eulogy. It was an edited version of one he could have given. He spoke about Devlin's courage as a soldier and how much he loved his foster parents, Bob and Mary Woodward. He also mentioned Holly: "Maybe she called to him in a dream, which is why he didn't want to wake up." Porter didn't share half as much he as could have, but he felt it was enough. Violet would be a prompt for Porter to think about his friend every day.

Just after the service Emma spoke to Porter. She wore an elegant black dress. Her melancholy face was bronzed and blooming with freckles, although she thought it prudent not to wear any make-up lest she wept and looked-like a raccoon from the make-up running.

"I'm not sure if you know but I met Michael for lunch, a couple of weeks before he passed away. I wonder if I should've noticed that something was wrong."

Porter immediately placed a hand on her shoulder and shook his head.

"You shouldn't blame yourself, for anything. Michael was Michael."

He was tempted to make the argument that, if not for her, Devlin would've ended his life sooner. But he thought better of it. Instead Porter recalled a couple of lines from *The Heart of the Matter*. Devlin had bought his friend a first edition of the novel, as a Christmas present.

"No human being can really understand another, and no one can arrange another's happiness."

Printed in Great Britain
by Amazon